F   Webb, Betty.

        The llama of death.

$24.95

		DATE	

The Llama
of Death

Books by Betty Webb

Gunn Zoo Mysteries
The Anteater of Death
The Koala of Death
The Llama of Death

Lena Jones Mysteries
Desert Noir
Desert Wives
Desert Shadows
Desert Run
Desert Cut
Desert Lost
Desert Wind

The Llama of Death

A Gunn Zoo Mystery

Betty Webb

Poisoned Pen Press

Library of Congress Catalog Card Number: 2012910481

ISBN: 9781464200663   Hardcover
      9781464200687   Trade Paperback

*Page 191. The song "Gathering Flowers for the Master's Bou-
quet" was written by Marvin Blumgardener in 1947. It was
recorded by Hank Williams and Kitty Wells that same year, and
is now being used as a ringtone.

Poisoned Pen Press
6962 E. First Ave., Ste. 103
Scottsdale, AZ 85251
www.poisonedpenpress.com
info@poisonedpenpress.com

Printed in the United States of America

Acknowledgments

Starting with the usual suspects, thanks a million to the ever-loyal and fierce Sheridan Street Irregulars, as well as the excellent Marge Purcell, Debra McCarthy, and Robert C. Kezer.

More kudos go to Mike Foley, a keeper at the Phoenix Zoo, who gave me the delicious quote about snake bites. Helpful regarding all things llama were Dave Salge and Alicia Santiago, of Queen Creek, Arizona, the delightful couple at the helm of Arizona Llama Rescue. To contact ALR, visit www.azllamarescue. org. Many thanks to Jane and L.G. Olson, who for a generous donation to the Arizona Cancer Center, let me use them as characters in this book; Jane, although married only once (and to the superlative L.G.), courageously allowed me to give her as many marriages as Teddy's mother! More thanks go out to Deborah Holt, a supporter of Murder on the Menu and other literacy projects in beautiful Wetumpka, Alabama, who became a zookeeper in this book. Thanks also to Paul Rago, of Brehm Vineyards, for taking time out of his busy schedule to educate me on the seasons of a vineyard.

The idea for *Llama* came from an article written by reporter Megan Boehnke, which appeared in the March 26, 2010 edition of the *Arizona Republic*; it revealed a situation similar to the one found in these pages, proving that truth *is* stranger than fiction. Pursuant to that, California attorney Bonnie L. Riley was helpful in guiding me through the resulting are-they-legally-married-or-not quagmire.

Last but not least, a rattle of the bones to that Renaissance Faire superstar Ded Bob, who gave me permission to use his handsome, if skeletal, self in these pages. If you're headed to one of the larger Faires, check out the Ded Bob Show; it'a killer.

Chapter One

"Alejandro, you spit in my face!"

He didn't answer, just glared.

I tried reasoning with him, keeping my voice steady while I wiped the spittle away. "Look, I know you're unhappy, but I'm unhappy, too. After all we've been through together there's no reason for you to treat me like this."

I ducked before he let fly again.

There's nothing more irritating than an irritated llama, but there's also nothing faster than a ducking zookeeper, so Alejandro's second spitball missed the top of my head by at least an inch. "Losing your touch, big fella?" Straightening up, I saw that the expression of disgust on his face had morphed into one of pure sweetness. What...?

"I only weigh thirty-five pounds, so can I have a ride?" piped a tiny voice.

By the gate stood a tow-headed child who barely reached my waist. "Llama rides costeth two yellow tickets, my lady," I said, my tongue cramping as it curled around the sixteenth-century phraseology the organizers of the Gunn Landing Renaissance Faire insisted upon. "Plus you musteth have your kind lady mother's permission." *Musteth*? Was that even a word?

The little girl's mother, who'd missed the llama spit-fest, smiled. "The jousting knights scared her, so I thought a llama ride would be more her speed. Llamas are calming, so I've heard."

Alejandro's ears, formerly laid back on his head, pricked forward. If I hadn't known better, I'd swear he was smiling.

Llamas play favorites. Alejandro adored children, but he wasn't crazy about adults, especially adults wearing outfits as ridiculous as mine. Billowing pink cotton skirt with too much lace and too many flounces, a plunging neckline that barely missed being X-rated, and a steel-ribbed bodice that would probably turn my face blue long before the day was over. And that net thingy the seamstress had called a "snood"? The only thing good about the contraption was that it kept my corkscrew red hair out of my eyes. Earlier this morning, after taking one look at me in my borrowed outfit, the seamstress—Maid Lucinda, she called herself—said, "Guess that will have to do." Then she'd turned her face away, but not before I heard her snicker.

So here I was, dressed up like some deranged sixteenth-century tart, working as a llama wrangler on the opening day of the Gunn Landing Renaissance Faire, when I should have been a mile away up the hill, tending to my usual rounds at the Gunn Zoo. I missed my friends: Lucy the giant anteater and her baby, Ricky; Wanchu the koala; even Marcus Aurelius, the mischievous lemur. Disgusted by my fate, I would have sworn a blue streak, but I couldn't remember the proper curses. Zounds? Forsooth? Earlier, I'd heard one of the knights—Sir Roland, I believe, although it was hard to tell under all that armor—snarl something pithy about a spotted toad wed to a warted hog, but the rest of his insult escaped me.

Trying to look as delighted as Alejandro now did, I smiled at the innocent little face looking up at me. "The llama's name is Sir Alejandro, my lady. If you're nice to him, he'll be nice to you. Uh, zounds."

She reached up a tiny hand and patted him on the nose.

Alejandro closed his eyes and hummed with pleasure.

"He's purring!" the child exclaimed.

"Most llamas make that sound when they're anxious, but he's different. He only makes it when he's happy, my lady. It doth appear you have truly stolen Sir Alejandro's heart. Forsooth and all that."

She beamed from ear to ear.

"Up you go, my lady." I heaved her onto Alejandro's saddle.

As soon as she settled in, we set off around the paddock. Alejandro continued to hum contentedly while I silently cursed my boss, Aster Edwina Gunn. Thanks to the old tyrant, I was up to my ankles in llama droppings, sweating like one of the Queen's royal swine in the hot California sun. Not to mention ducking spit.

◇◇◇

"Quit glowering, Teddy," Aster Edwina had snapped a week ago, after delivering my marching orders. "The Faire only runs four weekends and all the proceeds go to the San Sebastian County No Kill Animal Shelter, a cause dear to your heart."

"But my job at the zoo…"

"You'll miss four Saturdays and Sundays, that's all, and your duties will be taken care of by other zoo staff. On week days you'll stick to your normal schedule and even appear on that TV show of yours, *Teddy's Terrific* something or other. What name did we decide on?"

"*Anteaters to Zebras*, as you well know, since you're the one who roped me into doing it in the first place. But like I said, I'm much too busy at the zoo to play around as llama wrangler at the Renaissance Faire. We have that new orangutan fresh out of quarantine who's just started trusting me and the Grevy's zebra with the bad hoof. I'm the only person he'll let touch him."

She waved my protests away. "Costs on the No Kill Shelter have risen dramatically and we need the extra income the Faire will bring in. You'll make the perfect llama wrangler."

"What if it rains?"

"I won't let it."

Aster Edwina was only half joking. The wealthy old lady—she was somewhere in her eighties—was powerful enough to bully the weatherman. As head of the mighty Gunn Trust and doyenne of one of the wealthiest families on the Central California coast, she ruled over the Gunn Zoo, Gunn Castle, Gunn Vineyards, and dozens of other San Sebastian County properties and businesses, some of which included land my family owned. Or, rather, used to own before my felonious father, for reasons he alone knew, embezzled several million dollars, which allowed the Feds to swoop down and gobble up everything we held title to. Acreage, houses, boats, jewelry…Only my mother's subsequent remarriage to another multi-millionaire had saved us from living under a bridge with the rest of the homeless. I was a child when it happened, but the scandal taught me humility. Which is probably why I eventually gave in and allowed Aster Edwina to bully me into working the Faire.

◇◇◇

By the time the little girl finished her llama ride, it was past one o'clock and I was overdue for my lunch break, but Deborah Holt, my relief llama wrangler, still hadn't arrived. I couldn't leave Alejandro alone. For some reason the llama had developed a major hate-on for Henry the Eighth, or rather, for the Reverend Victor Emerson, who played the part of the much-married Tudor king. Given Alejandro's current mood, I wouldn't put it past him to jump the fence and gallop over to the Royal Pavilion and drown the roly-poly reverend in saliva.

Behind me, Alejandro grumbled.

"Don't start that again," I told him. "You're not the only person around here who's unhap…"

"Sorry I'm late," Deborah Holt's voice rang out. "But the leper twisted his ankle and I had to help him to the First Aid tent."

Deborah looked even more miserable than I. One of the zookeepers who worked the Friendly Farms enclosure at the Gunn Zoo, she was a near-beauty with honey-colored hair, clear skin, and bright blue eyes. Her ample bosom, almost shockingly revealed by her low-cut Renaissance gown, brought out the wolf in every man at the Faire. The lace hanky she'd sewn into her neckline during a fit of modesty hadn't helped.

"How are you bearing up?" I asked.

Her scowl was a perfect match for Alejandro's. "My breasts are thinking about bringing a class action suit for sexual harassment against every man at this God-forsaken place, that's how I'm doing. Has Alejandro calmed down yet? I hear you've had trouble with him."

"He really dislikes adults."

When she bobbed her head, her ample litigants-to-be bobbed along in time. "That's to be expected. We rescued him from a Carmel couple who were keeping him as a 'pet' in their tiny backyard. Whenever they threw a party, which from what I hear was almost every weekend, drunks would go out there and mess around with him, try to get him to drink beer, stupid stuff like that. His owner actually chipped the poor thing's front tooth ramming a beer bottle into his mouth."

I winced. No wonder Alejandro was so temperamental. "You ready to take over here? I'm starved. Any suggestions?"

"The Steak on a Stake is good and so are the turkey legs at Ye Olde Peasant's Place, but stay away from Dame Polly's Porridge Pot. Several people who ate there wound up heaving in the Royal Privies. The Health Department's on its way to check out Dame Polly's kitchen."

"Holy…Uh, zounds!"

She gave me a wry smile. "Just another day in Renaissance paradise."

Forewarned, I headed for Ye Restaurant Row. It being Saturday and the California weather as perfect as perfect gets, the Faire—spread over forty acres of pasturage downhill from the vast Gunn estate—was packed. Tourists and Renaissance-costumed characters wandered together along the High Street, the sawdust-covered main drag. High Street was lined on both sides with vendors hawking books, sculpture, garden gnomes, T-shirts, coffee mugs, blown glass, and all sorts of pseudo-medieval and Renaissance ware. Scents from the various stalls wafted to me on a gentle breeze: apples and cinnamon from Dame Dorothy's Dumplings, attar of roses from Sir Pompadour's Potpourri, the sour smell of beer from the King's Ale House.

Some of the stalls, such as the Royal Armory, which hawked replicas of medieval and Renaissance weapons, were owned by locals, but most businesses were run by professional vendors who travelled the rapidly growing Renaissance fair circuit.

At the far end of the High Street sat the wooden enclosure of the Royal Joust Arena, where I could hear the clangs as knights bashed each other with broadswords. Near the Faire's gated entrance rose two wooden entertainment stages, each featuring an assortment of musicians, magicians, dancers, and jesters. Located in a dogleg loop behind the Middleshire Stage were the rides and amusements such as the Flying Dutchman, Castle Siege, William Tell's Archery Range, DaVinci's Flying Machine, the Royal Maze, and the Throne Carousel. Although not historically accurate, there was no denying the Faire offered everyone a good time.

Everyone, that was, except we Gunn Zoo animal keepers who'd been roped into volunteering.

After purchasing a turkey leg the size of Arnold Schwartz-negger's bicep from Ye Olde Peasant's Place, I slipped through a nearby door cleverly disguised as a castle wall and into the back-stage area. This had been dubbed the Peasant's Retreat, a place where Faire workers and volunteers spent their off-hours and nights in individual tents or communal RVs. Back here courtly manners slipped away and contemporary speech replaced formal King's English. The gratis entertainment in the Peasant's Retreat wasn't half bad, either. Rumor had it that this evening, the Faire's musicians would perform an uncensored concert featuring songs popular with medieval and Renaissance peasantry. Aster Edwina had barred the more ribald of these from the day's public perfor-mance because their lyrics made gangsta rap sound sissy.

For now, Renaissance porn was the furthest thing from my mind. All I wanted was a quiet spot in the food tent where I could eat. Most of the picnic tables in the big tent were already full up with monks, wizards, and wenches, but I found a space at a table toward the rear. I settled myself on a wooden bench and began to gnaw.

"Well, if it isn't little Teddy Bentley!"

The chatter at the other tables ceased. I looked up to see King Henry the Eighth—a.k.a. Reverend Victor Emerson, all three hundred pounds of him—hovering over my shoulder. With his big moon face, hair even redder than mine, and belly the size of a water barrel, Victor bore such a strong resemblance to portraits of the old Tudor king that several fair-goers had queried him about his ancestry. Today he looked even more kingly in purple velvet robes, a garish crown, and a faux (I hoped) wolf fur-lined cape. He brandished a half-eaten turkey leg that made my own look spindly.

"Behead anyone lately, Your Majesty?" I asked.

Ignoring my frown, he sat down beside me. "You sound as sour as your mother." A mail-order reverend only, Victor was the proprietor of the San Sebastian Wedding Chapel. He had officiated at two of my mother's marriages, once in his basic minister's cassock, the other time dressed as Fat Elvis.

"My mother has a right to be cross," I told him. "Aster Edwina gave her the impression that she could have the role of Anne Boleyn, but you talked her out of it and turned the role over to Bambi O'Dair."

Victor gave me a smug smile. "Bambi wanted the part more. Besides, Caro's much too old to play Henry's second wife."

The talk at the other tables had resumed, but it paused again as everyone waited for my answer. Ignoring them, I leapt to my mother's defense. "Chronologically, perhaps, but Mother doesn't look a day older than Bambi."

"Only thanks to your mother's many cosmetic surgeries, which they didn't have back in the fifteen hundreds. Don't you think a queen's body should be as God created it?"

"Bambi's chest never saw an implant she didn't like!"

Two nearby monks snickered as Victor patted my hand condescendingly, tempting me to bonk him over the head with my turkey leg. "Your mother's a beautiful woman, Teddy, and an ambitious one, too, but young she's not. Anne Boleyn was little more than a teenager when she married Henry Tudor and not quite thirty-five when she died. But have no fear. I gave your mother the role of a lady-in-waiting. She'll still be part of the Royal Court."

"As if she'd be satisfied dancing attendance on Bambi. Where's your sense of customer loyalty, Victor? Doesn't the fact that my mother is a returning client at your wedding chapel count for anything?"

Grabbing a salt shaker from the middle of the table, he poured what appeared to be a half cup of salt on his turkey leg. "I officiated at Bambi's wedding to that Max Giffords person."

"And it lasted, what, ten months?"

He took a big bite out of the leg, then added more salt. "Don't go all prissy on me. That was one month longer than your mother's fourth marriage. Besides, I'm certain that Bambi will marry again, which would also make her a returning client. And she's a lot easier to work with."

"I'll grant that Mother can be a handful, but regardless, you shouldn't have cheated her out of the Anne Boleyn role. It disappointed her terribly."

"I'm not responsible for other people's feelings."

With no adequate comeback for such insensitivity coming from a reverend, albeit only a mail-order one, I turned away and concentrated on my turkey leg. Victor took the hint and did the same with his own. The lowered conversations behind us resumed to normalcy as we munched, if not companionably, at least without sniping at each other. Eventually Victor wiped his greasy face with a velvet sleeve and checked the time on his iPhone. New-fangled inventions such as watches were forbidden on the Renaissance Faire grounds because even the longest sleeves could slip and reveal them. Cell phones, however, could be safely tucked away in pockets.

"It's almost time for the Royal Progress." His manner and inflection segued into Renaissance-speak. "Best I be going, fair maid. It wouldst not do to keep the beauteous Bambi waiting. Adieu, 'til anon."

He kissed my hand, and before I could smack him, waddled off.

I wish I could say Victor's unwelcome visit put me off my feed but that would be a lie. Returning to my turkey leg, I found something primitively satisfying in tearing off long strips of meat using teeth as my only utensils. I was reflecting on the fact that we might not be as far from our Neanderthal ancestors as we thought when a soprano voice interrupted my gastronomical greed.

"What did that slug Victor Emerson say to you, Teddy? And for God's sake, wipe your mouth and hands. You look like something that crawled out of a cave."

The conversation behind me ceased again because the voice had belonged to Caroline Piper Bentley Hufgraff O'Brien Petersen. My mother. Although the wannabe queen looked gorgeous in her topaz satin gown, and her expensively highlighted chestnut hair swept back into a bejeweled snood, she didn't sound happy.

"Hi, Mom."

"How many times do I have to tell you not to call me that? It's Caro, remember. Caro! Answer my question, please."

"What was Henry the Eighth talking about? Hmm. Politics. Religion. The usual blather you'd expect from a Tudor." When her face darkened, I added, "Look, Mo…uh, Caro. I was sitting here minding my own business when Victor walked over and started in. And please, let's not have this conversation in public unless you want to make the gossip column of the *San Sebastian Gazette* again. That pirate over there is a reporter."

She ignored the warning. "Did my name come up?"

Reluctantly, I answered, "Yeesss…"

"In what context?"

"It was my own fault, really. I told him how wrong he'd been to…"

"He compared me to that cheap Bambi woman, didn't he?"

The monks began to giggle.

"Uh, he kinda, uh, did."

"And?"

"He, uh…He, uh…"

"Stop stuttering and tell me exactly what he said."

"That you were too old to be Anne Boleyn." I waited for the eruption.

One good thing about Caro; she never disappoints. "That ageist twit! I look every bit as young as Bambi and he has a nerve…"

She spewed on for the next few minutes, questioning the parentage of both Bambi and Victor, their rumored mating habits, and their possible congenital physical and mental deformities. Behind us, a collection of monks, minstrels, pirates, wizards, and wenches looked on, rapt.

"Furthermore," Caro finished, "Victor and that social-climbing hussy are lucky the Royal Armory's at the far end of the High Street, or I'd walk over, grab a sword and hack off both their heads."

With that, she flounced off.

"Nary a dull moment with yer lady mum, eh, Teddy?" called a nearby minstrel, still in character.

"Sometimes I miss dull," I muttered, dutifully separating the turkey leg from its wrapping paper. After tossing the remnants of my meal into the proper recycling barrels, I composed myself and re-entered the High Street.

It was too early to go back to Llama Rides so I walked toward the Royal Joust Arena, hoping to catch the last few minutes of one of the Faire's most popular events. Nothing was more exciting than seeing a fully-armored horseman ride full gallop toward another in an attempt to knock him off his horse with a long lance. By the time I arrived, however, the last joust of the program was over, and the arena was being set up for a medieval weapons demonstration. That sounded interesting, so I took a seat next to a large group of fellow Faire workers.

An array of wicked-looking weapons of slaughter were brought out one by one as an announcer explained their purpose over a loud speaker. For the mace demonstration, two armored knights from an earlier joust returned and flailed away at each other for a few minutes with spike-studded metal balls. Bangs, clangs, oohs and aaahs. Then came the pikes and halberds, long lances with hooks on the end used for unhorsing mounted knights, then stabbing them as they lay helpless on the ground.

"My, my, doesn't that look like fun," said Deanna Sazac, who was dressed as a female pirate. She and her husband Judd owned the *Chugalug*, which was berthed near my *Merilee* at Gunn Landing Harbor. Today they were taking turns manning the Gunn Zoo Information Booth.

"I'm surprised we don't see more broken bones," I answered.

She winced as a pike-wielder used the hook to drag the Black Knight to the ground. "Say, isn't that Yancy Haas?"

Once the Black Knight had been properly slaughtered, he came back from the dead to take his bow. When he raised his visor I saw that, yes, it was Yancy. Originally from nearby San Sebastian, he had moved to Los Angeles to work as a stuntman. While here visiting his parents, he'd apparently decided to make a few extra bucks as one of the Faire's paid actors. Not that the money could compare to Hollywood's.

The most popular demonstration turned out to be archery. First we saw an English longbow, wielded by Cary Keegan, who ran the Royal Armory booth, and then a crossbow. The crossbow may not have been as loud and flashy as the mace, pike, or broadsword, but it proved just as lethal. It also had the advantage of being a unisex weapon, as was obvious when Cary's wife, the frail-looking Melissa, hit the bull's eye on a target thirty yards away.

"Something like that might make Judd behave," Deanna said to me. The edge to her voice took the humor out of her comment. Were she and her husband fighting again?

Whatever was going on with the two, I took it as my cue to leave.

"Maybe I'll see you at the next joust," I said. "When is it?"

"Two-thirty," she answered. "But I'm coming back for the joust at four, that's when most of the other people working the

down in the back room, but they informed me that the dining nook could easily be re-assembled into a bed. Best of all, the RV was parked directly behind the castle wall, mere yards from the llama enclosure.

Cognizant of my own pets' needs, I called Linda Cushing, the owner of the *Tea 4 Two*, a sailboat-turned-houseboat berthed next to my *Merilee*. A long-time friend as well as harbor neighbor, she volunteered to care for Miss Priss, my cat, and DJ Bonz, my dog, before I had time to ask.

"I'll only be staying here tonight," I said. "Tomorrow evening I'll trailer Alejandro back to the zoo, then come home."

After Linda promised my pets plenty of food, love, and walkies, I ended the call and made Alejandro a soft bed of hay.

"All the comforts of home," I told him.

He hummed with pleasure, then began eating his bed.

Humming a similar melody, I headed back to the RV to enjoy an evening of mirth and bourbon with the Silly Slatterns.

◇◇◇

A loud racket woke me just after two.

"Wha…?" I lifted my head, blinking away dreams of Joe.

The noise intensified: a high keening sound, punctuated by a snarl, then a series of bark-like yips. Thuds. More yips.

The Slatterns stumbled into the room as I was untangling myself from the sheets. "What the hell's that, Teddy? Coyotes?"

"Dunno, but I'm going to find out."

"If it's coyotes, I mean, teeth and all that, shouldn't you call Security?" worried Petra.

"Security's got tasers," Tina added.

"Call them." I grabbed a cast iron skillet from the stove, and clad only in a borrowed nightshirt, ran out the door into the chill night air.

As I feared, the noise came from the direction of Llama Rides. Coyotes, which were common here in rural San Sebastian County, are solitary hunters, and the chances of one taking down a healthy llama weren't good. This is why sheepherders often use llamas as flock guards. While protecting their sheep, llamas had been known to stomp coyotes to death.

Feral dog packs were another story.

Hoping that wasn't the case, I almost knocked down the Faire's plywood castle in my clumsy rush through its door and into the darkness of High Street. If a dog pack was on the attack, I was in serious trouble, but at the moment I was more worried about Alejandro's safety than my own. Maybe the attacker was a lone dog. I hoped so because my only weapon was that cast iron skillet.

And my voice.

"Bad dog!" I yelled, my tone fierce. "Bad dog!"

Anyone experienced with dogs, even feral ones, knows that the human voice carries more weight than a frightened animal's cries. "Bad dog! Down, bad dog! Down!"

The barking yips continued, ever-increasing in urgency.

Not a coyote. Not a dog.

A terrified llama.

With no streetlights on the grounds and only a half-moon for illumination, the High Street was dark, but as I rushed up to Llama Rides I was able to make out a furry shape lying motionless inside the gate.

Alejandro?

Tears sprang to my eyes, but when I approached the prone form the yipping didn't stop. It continued even louder. Then, as if desperate for help, Alejandro emerged from the shadows and galloped to meet me.

Ipe-ack, ipe-ack! he barked. The second he reached me, he shoved his head into my chest, bleating out an almost human sob.

"Oh, Alejandro. Did my brave boy kill it?"

Normally, a llama will not go out of its way to kill an intruder, but he would use his strong, clawed feet in self-defense. If that's what Alejandro had done, he couldn't be blamed. Then I realized that the llama's attacker, whatever type of canine it had been, might not be dead, merely stunned. To be desperate enough to tackle something the size of a full-grown llama, it had either been starved or rabid. I couldn't see if Alejandro had any wounds, but the situation nevertheless called for caution. Taking him by his halter, I led him to the opposite end of the enclosure in case the animal got up again.

To my relief, I saw the bobbing of a flashlight and heard feet pounding toward me.

"Teddy! Are you all right?" I recognized the voice of Walt McAdams, the fireman who lived near me on the *Running Wild.* On vacation from the San Sebastian Fire Department, he had been hired as head of Faire Security.

"Yes, but be careful!" I shouted back. "We may have a rabid animal on our hands!"

Seconds later, Walt arrived with two more security guards armed with flashlights and tasers. They cautiously entered the llama enclosure and bent down to examine the still animal.

One guard gasped. The other turned away.

Walt looked stricken.

"What is it?" I asked. "Coyote? Dog?"

Walt's voice shook when he said, "It's…it's what's-his-name, the Henry the Eighth guy. He's dead."

Aghast, I turned to the llama. "Oh, Alejandro, what have you done?"

Chapter Two

In the dark, Victor Emerson's furry cape made the fallen man look like an animal, but once lit by several flashlights, Alejandro's victim was clearly human. Victor lay on his stomach with his arms outstretched. From the bit of clothing I could see, he was wearing pajamas. When the security guards rolled him over, the llama vented a catarrhal sound that could have been a sob. As for me, I was relieved that one of the guards had positioned himself between me and Victor. I had never liked the man but had no desire to see his dead face.

The guard closest to me made a gagging noise. Another swore.

"Uh, Teddy?" Walt's usually confident voice wavered even more. "Why don't you, uh, tie that animal up someplace and keep it out of the way. Seems it didn't have anything to do with this, ah, this situation. And as soon as you've got it secured, get the hell out of that pen. Duck under the fence so you don't track all over this area."

"Him," I snapped. "Alejandro's a 'him,' not an 'it.'" Nomenclature was a silly thing to be worried about at a time like this, but I'm a zookeeper, and to me, no animal is an "it." I started to lead the llama over to the hitching post at the back of the enclosure, then stopped. "Wait a minute, Walt. Are you saying Alejandro didn't stomp the poor guy to death?"

Now the security guards did an odd thing. In unison, they flicked off their flashlights, and with Walt leading the retreat, walked backwards until they had exited the enclosure.

"I'm calling Sheriff Rejas, Teddy," Walt said.

"You can't 'cause Joe's…he's…he's in Virginia," I stuttered, reminding him of my fiancé's whereabouts. "He's on that Homeland Security thing and…and he told me before he left that he might be out in the woods somewhere on some exercise and he can't be reached because they're clamping down a whatchacallit a…a news blackout or something like that on him and the other sheriffs and…and they took away everyone's cell phone so they can't talk or get calls and…and he won't get back until…" I stopped babbling and forced myself to think. "Did you check for a pulse?"

Walt nodded. "No pulse, fixed pupils, enough blood to float a boat. He's dead all right, but he didn't get llama-stomped. He's been shot in the jugular with some kind of arrow and he bled out."

Alejandro moaned. Or maybe he was mimicking me.

I swallowed. "In that case, I'd better remove Alejandro from the enclosure, too. Tell you what. I'll walk him over to the Camel Rides pen and stash him there. The camel didn't take well to the crowds, they usually don't, you know how they are, so his owner trailered him home and they won't be back. But that won't be a permanent solution. It's louder over there than here and Alejandro won't like that anymore than the camel did. Actually, I can't move him at all right now, because then Alejandro and I would be tromping all over the, um, crime scene. We shouldn't disturb it more than it already has been, because the authorities, well, you know, they don't like people messing with…"

"Stop babbling, Teddy. I've got the sheriff's office on my cell!"

I stopped babbling.

Time crawled as we waited for the authorities. Alejandro and I comforted each other while Walt and the other security guards huddled in the shadow of the big plywood castle. Shivering in the damp night air, I pressed myself against Alejandro's shaggy side. As if he understood, he looped his big head around and nuzzled me. Whatever tension had once existed between us was gone. We were two frightened creatures huddling together for warmth.

The guards tried to keep their voices down, but it was too late: the llama's cries had awakened Faire workers. One by one, they emerged from their tents and trailers onto the High Street to see what the fuss was about. For the most part they were respectful when they heard there had been a fatality, but the more curious of them surged forward for a better look. The guards pushed back, keeping them away from the enclosure's entrance. The onlookers whose costumes required fur capes were lucky; they'd thrown their capes over their nightclothes. Watching them, I realized that was what Victor must have done. He had wrapped his regal fur cloak around him before stepping outside.

But why leave his warm tent in the middle of the night in the first place?

A romantic encounter was the first thing that sprang to mind. Like many mail-order reverends, Victor had no church other than his little wedding chapel, and he wasn't in the business of delivering sinners from the clutches of Satan. Religiously speaking, he was free to play around. And he did. With considerable enthusiasm. Who could have been tonight's lucky lady? Victor was frequently seen squiring Bambi around town, but it was not unknown for him to be involved with several women at a time. What they saw in him was a mystery.

Soon the wail of sirens pierced the night. Minutes later, a herd of uniformed officers galloped toward us led by Deputy Elvin Dade, Joe's fifth-in-command.

"Where's the body?" he barked.

Walt, along with around thirty others, pointed to the furry lump on the ground.

"Get outta my way!" Elvin ordered, shouldering aside the security guards. He swaggered into the llama enclosure, circled the body several times, then knelt down and began pawing at it.

After watching him tug at the arrow implanted in Victor's neck, I yelled, "Hey, Elvin! Shouldn't you wait until the crime techs get here? You know, to check for fingerprints and stuff?"

"That's *Acting* Sheriff Dade to you, Teddy Bentley! And you stay out of this. You're not dealing with that indulgent boyfriend of yours now. Leave the crime detecting to people who know something about it."

He yanked on the arrow again, finally succeeding in pulling it out.

At the age of fifty-eight Elvin held more seniority than anyone else in the sheriff's office. He'd run for the top job twice, but Joe beat him each time. Not because of Elvin's abrasive personality, although I'm sure that factored in, but because the man was so full of himself he turned people off. Elvin had a temper, too, and all too often arrested people who annoyed him, whether they'd broken the law or not. Once he even tried to arrest my mother when her Mercedes CL beat his aging Ford Focus to a prime parking spot outside Sydd's Salad Supreme. Only the pleas of his hungry wife kept him from hauling Caro off in handcuffs.

If Elvin hadn't been the brother of California's powerful attorney general, Joe would have fired him years ago.

Still, given Elvin's less than pristine record as a peace officer, he was now in charge only because of a string of unfortunate events that not even a man as intelligent as Sheriff Joe Rejas could have foreseen. Two days earlier Head Deputy Stan Berringer, Joe's second-in-command, had suffered an attack of acute pancreatitis and lay hooked up to a glucose drip in San Sebastian County Hospital. Deputy Pete Rimstead, Joe's third-in-command, was recovering from a gunshot wound in the leg inflicted day before yesterday by a grandmother protesting the arrest of her teenage grandson for shoplifting. Ralph Wilson, Joe's fourth-in-command, had suddenly eloped with his girlfriend to Las Vegas. Or maybe it was Reno. Wherever he was, no one could find him, and thus—according to the command structure set down by the county commissioner—the officer with the most seniority then ascended to rank of acting sheriff.

Ergo, Joe's worst nightmare—Elvin Dade elevated to command.

"Look what I found!" Elvin crowed, standing up and brandishing the arrow. Whisking a handkerchief from his pocket, he proceeded to wipe it off.

Several other deputies actually groaned.

Aghast myself, I did a quick calculation. It was closing in on three o'clock here in California, which would make it around six in Virginia. Just in case the spooks at Homeland Security had changed their minds about cell phone confiscation, I would try to reach Joe anyway if I hadn't left my cell phone in the Silly Slatterns' RV. I looked over at Walt. Witness to the acting sheriff's incompetence, he was already punching in a number on his cell. Joe's, I hoped. I saw Walt's lips move for mere seconds, too short a time for a conversation. Voice mail.

Alejandro began muttering. Standing still for so long was getting on his nerves. I doubted he was wild about the smell of blood, either.

"Hang in there, big boy," I whispered. "This can't last forever."

Almost as if he'd heard, Elvin glanced over at me. "What the hell's that thing?"

"Llama. Name's Alejandro."

"Get it away from me before I shoot it."

Since the moronic man had already contaminated the crime scene beyond repair, I led Alejandro out of shooting range. I was tempted to transport him back to the zoo, never to return to the Faire. Only ghouls would turn up at the bloodied llama pen when the Faire opened, anyway. Then I remembered Aster Edwina's orders the day before: "Don't you give me any lip, Teddy. Conduct those llama rides or else!" God only knew what she meant by "or else." The irony here was that although I worked with bears, wolves, tigers, lions, and rhinos with nary a qualm, the old bat terrified me. Accepting the reality of my situation, I straightened my shoulders and led Alejandro to the deserted camel pen.

Halfway there, I ran into Melissa and Cary Keegan. The last time I'd seen them had been at the medieval weapons demonstration, when they were working with the longbow and crossbow. This realization made me stop so suddenly that Alejandro almost ran me down.

"What's happening, Teddy?" Melissa flowed toward me in a white, vaguely medieval nightgown, her waist-length black hair darker than the night itself. "Someone said there's been an accident."

I thought for a moment before I answered. "Is the Royal Armory missing any stock?"

Melissa started to answer, but Cary interrupted her. "Why do you ask?" The stormy expression on his face made me suspect that Melissa's answer would have been in the affirmative.

"Victor Emerson's dead." Given the size of the crowd at the crime scene, keeping it secret was a no-hoper, anyway.

Cary frowned. "Are you talking about that reverend guy who plays Henry the Eighth?"

"Yep. He had an arrow in his neck."

The two looked at each other. Melissa opened her mouth, but Cary shushed her again. "All our weapons are accounted for."

"But isn't that…?" Melissa suddenly winced as Cary's hand gripped her forearm tightly. Too tightly, I thought, for the first time noticing what a large man he was and how frail she seemed in comparison.

"There's nothing we can do about any of this," he told his wife, in a tone that wouldn't be argued with. "Let's go back to bed."

Melissa didn't argue.

I watched them walk toward their quarters behind the Armory until Alejandro bumped me impatiently with his nose.

"All right, all right," I said. "The camel pen it is. I'll get you some more hay, too. But promise me you won't spit on anyone tomorrow. Except for Acting Sheriff Elvin Dade. Spit on him all you want."

◇◇◇

After everything that had transpired, sleep proved impossible. I lay in the Silly Slatterns' RV with my eyes wide open, thinking about Victor. Who would have murdered such a harmless, if annoying, person? Although I'd never cared for the man myself, he had many fans, especially among those whose approach to marriage tended to be on the casual side. Until his dust-up with my mother over the Anne Boleyn situation, I had never known him to make an enemy since he'd moved to San Sebastian

County. Even women he once dated bore him no ill will. Maybe it was his gift of gab. He had been slick, no doubt about it.

I also couldn't stop thinking about the arrow Elvin pulled from Victor's neck. Something seemed "off" about it. While attending Miss Pridewell's Academy, I was on the archery team, yet never saw an arrow like it. For starters, the thing appeared to be less than a foot long, which was much shorter than the standard archery arrow. In fact, it had looked almost like...

A crossbow bolt.

Sunrise found me still staring up at the ceiling of the Silly Slattern's RV. Somehow I managed to haul myself out of bed, clean off in a tiny shower stall, and dress in my Renaissance duds without ripping the fabric. This time, however, I dispensed with the corset. I felt miserable enough already.

Hoping against hope, I punched in Joe's number on my cell, but the call rolled over to voice mail. Good ol' Homeland Security and their no-phones rule. I left a message anyway.

"Elvin tromped all over the crime scene and then pulled the arrow right out of Victor's neck, Joe. If a miracle happens and Homeland Security gives you your cellphone back, please call that foolish man and give him a talking to. Victor was horribly murdered, and the way Elvin's going he'll have the case so screwed up by the time you get back home it'll take you twice as long to solve it. Love you. Call me as soon as they let you. And for God's sake, call Elvin and put some sense into him!"

I rang off wondering when Joe would get my message. What was Homeland Security doing with him and the other sheriffs, anyway? Were they bivouacking in the Virginia woods, or sitting in stuffy meeting rooms listening to FBI agents drone on and on about suspicious-looking Middle Easterners? Remembering Ted Kozinski, Timothy McVeigh, and Anders Brevik, I hoped they would warn them about suspicious-looking Anglo-Saxons, too.

Since there was nothing more I could do at the moment I left for the camel pen. This early in the morning few people were up and about. The vendors' shops were still closed, except for Ye Queen's Bakery, which was serving breakfast.

Four miles inland, this narrow valley seldom suffered heavy bouts of the morning fog that plagued the coast, but today a few wisps had made it over the surrounding hills from the Pacific. Thanks to my low-cut bodice, the damp chilled me, and I was cursing under my breath by the time I reached Alejandro. Knowing how sensitive he was, I forced a cheerful note into my voice.

"Miss me, sweetie?"

A soft chuffle assured me that he did.

After giving him a friendly ear-scratch, I dished out his morning meal of alfalfa pellets mixed with oat hay topped with a sprinkling of chopped carrots. Llamas are modified ruminants with three stomach compartments. They chew their food well, swallow, then bring it up again later for another round of chewing. Unlike cows, they don't have a fourth stomach compartment, so colic can be a problem. When dealing with domesticated llamas, proper food measurement is critical so as always, I took great care with the proportions.

Alejandro quickly polished off his breakfast, then walked over to nuzzle my ear. All signs of yesterday's spit-fest vanished, he was now in his llama-ish way, declaring me his BFF.

"Love you, too," I crooned.

For the next hour I swept llama turds out of the enclosure and took care of all the other chores necessary to keep a llama happy, which wasn't much different than my job at the zoo. Work finally accomplished, I set off for Alejandro's previous habitat to get the LLAMA RIDES sign and transfer it to his new digs. The entire enclosure was now blocked off by yellow police tape. At least Elvin got that part right. Even better, he had posted a deputy I knew at the entrance. Emilio Gutierrez was an old friend of mine who descended from one of my great-great-great grandfather's vaqueros in the halcyon days when we Bentleys owned most of San Sebastian County. A string of bad investments, lawsuits, and the Depression had changed all that.

"Hola, Teddy!"

"*Buenos dias*, Emilio. Bad scene last night, wasn't it?"

He pulled a face. "Made even worse by our inglorious leader. We're counting the hours until Sheriff Joe gets back."

If intelligence mattered as much as seniority, the very bright Emilio—who had served only four years with the Sheriff's Department—would now be the acting sheriff of San Sebastian County, but thanks to bureaucratic short-sightedness, he wasn't.

"Have you tried to reach Joe?" I asked him.

His face grew longer. "Yeah. And so has every other deputy in the county. I called Homeland Security itself, not that it did any good. The agent I talked to said that unless there was a dire emergency—and he didn't consider one measly murder an emergency—none of the sheriffs could be reached until their training sessions are completed. Which means Joe has no idea what we're going through, and he won't until they give him his cellphone back. Heck, I even called the state police about our situation, but because of jurisdictional issues, they can't override Elvin no matter how goofy he gets. Unless he actually breaks the law, that is, and it's not illegal to act like an ass. The county commissioner is standing firm on the seniority issue, too, so we're screwed." He sighed. "I hear you're set up at Camel Rides now. You need your sign?"

"That, plus any more information you care to give me."

"No problemo."

As I detached LLAMA RIDES from the post it had been hammered onto, he filled me in on Acting Sheriff Elvin Dade's latest misadventures.

Elvin was moving through the Peasant's Retreat like a hurricane, Emilio told me, rousting sleepy people and demanding to know where they were and what they were doing at two in the morning. Everyone except Walt McAdams and the other security guards claimed they had been asleep. When Walt confessed he had been less than three hundred yards from the crime scene when the alarm was raised, Elvin had all but pulled out a rubber hose to work him over.

"Geez, Teddy, he put Walt through such a grilling I thought he was gonna arrest him right then and there," Emilio said. "But after Walt told him you reached the body before he did, Elvin started carrying on about you, yelling that you had no business tramping all over the crime scene, that you…"

"I heard screams. What was I supposed to do, roll over and go back to sleep?"

"Of course not, but logic isn't Elvin's thing. You'd be sitting in an interview room down at the station right now except for what Walt said next." He paused for dramatic effect.

"Which was?"

"He claimed he'd seen a ghost."

I blinked. "Did you say, 'ghost'?"

"Can you believe it? First, somebody's been out in the middle of the night playing bows and arrows, Walt sees ghosts, Henry the Eighth winds up dead. You can't make this stuff up. So yeah, Walt saw a ghost, or at least something pale and filmy floating around near that Ye Olde Imagery place."

Ye Olde Imagery was the photo booth where Faire-goers could pose in medieval or Renaissance garb. It was located at the north end of High Street between the Gunn Zoo Information Booth and the Royal Armory. Picturing it, I remembered Melissa Keegan's filmy nightgown. Her black hair could have blended into the shadows, but her white gown could easily have been seen as a ghostly apparition. Victor had been killed by a crossbow dart, and the Armory not only stocked working crossbows, but their ammunition as well. Melissa's demonstration yesterday in the jousting arena proved she was skilled with the weapon, but for the life of me I couldn't see her as a murderer. Besides, it was well known around the county that she was too timid to even talk back to her bossy husband, let alone kill someone she knew only in passing.

"Do you know where Elvin is now?" I asked Emilio. "As much as I hate the idea, I need to tell him something."

Emilio jerked his head in the direction of the RV parking area. "He's still back there. My advice is to stay out of his way, but do what you have to do."

I tucked the LLAMA RIDES sign under my arm and headed for Peasant's Retreat. Finding Elvin was easy; all I had to do was follow the cries of outrage.

He was outside the RV shared by Deanna and Judd Sazac, who took turns manning the Information Booth. Standing next to them were Howie Fife, the Faire's teenage "leper," whose injured ankle remained wrapped in bandages, and Dr. Willis Pierce, head of the Drama Department at San Sebastian Community College. Dr. Pierce had been roaming the Faire dressed as Shakespeare, quoting the sonnets and handing out flyers advertising the school's upcoming production of *Much Ado About Nothing*. The four of them were strung out along the side of the Sazacs' motor home like suspects in a lineup. The adults merely looked miffed but seventeen-year-old Howie appeared petrified.

"What do you mean, your costume disappeared and you didn't tell anyone?" Elvin screamed at the kid.

"I…I…"

"Quiet, Howie," Dr. Pierce snapped. "You don't have to tell Deputy Dade anything. You're a minor. *Ex parentis*. Keep silent until your mother gets back with breakfast."

"Oh, so you're a lawyer now, Pierce?" Elvin sneered. "Just because you're some fancy-pants college teacher doesn't mean you know what you're talking about."

Pierce rolled his eyes. "'The fool doth think he is wise, but the wise man knows himself to be a fool.' *As You Like It*, Act V, Scene I."

Rightly suspecting he'd been insulted, Elvin scowled. "What's that supposed to mean?"

"It's a quote from a play," I said, jumping in. "Elvin, before you question these folks any further, I have important information for you."

He transferred his scowl to me. "Teddy Bentley, did I or did I not tell you to address me as Acting Sheriff Dade?"

If Pierce rolled his eyes any further, they'd unscrew from his head. Averting my own eyes from that fascinating display, I answered, "Sorry, Acting Sheriff Dade. It's just that I…"

"Let me guess. You want to stick your nose in another murder case. Go back to your big hairy pet."

I threw a despairing glance at Dr. Pierce, who rolled his eyes again. As I walked away the other deputies gave me sympathetic looks. They didn't like the situation, either, but there was little they could do about it.

On the way to the Queen's Bakery I ran into Ada Fife, Howie's mother. She carried a tray loaded with muffins and coffee, and was walking slowly so as not to drop or spill anything.

"Ada, Elvin Dade is giving Howie a bad time."

She looked so startled she almost dropped the tray. "What? Are you sure?"

"I'm afraid so. Dr. Pierce is trying to protect him, but you've lived here long enough to know what a dunderhead Elvin is. He's asking Howie all sorts of questions, so you'd better..."

I wasn't finished with my sentence before Ada hustled off toward the RV parking area, coffee sloshing as she ran.

A few minutes later I'd purchased my own coffee and a bran muffin the size of a soccer ball. By now it was almost eight, and even local Faire workers who had been lucky enough to spend the night in their own beds at home were trickling in. The day was warming up and the remnants of the morning fog burned off. When I entered the food tent, everyone was talking about last night's events.

"I heard the guy was shot," said a rotund jester I didn't recognize. In his yellow and orange costume, he looked like an overripe peach.

"My money's on a stabbing," a sleepy-eyed monk offered. "I didn't hear any shots."

"Considering what you were up to with that blonde last night, you wouldn't have heard the charge of the Light Brigade."

The monk snickered. "Methinks I detect a note of jealousy."

"Next time, take it outside. As a favor to me."

"Anything to make the court jester happy." The monk's face grew serious. "Speaking of court, how's the Royal Progress going to be handled today? No king, no Progress?"

The jester brushed away a fly. "The buzz going around is that they asked that Shakespeare guy from the college to step in, seeing as how he's so good at the lingo. He's the right height, if not weight, but I imagine pillows will help with that."

"The King is dead, long live the King."

I was a quarter way through my muffin when Melissa and Cary Keegan sat down across from me. The couple manned the Royal Armory and ran a mail order medieval and Goth weapons company from their house in San Sebastian. From spring to fall they travelled the circuit from Renaissance faire to Renaissance faire throughout the west to sell their wicked-looking wares, spending almost as much time in their RV than at home. I noticed that even though it had a well-equipped kitchen, they had purchased coffee and rolls from the bakery. The better to hear gossip about last night?

Given Cary's shoulder-length black hair, multiple ear studs and nose rings, he looked like Satan on his way to collect a soul. He was study in black: black beard, black fingernail polish, black leather vest, black satin shirt, black leather pants, and black leather boots. All he needed to complete the resemblance to Old Scratch was a forked tail.

Melissa wore black, too, but on her it wasn't scary. The bodice of her long ebony dress barely covered her milk-white breasts, and her matching eye shadow and lipstick played up her flawless skin. The monk and jester almost fell off their bench ogling her. When Cary shot them a look they hurriedly returned their attentions to their muffins.

"Cops arrest anyone yet?" Cary asked me as soon as he sat down, confirming my suspicions.

"You mean Acting Sheriff Dade? Not that I know of."

"I thought he was quite rude when he questioned us this morning," Melissa said, her voice a vulnerable soprano. "He's not a very nice man, is he?"

"Nice" not being a word normally associated with Elvin Dade, I made no reply.

"When we left the RV this morning," she continued, "I heard a couple of the ladies-in-waiting talking. One of them said she'd gone down to the llama pen when she heard all the noise. She got close enough to see everything and she said it looked to her like a crossbow dart killed Victor, but I don't see how…"

"That's enough, Melissa," her husband said.

"But Cary, that missing crossbow, it wasn't my fault! I keep as close an eye on our stock as possible, but with all I had to do…"

"Quiet!" he hissed.

"Don't you see that…"

"Melissa," I said, "When Elvin Dade finds out about the missing crossbow he might want to talk to you again, so you'd better get your story straight."

"Mind your own business, Teddy," Cary snapped. Then, to his wife, "Time to open the booth."

"But I've only started drinking my coffee. And I haven't touched my muffin." Melissa couldn't have sounded more mournful if her dog had just died.

He frowned. "Bring it with you. On second thought, leave it here. I don't want it slopping all over the stock."

Ignoring her protests, he dragged her away.

"That brute doesn't deserve her," the monk said to the jester.

"I thought you preferred blondes," the jester parried, as he helped himself to Melissa's leftovers.

"Depends on the brunette."

Looking around, I saw that Cary's behavior had had the same effect on all the men. The women appeared more puzzled than outraged. Especially Speaks-To-Souls, who had entered the big tent with her greyhounds in time to catch the end of the conversation. Spotting me, the animal psychic came over to my table.

"What did you think of that little scene?" She smoothed her white abbess robe and sat down carefully, greyhounds at her feet.

"The monk said it best, Cary's a brute."

"Making Melissa a damsel in distress?"

Her tone surprised me. "That's what it looked like to me."

"Yes, it did, didn't it?"

Uncomfortable, I changed the subject. After we shared a thorough rehashing of last night's events, Speaks-To-Souls mused, "I wonder what Victor was doing in the llama enclosure."

I had wondered, too, before remembering that Victor once officiated at a wedding between a couple of San Sebastian llama owners who brought along their two llamas to serve as best man and maid of honor. The local newspaper ran an article about their nuptials, illustrated with a picture of the bride and groom in formal wedding attire posed between the llamas. It was my guess that besides the vows themselves, there had been a certain amount of conversation between all parties about the animals' frequent use as herd guards.

"Maybe Victor thought Alejandro would protect him," I said.

"Isn't Alejandro a spitter?"

"Getting spit on's better than a crossbow dart in the neck. Besides, I doubt if he knew about Alejandro's dislike of adults."

"Hmm."

I raised an eyebrow. "Hmm?"

"Well, we'll see, won't we? Which brings me to the main reason I wanted to talk to you. Have you seen your mother this morning?"

"Caro? No, why?"

"You might want to give her a call."

"I'm sure I'll see her sometime today. She's supposed to take part in this morning's Royal Progress."

"Call her anyway. When I was walking over here, I passed Bambi O'Dair. She was talking to Deputy what's-his-name, and I didn't like what I heard."

"Elvin Dade. And he prefers being addressed as Acting Sheriff Dade."

A faint smile from Speaks-To-Souls.

"Anyway, why should anything Bambi says worry you?" I asked. "She's the kind of blonde that gives all blondes a bad name. She…" I stopped, remembering the conversation between the jester and the monk. The monk had spent a noisy night with a blonde. Bambi, perchance? The woman did have a reputation for being free with her affections.

Speaks-To-Souls interrupted my thoughts. "I heard Bambi tell Elvin Dade that your mother threatened to kill Victor. Behead him, I think."

I laughed. "Caro's always running her mouth. It doesn't mean a thing."

"Does Elvin Dade know that?"

"He should, since he's known her all her life. Went to high school with her, dated her once, even asked her out again one time when she was between marriages, the second and third ones, I think. Or was it the third and fourth? Mother's been married so many times it's hard to keep track. No, it had to be between the second and third, because not long afterward, Elvin married Wynona Foster from over in Castroville, and they've been together for, what, fifteen years? Twenty? As a matter of fact, Victor officiated at their wedding. This was before Wynona got religion, and still thought one reverend was as good as another. But since they were all dressed normally and didn't bring any animals with them, they didn't get their picture in the paper. She's younger than Elvin, but it wasn't like she was a child bride or anything, so there was no story there."

Speaks-To-Souls face hadn't lost its solemnity. "Caro needs to know what Bambi's been saying, Teddy."

I glanced at my watch. "She'll be driving in from Gunn Landing any minute. I'll stop by the Royal Pavilion and tell her to turn her mouth off, at least until all this blows over."

I probably should have taken Speaks-To-Souls' advice and called Caro right away, not that it would have made any difference. By the time the Faire opened for the Sunday crowds, Acting Sheriff Elvin Dade had already placed my mother under arrest.

Chapter Three

I should have known something was wrong on Sunday when Caro didn't show up for the King's Progress. I have two excuses. One: sick as it sounds, murder is good publicity. The Faire was twice as crowded as yesterday, and given the business boom in Llama Rides, I had no time to hunt my mother down. Two: sometime during the morning my cell phone died and I was too busy to notice. Between the hectic work and a cell phone too dead to chirp, I remained blissfully unaware of my mother's situation until the Faire closed for the weekend, and I had trailered Alejandro back to the zoo, then returned to my home in Gunn Landing Harbor.

The village of Gunn Landing lies a few miles north of Monterey and sits on a quarter-mile-wide strip between the Pacific Ocean and the coast highway. The village is so small that most residents, such as myself, live on boats in the harbor. We're called liveaboarders, a clumsy word for describing people whose lives are ruled by the tides and whose diets are rich in fresh fish. My own floating home is the *Merilee*, a refitted thirty-four foot trawler berthed at the southern end of the harbor.

A thirty-four foot boat sounds roomy enough, especially since it's almost twelve feet wide at the beam, but the actual walking-around room is less than twenty feet. The rest of the boat's interior was taken up by the bulkheads, cabinets, forward and aft bunks, and the galley with its built-in eating area. Houseboat living isn't for claustrophobes.

But it can be soothing. When I first came into possession of the *Merliee* after my return from San Francisco, I replaced the *Merilee*'s former party boat decor. Now the forward cabin bunk was covered with a pale blue spread and plump cushions depicting dolphins and whales. The aft bedroom, where my pets and I slept, boasted an otter theme. Small though my boat is, living aboard is no hardship. Imagine waking to the pitter-patter of pelicans waddling around on your roof, or cries of seagulls following the fishing boats out to sea. No matter what I've gone through during the day, watching the sun set from the *Merilee*'s deck brings peace to my soul.

Not tonight, though.

As I stepped aboard the *Merilee*, the sun had already dipped into the Pacific, fog was rolling in, and the other liveaboarders were battening down their hatches for the evening. Bluish TV light flickered from nearby portholes. From the boat next to mine, I heard Wolf Blitzer delivering the evening news. Taxes were up, income was down, same old same old. Tuning out, I concentrated on the good things of life: my furry companions.

When I entered the cabin, DJ Bonz, the three-legged terrier mix I'd rescued from Death Row at the pound, rushed to meet me. *Love ya, love ya, gimme food, gimme walkies*, he yipped. Miss Priss, the one-eyed Persian mix adopted from the same pound, merely stalked over to her bowl and stared at me as haughtily as a one-eyed cat can stare. I fed them both, then sat in the galley and watched them eat. The tide was going out, rocking the *Merilee* ever so gently. Above the slurps and gulps of my pets, I could hear the soft shush-shush of the waves against her hull. Serenaded by the sea, I began to nod off, only to be startled back into wakefulness when Bonz jumped into my lap and licked my face.

Walkies! Walkies!

"Oh, Bonz, you're so subtle." Since he was in such a hurry, I put off changing out of my Renaissance duds and took him for his walk.

Gunn Landing Park, located on the other side of the harbor's parking lot, was empty except for three other liveaboarders walking their own dogs. We waved at each other through the thickening fog, but other than that, kept our distance. Linda Cushing had obviously followed through on her promise to care for my animals, because Bonz had little to do other than mark his territory. Less than ten minutes after I left the *Merilee* we returned, only to find Linda, my elderly neighbor, standing on the deck. She wore an anxious expression and held an open can of dog food in her hand.

"Oh, thank heaven, there he is!" she exclaimed. "I was afraid he'd gotten out somehow. But what in the world are you doing here, Teddy? I thought for sure you'd be at the jail."

"To visit Joe? He's away on that Homeland Security thing."

She gave me a peculiar look. "No, Teddy. To see your mother."

"To see Caro? What do you mean?"

The odd look transformed into one of pity. "You don't know, do you?"

"What don't I know?"

She glanced at her watch. "If you leave right now, you'll get to the jail in time for evening visiting hours. I'm sure Caro can tell you more than I can. If you want, I'll even drive you over there. Maybe that's best, seeing as how you're bound to be pretty upset and all. What do you think?"

I've always liked Linda, but I was getting tired of these guessing games. Normally a forthright person—too much so, for some people—tonight she would have won a gold medal for obtuseness. "For the last time, Linda, what don't I know and what's it got to do with Caro?"

She reached over and grabbed Bonz's leash. "I'll settle him in, because I want you to get in that truck of yours right now and head for the San Sebastian jail. That stupid man Sheriff Joe left in charge has gone and arrested her."

"Joe didn't leave Elvin in ch…Wait a minute. Did you just say that Elvin arrested my mother?"

"I'm afraid so."

"What the hell for?"

"For murdering that guy who ran the wedding chapel. At least that's what the local news said. At first I couldn't believe it, because, well, we all know what Caro's like, don't we, but she's not really crazy enough to kill anyone. At least I don't think she is. Why, I've known her for years and the worst thing you can say about…"

"Gotta go!"

As I ran for my truck, her voice trailed after me, "…her is that she's an awful snob."

◇◇◇

I made the fifteen-mile drive inland in record time. Five minutes after walking into the San Sebastian County Jail, I sat facing my mother through a Plexiglas window in the visitors' area. She was upset, but not for the reasons you would think.

"It's appalling, Theodora, simply appalling. This morning, not realizing that I'd be wearing a vulgar orange jumpsuit so shapeless it could have been made by a blind tailor, I had a Tawny Pink mani/pedi because the subdued hues would look so cunning with my lavender lady-in-waiting gown. Now look at me. If I'd known what lay in store, I would have opted for something in the bronze family like that Sun-Kissed Copper I've been eyeing. You know who I blame for all this? That precious fiancé of yours, that's who, for being tasteless enough to buy this nasty thing. Orange, I tell you. Orange!"

Folding her arms across her surgically-assisted chest, she sat back on the other side of the Plexiglass with an expression of triumph, having scored another one against Joe.

"Clashing colors should be the least of your worries. Here you are, sitting in jail, about to be charged with murder. For Pete's sake, Moth…"

"How many times do I have to tell you to call me Caro!"

I had to count to ten before I could speak. "Caro, please tell me you at least called an attorney."

For a moment, a fleeting moment, an expression of concern crossed her face. "As to that, I used up all the calls allowed me trying to reach you. After my sixth attempt, that vile Elvin had me locked up in a cell. Which reminds me. Did you know that jails furnish their cells with blue plastic mattresses? You can imagine how that looks next to an orange jumpsuit. No sheets or pillows, either, just a nasty blanket some homeless person probably threw away."

I took a deep breath. "Then I'll call an attorney for you. You're due in court for a bail hearing tomorrow."

"Don't be ridiculous. Why should I waste good money because of a fool like Elvin?"

"Caro, don't you understand how much trouble you're in?"

"Elvin has no sense, Theodora. Surely you can see that."

This was impossible. "Mo…Uh, Caro, why don't you tell me what happened? There must have been a terrible mistake, because there's no way you would kill anyone, let alone Victor Emerson."

"That's the first time you've said something sensible. If I were going to kill anyone it would be that simpering creature who calls herself Bambi. She drives a pink Cadillac, can you possibly get any more vulgar than that? Pink! And have you seen her breasts? They remind me of that old Ripley cartoon, *Believe It Or Not*."

Before I could stop myself, I said, "Bambi's only one cup size larger than you."

"Two. And on her, they look cheap. She probably went to some bargain-basement surgeon, whereas I use only the best. Are you sure you don't want a little work done, Theodora? There should be lush bosoms peeking out from that Faire dress of yours, but all I can see are two little bumps. Having your best interests at heart, I'd be glad to foot the bill."

Whenever I try to have a serious conversation with my mother, she always goes off on a tangent. Mother has a brain, but it's rusty from disuse. This is what happens when a woman is in the habit of getting by on her looks. In her late fifties—I could never pin her down on her exact age—she is still so beautiful that her ex-husbands come running whenever she crooks a manicured finger. In fact, getting married to, then divorced by Caro, has become an odd sort of status symbol among the men

then stepped out into the chilly air. While I'd been at the jail, night had fallen and it was full dark. With rush hour over, or what passes for rush hour in this sparsely populated section of the county, it could be hours before anyone else came along, so I decided to hike up the hill to Gunn Castle and use one of the phones there. Mind you, I was still wearing my wannabe "buxom wench" garb from the Faire, which would hamper my climb, yet I had little choice. Caro needed an attorney and she needed one now.

Hitching up my dress, I abandoned the truck and set off.

The Gunn Estate is a large one. Several hundred acres of vineyard stretched before me, the earth beneath the vines cold and damp. But to continue on foot to the side road that paralleled the estate and wound its way around the hill to finish up at the zoo would double the distance. So into the muck I stepped.

A half-hour later I arrived on Aster Edwina Gunn's stately doorstep. I felt like hell and looked it, too. My feet were covered in mud and my long skirt was wet to the waist.

"Why, Miss Bentley," said Mrs. McGinty, the housekeeper, when she answered the door. "What a nice surprise."

"Not for me," I muttered, entering the vast marble entryway. It was still flanked by the same two suits of armor that had terrified me as a young girl, and they looked just as menacing now as they had then. "I hiked up here through the vineyard and got bogged down in the mud." At her questioning look, I added, "Flat tire. The nearest phone's in the library, right? I need to call an attorney. Then AAA."

Mrs. McGinty's face took on a sorrowful expression. "Car trouble can happen in the most inconvenient places. And I take it you're calling an attorney for your mother? We here at the castle all heard about Mrs. Bentley..." Confusion chased the sorrowful expression away. "Mrs. er..."

Not for the first time I wished Caro would stop changing her name every time she got married. "My mother's current last name is..." I had to think a moment. "...ah, it's Mrs. Petersen now. For a while, anyway. Yes, Caro's in trouble, and it's serious.

She needs the best lawyer I can find and as fast as I can get him over to the jail."

"Might I suggest Albert Grissom, at Hamilton, Lawler and Grissom? He successfully handled some recent unpleasant- ness for the family, and I'm certain he'll do the same for your mother." Reaching into her pocket, she pulled out a cell phone and handed it to me. "Given your muddy feet, using the phone in the library isn't a good idea. Aster Edwina had the Aubusson rugs cleaned the other day, and you know how she is." With the steely grip of a nightclub bouncer, she dope-walked me past the armor and over to a massive Jacobean armchair. "While you make your calls, I'll fetch a water basin and towels. And some hot chocolate. You're shivering."

Before I could say "Don't trouble yourself on my account," she bustled off.

First things first. I called the attorney, and after answering a few uncomfortable questions, many of them financial, he prom- ised to be at the courthouse first thing tomorrow morning. Then I called AAA. No, I wouldn't be with the truck. No, I couldn't remember the license number, but I was certain it was the only elderly Nissan pickup mired in a ditch on Old Bentley Road ten miles west of San Sebastian. Yes, I'm an AAA member, yes, haul it to the nearest open garage, yes, I know that's probably in Monterey, yes, here's my membership number, yes, you have a nice day, too.

When Mrs. McGinty returned with the promised comforts, Aster Edwina Gunn was right behind her.

"What have you gotten yourself into now, Theodora?" the old harridan asked, as Mrs. McGinty wrapped a heavy blanket around my shoulders.

"Mud."

"I'm not blind. But whatever for?"

"Truck broke down." I took a deep swig of hot chocolate.

"Not trailering that poor llama, I hope. If you've let anything happen to him your head will roll." Despite her advanced age and wealth, Aster Edwina micro-managed the zoo and all its animals and employees with the energy and attention to detail of a much younger person.

"Alejandro's safe at the zoo. I took him there as soon as the Faire closed."

"He'd better be all right. I have a soft spot for that animal. Unlike humans, he's honest about his feelings." When she smiled, she looked like a hawk about to pounce on a mouse. Not even time had softened her features. "But what's all this I hear about Caro murdering Victor Emerson?"

"She didn't."

"So you say."

"Yes, I do say, and so would you if you gave it any thought. For heaven's sake, Aster Edwina, you've known Mother since she was a child. Have you ever known her to hurt anyone?"

Never one to let a "gotcha" moment pass, Aster Edwina flashed me a look of triumph. "If you'll remember, Theodora, she once delivered a roundhouse right to my nose, almost breaking it. Quite an arm your mother has."

Oops. I'd forgotten that long-ago nose bashing incident. "She only hit you because you'd spanked me with a riding crop."

"Which I had every right to do since I caught you sneaking into my vineyard." She looked at my feet. "Oh, my, do I detect a pattern here? In case you don't remember, you were swiping grapes. Repeatedly. For weeks. Have you resumed your thieving practices? Anyway, Caro was always too lenient with you, and it was time somebody taught you a lesson. Now tell me, how is your mother? Is she confortable? I hear the facilities at the San Sebastian County Jail are less than stellar."

I know when to holler uncle. As Mrs. McGinty took off my muddy shoes and scrubbed my filthy feet, I brought Aster Edwina up to date, leaving out all that business about color palettes. She listened carefully until I finished, then pronounced Elvin Dade an unmitigated idiot.

"By the time Sheriff Rejas gets back from Washington, Elvin will have the county knee-deep in lawsuits," she said. "The ninny should have been forcibly retired years ago. It's unfortunate that he's the attorney general's brother. Proves the old saying that every family has its idiot, doesn't it?"

I agreed, not that it did any good. Although Caro's arrest had been without due cause, she was still trapped in a six by nine cell for the night. "I plan to be in the courtroom tomorrow when the judge sets bail. Then I'll drive her home."

"No you won't."

"What do you mean? Of course I'll be there for her."

"Show up at work or get fired. With so many zookeepers on vacation, we're short-handed enough as it is."

"But my mother..."

Aster Edwina interrupted before I could tell her Caro needed her make-up kit. "Don't be such a worry-wart, Theodora. You called Albert Grissom, didn't you? Brilliant attorney, brilliant. He'll have her out of that cell in a heartbeat."

I began to relax. Aster Edwina might be pitiless, but she's always right.

Most of the time, anyway.

In the end, the old woman softened enough to let her chauffeur take me home. During the drive down Old Bentley Road, we found ourselves stuck behind the tow truck hauling my battered Nissan.

The poor thing looked as depressed as I felt.

Chapter Four

The next morning one of my liveaboard neightbors gave me a lift to Monterey, and I picked up my Nissan. Then, taking Aster Edwina's threat seriously, I worked my usual shift at the Gunn Zoo. In between frantic calls to Caro's attorney on the cellphone I'd finally recharged, I fed tigers, shoveled anteater poop, and estimated how far along in her pregnancy Wanchu the koala might be. I wasn't only covering for one zookeeper, but two. Jack Spence, the bear keeper, was in Africa with Robin Chase, the big cats keeper, and rumor had it that romance was in the air.

Romance was in the air at the zoo, too, springtime being breeding time for thousands of species. Take the Galapagos tortoises, for instance. Big Tim was busy knocking up Big Lil, and the noise they made while mating horrified some prim zoo visitors.

"Make them stop!" begged a Rotarian-type male as I trundled by with a wheelbarrow full of anteater dung. The man looked like he was about to have a heart attack. "They're upsetting my children."

Oh, no, they weren't. The man's three kids, ranging in ages from around five to ten, were loving the triple-X display.

The Devil in me was tempted to send Shy Dad over to the Argentine duck enclosure, where the sixteen-inch-long male, in accordance with his species, had been busy all morning lassoing various females with his seventeen-inch-long, retractable penis.

But the Angel in me overcame my naughty side, and I merely answered, "Sir, it would be very difficult to stop an eight-hundred-pound tortoise from doing anything it wants, but even if I could, that would mean we wouldn't get any cute little Galapagos babies, would we?"

The wheelbarrow and I moved on.

The blue-footed boobies were at it, too, but theirs was a more restrained ritual. While emitting high whistles, the male marched around in a small circle, lifting his big blue feet up in the air as high as they would go while the female judged the angle of the lift. Unimpressed, she waddled away.

"Hang in there, big fella," I called. "Women have been known to change their minds."

As if he understood, the male waddled after her, still lifting his feet with the energy of a drum major on crack.

A few feet away from the boobies' enclosure, I stopped in the shade of a looming eucalyptus tree, pulled out my finally recharged cell, and called Albert Grissom again. When the attorney picked up, he sounded testy.

"No, Teddy, the hearing hasn't started yet, and haven't I told you a dozen times I'll call you as soon as it's over? You do realize, don't you, that I'll have to turn my cell off the minute I get into that courtroom?" Impatience roughed his pleasant tenor.

After I apologized, his voice softened and he added, "Between you and me and the lamppost, I'm hoping your mother keeps her mouth shut during the hearing. When I met with her this morning, she didn't come across as the most reasonable person. If you don't mind my asking, what is a color palette?"

I groaned. "Try to keep her quiet, that's all I'm asking. As for color palettes, it has something to do with a pink mani/pedi clashing with orange."

"As in jail jumpsuits?"

"Exactly."

He chortled. "She is beautifully groomed." The roughness had disappeared from his voice.

"You wouldn't happen to be single, would you, Mr. Grissom?"

"My divorce was final last month. Why?"

"If your annual income is in the seven-digit range or higher, I'd advise you to give my mother a wide berth after today's court proceedings."

"I don't understand."

"You will."

We rang off and I resumed my duties.

I've always seen the Gunn Zoo as the one perfect place in a naughty world. The three-hundred-acre private zoo—founded by Aster Edwina's father—is home to more than fifteen hundred species, ranging from anteaters to zebras, all exhibited in large enclosures that mimic their natural habitats. Among the zoo's collections are endangered animals such as snow leopards, Asian rhinos, red pandas, Bengal tigers, Andean bears, wooly leumurs, and cheetahs. At the back of the zoo, but not open to the public, is the one-hundred acre elephant sanctuary, where both African and Asian elephants roam free.

Working here is a privilege. No matter how irritating Aster Edwina can be, not one of her zookeepers would work anywhere else. Not only is the zoo large, but it is one of the most beautiful in Central California. More than three miles of walking trails weave in and out of eucalyptus forests, sun-dappled hills, and lush, bird-songed valleys. Every day here is a day spent in Eden.

But even in Eden there are chores.

And trouble.

After spending the next hour feeding, sweeping, and changing bedding in various enclosures, my mother's attorney still hadn't called back. To calm my nerves, I wandered over to Friendly Farm. Alejandro was on exhibit in the barnyard, surrounded by chickens, pygmy goats, and children. He looked happy. Not wanting to disturb him by my adult presence, I began to back away, but he caught sight of me.

"Maaa-yah!" he called, his head going up, ears pricked. Careful not to step on tiny toes, he moved forward until he was within spitting distance.

"Alejandro, please don't…"

He didn't. Instead, he nuzzled my neck. "Maaa, maaa."

"I love you too, Alejandro," I whispered. "We've been through a lot together, haven't we?"

"Maaa."

"I'm worried about Caro, you know."

"Maaa?"

"She's wily, but not always smart."

"Maaa." He nuzzled my neck again, offering comfort in that special way llamas can.

By this time, the children in the Friendly Farm enclosure had realized a species-to-species conversation was going on, so they came over to take part, trailed by two pygmy goats and a chicken.

"Does she know what you're saying?" asked a little boy of around four.

"He's a he, and his name's Alejandro. He probably doesn't understand my exact words, but llamas are very good at sensing our feelings. That's why people like them so much."

"Does he bite?"

"Never. Especially not children."

"Alejandro looks worried," said a slightly older girl who looked enough like the boy to be his sister.

"See what I mean about llamas sensing our feelings? I was worried about something, and he picked up on that."

She frowned. "What are you worried about?"

Rule Number One for zookeepers: never bother the visitors with your personal problems, even if you're bleeding profusely or your mother's been jailed. "I'm worried it might rain."

The children looked up at a cloudless sky. "I think you can stop worrying," the little girl said.

I looked up. "Oh. I think you're right. Smart girl!"

As the child congratulated herself on her superior intelligence, my cell phone chirped. Alejandro cocked his head. "Eep?"

"Excuse me, ladies and gentlemen and llama, but I must take this call." With that I hurried to a more isolated place in the exhibit.

It was Albert Grissom with bad news. Bail had been denied. Not because of the murder charge—Judge Feinstein, knowing Deputy Elvin Dade personally, scoffed at the arrest—but because Caro's subsequent behavior in the courtroom gave him no choice.

"Teddy," Grissom moaned, "The minute Judge Feinstein ruled your mother be released, she jumped up and began a tirade about conditions at the jail. When he tried to shush her, she accused him of being the unwitting pawn of an evil empire set up to guarantee the comfort of the upper classes at the detriment of the lower. She then turned around to the other prisoners who were awaiting the deposition of their cases and urged them to free themselves from their chains and unite to overthrow the class system."

My mouth dropped so low it was a miracle my lower lip didn't scoop up goat droppings. "That…that doesn't sound like Caro."

"You should have seen the fire in her eyes!" Grissom said, admiringly. "Unfortunately, Judge Feinstein was unimpressed, especially when the gangbangers behind your mother began rattling their shackles and shouting 'Fight the power!'" His voice took on a mournful quality. "The judge actually sentenced that magnificent woman to thirty days for incitement to riot."

What an ass, and I don't mean the judge. Grissom had obviously fallen under Caro's spell, becoming more fan boy than lawyer.

"Mr. Grissom, do you have any female attorneys in your office?"

"Call me Al, Teddy. Yes, why do you ask?"

"I want a woman handling my mother's case from now on."

"Surely you don't mean that."

After thinking carefully about my answer, I said, "Look, Mr. Gri…uh, Al, you're such a well-known attorney and all, as well as high-priced—justly, I hasten to add, considering your many achievements in California jurisprudence—but I think we need someone less expensive." And everybody knows women work cheaper than men; I had the paycheck to prove it.

"No problem, Teddy. I'll work pro bono."

Poor sap. I might as well start calling him "Dad" right now, because Caro knew a sucker when she saw one. Accepting the inevitable, I said, "Well, Al, do what you can for her. Caro has a tendency to be her own worst enemy."

"I understand. People with strong beliefs in social justice often behave that way, thus they become true martyrs."

Somehow I refrained from laughing. The only time Caro had ever felt martyred was the time she wore a pair of five inch Fendi pumps to meet the Duke and Duchess of Cambridge at the Pebble Beach National Pro-Am.

Chapter Five

After ending the call with Caro's attorney, I looked at my watch. Lunchtime. Normally, the San Sebastian County Jail was a half-hour's drive away, but my Nissan's new tires made it more zippy, so twenty minutes later, I was arguing with my mother through the Plexiglas barrier.

"What in the world do you think you're doing with this 'overthrow the class system' business, Caro? You never gave a hoot about the underprivileged before."

"Soledad Rodriguez has opened my eyes. Did you know that..."

"Soledad Rodriguez!" I yelped. "Surely you're not talking about the woman who heads up that Female Devils gang!"

"Their proper name is Demonios Femeninos, Theodora, and I'll thank you to remember that. And it's more like a sorority than a gang."

When she leaned back and crossed her arms in disapproval, I noticed her manicure now matched her orange jumpsuit, although the job looked rushed. "Who did your nails?"

"My cellmate. She doesn't understand cuticles."

"Where'd you get the nail polish? That's not something the jail normally keeps on hand."

"Al brought..."

"Al who?"

A scowl. "Albert Grissom, of course. My attorney. Please try to pay attention, Theodora. Anyway, dear Al brought me a complete manicure kit, just as I requested. The corrections officer had to take away the metal nail file, but she let me keep the emery boards. Perhaps the color selection isn't all I could wish for, he must have picked it up at some discount drugstore, but when you're fighting the power you have to make sacrifices."

"Your lawyer brought you a manicure kit and the guards let you keep it?"

"That's what I said."

"Why?"

"Why what?"

"Why did the guards let you keep a manicure kit?" Food I could understand. Magazines, books, a Bible, the Koran, the Ark of the Covenant. But a manicure kit?

"Guard. Singular. A lovely girl named Annabelle, whose mother once worked for your father's firm. Before he embezzled all that money, which he should never have done, at least that's what the Federal prosecutor said, although I think…"

"Stick to the subject at hand."

She gave me a look. "I swear, Teddy, sometimes I despair of your temper. Let's see, what were we talking about before you turned into Mr. Hyde? Oh, yes, Annabelle. Surely you don't hold to the antiquated belief that all jail guards should be male. If so, let me set you straight. Fully one-third of the corrections officers here are female and they understand the necessity for every woman to put her best foot forward, especially when incarcerated by the male-dominated ruling class."

This time I counted to ten before I spoke. It didn't help. "So you are telling me that your attorney brought you a manicure kit and that your cellmate did your nails but she doesn't understand cuticles. What does your cellmate do for a living, drive getaway cars?"

"Hardly. Soledad is a…"

"Soledad Rodriguez is your cellmate?!"

A disapproving frown. "I'll have you know she's never been convicted of anything other than a misdemeanor."

"What was that for? Bank robbery with plastic explosives and a machete?"

"Bank robbery is a felony, you foolish child. No, poor Soledad was convicted of littering for passing out fliers at the La Raza Parade last year. The judge actually gave her thirty days, which I find outrageous."

"What did the fliers say? '*Arise, revolt, and behead?*'"

She pursed her perfect lips and folded her arms in front of her, the very picture of a disapproving parent. "Considering the circumstances, Theodora, I find your sarcasm to be sorely out of place. The fliers merely announced the grand opening of her uncle's new auto parts store."

"Soledad was charged with a misdemeanor for that?"

"Some of the fliers blew away in the wind. Well, maybe a lot of them did."

Aha. Not for nothing had the city of San Sebastian won the coveted title "The Cleanest Small Town in Central California" the past three years in a row. In San Sebastian, litterers were considered only slightly less reprehensible than serial killers. However, given Demonios Femeninos' fearsome reputation, the misdemeanor charge was probably the law's way of getting the gang leader off the streets. For a while, at least.

"What's she in for now? Re-littering?"

"She's awaiting trial."

"For what?"

"Homicide. But the man was already dead when she got there."

Not only was my mother in jail, but she was being housed with a probable murderer. "Who'd she kill?"

"Didn't I tell you that the man was already dead?"

With some difficulty, I kept my voice steady. "Then who was the already-dead-man she didn't kill?"

"Your lack of knowledge of current events is appalling, Theodora. You should spend more time reading the newspapers."

"I've been busy. Who was it?"

Mother shifted her eyes to her orange nails, then to the corrections officer standing behind her, back to her nails, then to a spot somewhere beyond my left shoulder. Speaking to the air, she said, "The victim was Duane Langer."

Now I remembered. Last week Langer, the titular head of Viking Vengeance, had been found shot to death in a San Sebastian alleyway. And wasn't there something…"Mother, wasn't Soledad Rodriguez found standing over him with the murder weapon in her hand? And didn't all this happen on Demonios Femeninos' turf, where Viking Vengeance was forbidden to go?"

"It's Caro."

"Excuse me?"

"How many times do I have to remind you to call me Caro?"

Oh, for the love of…

Here my mother was, locked up in jail for the next thirty days, her cellmate was a suspected murderer, and all she cared about was her color palatte and what she considered was the proper way to address her.

"Okay. Caro."

She sniffed in satisfaction. "Yes, if you must know, Soledad admits she was holding the gun, and that he was on her gang's turf, and furthermore, I really don't care who killed the despicable Duane. Be that as it may, Theodora. I want you to…"

"You want me to tell your attorney to bring your furs and jewelry?"

"No, Miss Sass. Al doesn't have entrée to my house, not yet, anyway, so I need you to go over there and pick up my Le Bleu Crème Pour le Visage. The air in this place is so dry I despair of my complexion."

"Considering that you're sitting in jail, what does it matter what your complexion looks like?"

She gave me a look of disbelief. "In the eyes of a man, a woman's years are like dog years. By the way, while you're at the house, get Feroz Guerro and drive him back to your boat. The maid's been taking care of him, but I'd rather have him stay with you for the duration now that the ruling class had decided to keep me locked up for a month simply for exercising my civil rights to free speech."

"For inciting a riot, you mean."

"Whatever."

◇◇◇

Another thing I like about animals is that, unlike people, you can always count on them. Granted, in some cases that means you can count on them to bite your eyes out, but at least you're fore-warned enough to safeguard against such behavior. Take Maharaja, for instance, our five hundred pound Bengal tiger. As I guided my wheelbarrow into the protected area behind his enclosure, he attempted to claw my arm off through the bars separating us.

"Missed again, big boy," I said, happy to see him so feisty.

He snarled.

"My, what big teeth you have."

Threat duly delivered, he sat back and watched in eager anticipation while I readied his daily bloodsicle.

Tigers are predators. Unless given something to exercise their I'm-gonna-kill-and-eat-you instincts they grow bored, and a bored tiger is a doubly dangerous tiger. Thus Maharaja's beloved bloodsicle, a frozen half-pound tube of cow blood infused with turkey strips.

Maharaja knew the drill. As soon as I attached the bloodsicle to a long bungee cord, he padded over to the thick gate that led to his night house. Once it slid open, he entered. The gate immediately shut, but I could still hear him pacing and snarling and grumbling as I hurried into his enclosure and made my way to the live oak that stood in the middle. While a curious group of zoo visitors gathered to watch, I hung the bungee cord from one of the higher limbs so Maharaja would have to work to get at his bloodsicle. Once it was secured I returned to the protected area and pressed the remote control button that opened his gate.

The crowd ooohed and aaahed as the big Bengal rushed out with a mighty roar and made straight for the bloodsicle. He leaped into the air, and with the swing of a huge paw, snagged a fist-sized chunk of iced blood. After making quick work of it he leaped again, this time coming away with only a finger-sized bite.

"Better luck next time," I called, leaving.

Behind me, a louder chorus of ooooh's informed me that he had made a more successful leap.

Zoo visitors frequently ask me why we make getting at food so difficult for our animals, even the less-lethal ones like the tiny squirrel monkeys over in Monkey Mania. We're not trying to frustrate them or tire them out, which in the case of the Bengals is not a bad idea, but we want to keep our animals healthy. Enclosures at the Gunn Zoo are quite large and designed to mimic an animal's native territory, but they still cannot be as large as an unfenced jungle or savannah where animals can roam and run for miles every day.

All wild animals work for their food. In the case of the big cats, that means running down a gazelle or zebra. For elephants, it means stretching their trunks high in the air to pick the foliage off trees. Constant activity in the wild keeps animals mentally alert, their circulation healthy, and their muscles toned. Zoos match these natural workouts by something called behavioral enrichment, a series of cleverly designed food stations in each enclosure, where in order to get food, animals must make the same types of physical movements they would make in the wild. Thus our big cats leap for treats, and elephants stretch to obtain hay from bales hung from tall eucalyptus trees.

Practicing behavioral enrichment is especially fun with the squirrel monkeys. In their case, it not only means coaxing them to climb, but figuring out ways to make them use their fingers and brains. For them, we had created an ongoing, ever-changing game of Hide and Seek. Later today, I would stash a mixture of dried crickets and fresh fruit into camouflaged boxes throughout their enclosure in order to get them off their little rumps.

But first I needed to visit Maharani. Having gone off heat, Maharaja's mate now occupied the enclosure next door. Bengals are solitary animals; after their brief but frenzied mating encounters, the pair lost interest in each other. Therefore the impregnated Maharani was left alone with her very own bloodsicle.

Environmental enrichment of a different sort took place in the cheetah brothers' digs. While Abasi and Akida looked on from the other side of the gate, I attached part of a beef haunch to a motorized pulley, then flicked the switch and sent the carcass on a thirty-mile-per-hour trip around their enclosure. Once I took myself to safety and opened the gate, the cheetahs joyfully bounded after it. Akida, the quicker of the two, brought down their prey as it neared the second turn, delighting both me and the crowd gathered to watch.

Compared to that, hiding dried crickets and fruit from the monkeys was no big deal.

By the time my rounds took me to Friendly Farm, the pleasure I took in caring for my four-legged friends had made me forget about my mother's woes. But when Alejandro trotted over to me I had a brief flashback of Victor Emerson lying dead at his feet. I tried not to convey my unhappiness to Alejandro while refreshing the water in the barnyard's big trough, but llamas are sensitive creatures and little gets past them.

"Errr?" he asked, nuzzling my neck in an apparent attempt to comfort me.

"I was thinking about how sad it is, what happened to poor Victor."

"Maaam" More nuzzling.

"Who killed him, Alejandro?"

"Maaam."

I scratched his ears. "No, Mother's off the hook for that."

"Maaam." He lowered his head and gently butted my chest.

"But she's still in jail."

I was about to tell him how much I missed Joe when a group of children entering the barnyard caught his attention. He raised his head and flicked his ears toward the piping voices. His big brown eyes gazed at me soulfully. "Eeep?"

"Sure, go play with them. I know how much you love kids."

As if he understood, he turned away and trotted toward the children, humming happily.

After I had added fresh hay to his manger, then returned the wheelbarrow to the equipment shed, I noticed that the Reptile House across the way and the area surrounding it were being cordoned off by yellow warning tape. Concerned, I approached Phil Holt, who was married to my friend Deborah, who worked at Friendly Farms. The head reptile keeper's gaunt face looked stricken.

"Has there been an accident?" I asked.

"Not yet," he said, his voice edgy. "But Sssybil's missing. She wasn't in her exhibit when I went to feed her a few minutes ago. Apparently the bottom hinge on her door rusted through, and she managed to get out through a small opening. We were about to call a Code Red and clear everyone out of the zoo, but then Nicci here..." he motioned toward another worried-looking zookeeper, "saw signs she was heading for the vineyard."

The Reptile House backed up on the huge Gunn Vineyard, which was good in that Sssybil, a four-foot-long Mojave rattle-snake, wouldn't be injecting her venom into some unfortunate Gunn Zoo visitor. But it was bad in that one of Aster Edwina's workers might get bitten or instead, kill Sssybil in what he saw as self-defense. June wasn't a busy time for the vineyard but on the way to work this morning I saw several men pulling weeds between the rows.

The venom of a Mojave rattlesnake is highly potent, ten times more toxic than any of the other eighteen species of North American rattlesnakes. To get fanged by one is a serious matter. The venom not only keeps a victim's blood from clotting, but it also contains a neurotoxin that causes respiratory paralysis if the victim isn't immediately treated with antivenom. Even then, there will be a certain amount of necrosis, possibly resulting in the loss of fingers or even a hand.

And yes, snake bites were usually on the hand, a man's hand to be exact, because men were more quick to prove their machismo than women. The joke among herpetologists was that the words most commonly heard before a snake bite were, "Hold my beer and watch this!"

I hoped Aster Edwina's vineyard workers had more sense. "Did you call Aster Edwina for permission to search her property?" I asked Phil.

"We contacted her immediately and since she knows what's up with these Mojaves she said yes. Several keepers have volunteered for the hunt, but until we find her, this area has to stay off limits. The chance is slim that she might get hungry and return on her own, because that vineyard's filled with snake food. Mice, ground squirrels, lizards, what have you, it's got them all. And fresh, not freeze-dried, like she gets here."

As much as I wanted to join the search party there was already too much on my plate. I wished Phil good luck and continued my chores.

The rest of my workday passed quickly and six o'clock found me still in my zoo uniform, letting myself into Caro's house in Gunn Landing's Old Town, the wealthy enclave sitting high on a hill overlooking the Pacific Ocean. Feroz Guerrero, Caro's miniscule Chihuahua, met me at the door. He kept me trapped in the hall until he'd explored every strange odor on my clothes: eau de monkey, cheetah, tiger, llama, anteater, koala, sheep, chicken, and goat.

Pulling a tan lip away from an incisor in a tiny sneer, he asked, "Aark?"

"Yes, Feroz, I'm afraid I stepped in goat dung at Friendly Farm. I'll try to be more careful next time, but you know how it is. When you're busy, you don't always watch where you're going."

"Aark!"

"You can say that again."

Once I'd been thoroughly sniffed, Feroz allowed me access to the kitchen, where I found Eunice Snow, my mother's new maid, weeping at the kitchen table. Unlike her predecessor, she was young, no more than thirty.

"Hi, Miss Bentley," she sobbed.

"Er, hi. Is there anything I can do to help?"

She looked up at me through reddened blue eyes framed by straggly blond hair. "You can get Miss Caro out of prison. She'll wilt in there. I know."

"Jail," I corrected. I did not want to know how Eunice knew anything about the depression that usually follows incarceration, because I suspected I might not like the answer. Mother had a decidedly spotty record with household help. Last year she'd gone through five maids. This year, although it was only June, three had already walked out on her. Of late she'd become so desperate for help she no longer checked references, just hired whomever was ill-informed enough to apply for the job.

"Actually, the jail didn't seem all that bad to me," I said, attempting to cheer Eunice up. "There's a rec room with a TV for people not charged with violent offenses. And the corrections officers are even letting Caro keep part of a manicure kit. Besides, she'll only be in jail for thirty days, not life."

"Prison is torment. It breaks your spirit."

"Hmm."

Perhaps sensing the way my suspicious mind had begun to work, she added, "I'm also upset over poor Reverend Emerson's death. He married me and Bucky a couple years ago. Bucky thought that little church of his was cute."

"Chapel."

"That's what I said, church."

Deciding not to enlighten her on the many differences between a wedding chapel and a church, I said, "Mother wanted me to pick up Feroz, so if you'll show me…"

"I'm pregnant again, too."

Here I'd been thinking she was just fat. "Congratulations."

"Bucky wants a big family."

"Oh?"

"Our twins were born last Christmas day. Bucella and Bucky, Jr."

"My, wasn't that a merry Christmas!" Feroz nipped at me when I picked up his bowl, but working with tigers had given me quick reflexes, so his teeth closed on empty air.

"Yeah, we were all real happy then, but Bucky got laid off last week."

"I'm so sorry. Do you know where Feroz's leash is?"

"Second drawer from the left. With your mom in jail and you taking the dog, will she still need me here even though things don't get messed up like they usually do? I can dust. And mop. Maybe organize the basement, where all that junk is thrown together—chairs, lamps, clothes, and what all. I really need this job, Miss Theodora. Mine's our only paycheck until Bucky finds work. If Miss Caro decides not to use me while she's in jail, I don't know what'll happen." She snuffled, dabbed at her eyes. "We're already behind on our rent."

"What does Mr. Snow do?"

"He's good with cars and things."

I thought a moment. "Does 'things' include scraping barnacles off boats?" The *Merilee* had collected a few; same with the *Tea 4 Two*, the *Running Wild*, the *Minnie*, and a few other boats moored at the harbor. Maybe I could throw some work his way.

My plan faded when Eunice asked, "What's a barnacle?"

Feroz hopped up and down, trying to grab the leash. Taking pity, I snapped it to his collar. He tugged toward the door with surprising strength. Time to go.

"Eunice, give me your home phone number, or your cell, whichever. I'll ask my friends if they need some help or know anyone who does."

"We'd be so grateful, Miss Theodora." Lowering her voice, she added, "Bucky's parole officer said that if he's not working by the end of the month, he'll have to go back to prison. And prison makes you…"

"Wilt," I filled in, unhappily.

◇◇◇

After a brief walk in Gunn Landing Park, Feroz established himself as captain of the *Merilee*. While DJ Bonz and Miss Priss took refuge in the forward sleeping area, the Chihuahua swaggered back and forth through my small boat as if it belonged to him.

"Better watch yourself, Feroz," I warned him. "Pride goeth before a fall."

Come to think of it, I'd better watch out, too. Here I had been priding myself on my ability to help with the Snows' dire financial situation, when all along, Eunice's out-of-work husband was a convicted felon, not that there's anything wrong with that.

But husbands often paw through their wives' handbags, and what would happen if during a cursory pawing, Bucky found my mother's house key? When I ran a brief mental inventory of the contents of Caro's bedroom safe, I came up with eight diamond solitaires ranging from two to six carats, and an emerald-and-diamond necklace with matching earrings—all gifts from various husbands. That inventory didn't include the furs in her closet, a PETA nightmare of sable, mink, and ermine.

In order to keep Caro's inventory at its present level, I decided Bucky Snow needed a job, and fast. While Feroz continued his reign of terror, I fished my cell phone out of my pocket and made some calls.

Time flies when you're setting up job interviews for ex-cons, but I was eventually able to call Eunice with good news. The San Sebastian Cinema needed an usher, someone who was as good with a broom as he was throwing out disruptive teens. Given Mr. Snow's prison experience, I figured he would be perfect. Before I ended the call, it occurred to me to ask Eunice what had landed her husband in prison in the first place.

"Grand theft auto," she answered.

Good news, since the San Sebastian Cinema wasn't a drive-in.

Minutes later, DJ Bonz's frenzied barking reminded me of something I had forgotten in my rush to find Bucky a job. My own dog needed his evening walk. Ignoring Feroz's jealous snarls, I snapped Bonz's leash onto his collar and started off.

Evenings are my favorite time at Gunn Landing Harbor. While I'd been on the phone, a thick fog rolled in, enveloping me and my three-legged terrier in a vast cocoon of gray. The usual night sounds were softened. The foghorn on the break-water muted to a moan, the warning bell on a channel buoy pealed more discreetly, and the incoming tide whispered instead of roared.

After being cooped up all day, the three-legged mutt took his time, piddling on this Monterey pine, squatting under the next. Eventually he signaled he was ready to return to the *Merilee* and his evening dinner, so we headed back. As we were about to cross the parking lot that separated the park from the boat slips, he barked at a dark shape looming toward us through the fog. A smaller dark shape trailing the larger one yipped back.

"Who goes there?" the big shape called. "Friend or foe?"

It was Albert Grissom, lawyer to the less-than-downtrodden. Not surprised at his defense attorney theatrics, I called back, "Friend of a friend. I'm Teddy Bentley, Caro's daughter, and my companion is DJ Bonz, my trusty Heinz 57. Who's the little charmer with you?"

Al emerged from the fog with a Chihuahua even tinier than Feroz. She wore a doggy diaper, which signaled she was in season. When she reached Bonz, she indicated more than casual interest, so Al bent down and scooped her up.

"DJ Bonz, meet the lusty Golden Honey Veracruz de la Sonora, Vera to her friends, of which she has more than she needs right now." Smiling, he added, "I plan to breed her, but only to a gentleman I deem worthy of her favors. No disrespect intended."

Poor Bonz. Unlucky in the leg department, unlucky in love.

While Bonz mournfully eyed the lusty Vera, Al and I talked dogs. Once that subject was exhausted, we talked Caro.

"Theodora, I was going to call you this evening, so it's fortuitous that we ran into each other. A source of mine at the sheriff's office said Elvin Dade is still trying to drum up evidence against your mother for the Victor Emerson murder." His mouth turned down and a line formed between his eyebrows. "I find that worrying. In fact, my source says Elvin is downright obsessed with the idea of Caro's guilt. Is there a history between the two? Something I should know about? I'm speaking as her attorney, of course, not as, well, someone who, ah, who…" His blush travelled all the way to the tips of his ears.

There was a history, all right. According to Caro, Elvin Dade had pretty much stalked her during their high school years. Not knowing as much about men then as she did now, she accepted a soda date with him, naively believing it would scratch his itch. Her ploy didn't work. On the way home Elvin attempted to kiss her, among other things. The groping stopped only when she grabbed his ear and twisted it until it bled. Thinking quickly, she hopped out of the car and ran up to an elderly couple, pleading for assistance. Unfortunately for Elvin, the elderly man turned out to be a retired California Highway Patrol officer. After reading the randy teenager the riot act, the ex-cop called Elvin's parents and told them how badly their darling boy had behaved. Elvin was grounded for a month and his driving privileges were revoked for the rest of the school year. For a teenage boy, that was tantamount to a life sentence.

When I finished relating this sorry story to Grissom, the attorney's face shone with admiration. "What fire your mother has!"

"You could call it that."

"We have to protect that wonderful woman from herself, Theodora."

"Teddy."

"Ah, yes. Teddy. Can I rely on your help?"

"Certainly."

But could either of us rely on Caro?

◇◇◇

The idea of my mother as Jean Valjean relentlessly pursued through the California sewers by a Javert who strongly resembled Elvin Dade kept me awake half the night. The gentle bobbing of the *Merilee* didn't soothe me, nor did the sleepy call of a gull nearby. Not even the warm bodies of Miss Priss, DJ Bonz, and Feroz Guerro snuggled near my feet eased my anxiety.

The only person who could have helped remained somewhere in the Virginia woods, playing spy games with Homeland Security.

Chapter Six

I awoke at four knowing exactly what I had to do. If Elvin Dade was too focused on Caro to catch Reverend Victor Petersen's real killer, I would catch him myself. Yes, chasing killers could be dangerous, but previous run-ins with homicidal types had taught me the value of caution.

While taking the dogs out for their pre-dawn walk, I replayed the night of the murder in my head: Alejandro's screams; Victor Emerson lying dead in his royal robes at the llama's feet; Elvin screwing up the forensics before the other deputies could stop him; the pandemonium as dozens of Faire workers descended upon the murder scene. In my mind's eye, I could see their faces. Melissa Keegan's terrified expression as Cary, her thuggish husband, jerked her away from the scene. The near-panic of young Howie Fife, the Faire's leper. Deanna and Judd Sazac, part-time liveaboarders who unaccountably seemed to be arguing even as Victor's body cooled. They were all part of the crowd of assorted monks, minstrels, and peasants who arrived at the crime scene moments after me. But that meant nothing. Killers often returned to the scene of the crime to gloat.

Which of them wanted Victor dead, and why? As far as I knew, Victor had never caused trouble for anyone, unless, of course, I counted that Anne Boleyn dust-up with my mother. Then I remembered something else to take into account: Victor wasn't just a mail-order reverend with a tacky wedding chapel—he was also a notary public. That meant he was frequently called upon to notarize all sorts of legal documents, ranging from real estate transactions to wills. Maybe he had inadvertently put his stamp on a transaction that turned out to be fraudulent. Or maybe he'd merely offended a Faire worker and that person had taken his late-night revenge.

One thing was certain. I needed to learn more about Victor Petersen.

As soon as I returned the dogs to the *Merilee* my cell phone chimed the opening measure to "Born Free." It wasn't even five yet, but caller ID informed me that the doyenne of San Sebastian County was on the line. Groaning, I answered.

"I'm not due at the zoo until six, Aster Edwina, so whatever you want, can't it wait until..."

"Hi, sweetheart," my felonious father interrupted. "I knew you'd already be up, taking care of some animal. What's all this I hear about your mother? Is she really being charged with murder?"

I looked at my cell again. Yes, that was definitely one of Gunn Castle's phone numbers. "Dad, what the heck are you doing back in the States?"

During my childhood, my father embezzled millions from his partners at Bentley, Bentley, Haight & Busby. Since then, he had become quite the globe-trotter, but his usual domicile was somewhere in Costa Rica, a country known for being slow to extradite its tax-paying guests back to the States. The Feds still had a cell waiting, and the thought of Dad on American soil scared me half to death.

He sounded perfectly at ease. "As soon as I heard about your mother, I hitched a plane ride with a friend whose name I can't reveal since he's an even bigger crook than I. Aster Edwina was kind enough to hide me here in the castle for the duration. Well, enough of the niceties. Is your mother being represented by counsel? If so, how good is he? Or she."

If not always honest, dear old Dad was always politically correct. "Mother is well-represented. Maybe too well, if you get my drift."

Brief silence at the other end, then, "Single man with money?"

"How well you know her."

"Let's change the subject."

It might have been my imagination, but I thought he sounded jealous. "So how's the weather in Costa Rica? Warm?"

"Humid. And the howler monkey who lives in the tree outside my villa screams all night. To return to an even more unpleasant subject, how honest is your mother's attorney?"

"I've never heard of Albert Grissom being mixed up with anything shady."

"That's not good," he said.

"Why?"

"Because sometimes it takes a crook to catch a crook."

I digested that for a moment. "Please don't tell me you're thinking of investigating Victor Petersen's murder yourself. Leave it to the police. They know what they're doing."

"Teddy, you've got your fingers crossed behind your back, don't you?"

I uncrossed them. "Listen, Dad…"

"Aster Edwina told me that sheriff boyfriend of yours is out in the D.C. area doing something with Homeland Security, and in his absence, the ever-foolish Elvin Dade—by a series of flukes—has taken over. Imagine! Trying to pin a murder on Caro when the whole county knows she wouldn't hurt a fly. Well, not unless the fly stung or bit you. Which is it?"

"Which is what?"

"Flies. Sting or bite?"

Talking to my father can be as irritating as talking to my mother. "Most flies don't have stingers, but their jaws work in a sideways motion, causing great pain and sometimes even…"

"Good to know. Anyway, this thing with Elvin Dade, it's nothing more than a personal vendetta. Your mother told me all about the time she was foolish enough to go out with him and what happened, told all the ghastly details, including a few I'll bet you don't know about. Take my word for it, Elvin's out for blood."

"He's married now. More or less happily, I've heard." I wasn't trying to defend the man; I simply wanted my dad to get the hell out of Dodge before the Feds showed up.

"Happily married or not, men never forgive that kind of public humiliation. Especially at the hands of a woman."

"When Joe gets back, that'll all change." I hoped. While Joe was definitely a law-and-order type, he had common sense. And uncommonly strong arms, the better to hold me with and…

Dad's voice interrupted my erotic fantasy. "Hate to burst your bubble, kid, but Aster Edwina, who around here has more power than God, already called several higher-ups in Homeland Security about the situation here. Even she couldn't get them to release Joe early. They wouldn't let him have his cell phone back, either, saying that national security was more important than whatever little problem San Sebastian County is having."

Before I could point out the outrageousness of the agency's position, he said. "Shush. As if that's not bad enough, Aster Edwina also found out Joe won't be back for at least another week—maybe more—which will give Elvin plenty of time to fabricate evidence against your mother. I can't allow that to happen. The only good news here is that she's locked up safe in jail on that incitement to riot charge and can't get herself into any more trouble."

"This is all about guilt, isn't it?"

"She's not guilty!"

"I'm talking about your guilt, Dad. For embezzling all that money and leaving her destitute. Remember when the Feds swooped down and took the house, the cars, the…"

"Have a nice day, Teddy. They still say that in California, don't they?"

"All the time, but…"

Dial tone.

◇◇◇

For the next few hours, my concerns about my parents receded into the background while I buried myself in work. On Tuesdays I appeared on *Anteaters to Zebras*, my live television segment on the early morning television show, *Good Morning, San Sebastian*. The job wasn't as onerous as it had once been now that the program had a new anchor, who—unlike the previous anchor—had enough sense not to grab at an animal no matter how loveable it appeared. Ariel Gonzales was an ex-Marine and a highly-decorated veteran of the Iraqi War. The perfect early morning host.

Today's all-Africa segment on *Anteaters to Zebras* went well while I showed off Gloria, a loveable meerkat, followed by Jinks, a leash-trained jackal. But then came Roscoe, the Gunn Zoo's adolescent honey badger. Last week I had tried to convince Aster Edwina Gunn that a honey badger's temperament wasn't suitable for live TV, but the old lady had been adamant.

"Teddy, ever since that clever 'Honey Badger Don't Care' video ran on YouTube, Roscoe's become quite the star. I'd like to raise his profile even further, enough so that…."

"Uh, Aster Edwina, I don't think…"

"…we can lure a young female honey badger over from the National Zoo, where they have an extra. I envision a honey badger breeding program…"

"But…"

"…that will be the envy of the Association of Zoos and Aquariums."

"Roscoe bites, Aster Edwina."

She merely smiled. "You are a zookeeper, aren't you? Deal with it."

So here I sat in front of a live TV camera, holding a more-or-less subdued honey badger on my lap. I was gloved and had a good grip on his thick collar, but given past incidents, I wasn't taking any chances. A honey badger's skin is so loose no collar should be considered escape-proof.

"With Roscoe's white stripe down his back, he resembles a skunk," Ariel said, smiling down at him, then up at the camera. "Are skunks and honey badgers related?"

"An astute observation, Ariel," I chirped. "Both animals are members of the polecat family—weasels and skunks, if you will. Notice his strong odor?"

"Now that you mention it, the air in here has become rather ripe."

"No kidding. But unlike skunks, a honey badger doesn't spray its enemies. It just kills and eats them."

"How fierce! Can you tame a honey badger, Teddy? He sounds like he'd make a fine guard dog. Or should I say, 'guard badger?'"

"Roscoe is as tame as a honey badger ever gets, which isn't much. Did I mention that they're also related to wolverines? Wolverines can bring down a moose. That aside, Roscoe does settle down somewhat when we put on his collar. He's figured out that every time we do that, food shortly follows. Honey badgers are very intelligent animals."

Roscoe had been collared for almost a half hour now and if he wasn't fed soon, there'd be trouble. Bernice Unser, one of the Gunn Zoo's volunteers, waited in the Green Room with an entire raw chicken we had brought to reward him the minute we left the set, but Ariel didn't appear ready to bring *Anteaters to Zebras* to a close.

"You mentioned enemies, Teddy. Do honey badgers have many?"

Keeping a firm grip on my little charge, I said, "Oh, sure. Snakes. Hyenas. Lions. But even those animals usually have more sense than to mess with these guys. Honey badgers are the most fearless creatures on earth. For instance, if Roscoe here decided you represented a threat he wouldn't be frightened, he'd just see you as lunch. Another interesting thing about honey badgers is that unlike most animals, they devour all parts of their prey— flesh, hair, skin, teeth, feathers, even bones. They've even been known to dig up human corpses and…"

Ariel beamed at the camera. "And now a word from our new sponsor, San Sebastian's very own Speaks-To-Souls. If your pet's been acting out, his past life could be the problem. Let Speaks-To-Souls, a certified animal psychic, get to the root of the matter in the Past Life Regression Room. And look for Speaks-To-Souls and her rescued greyhounds appearing this weekend at the Gunn Landing Renaissance Faire. Huzzah!"

Once Speaks-To-Souls' phone number and store address flashed across the monitor, Ariel turned her attention back to the honey badger. "Ever wonder who Roscoe was in his previous life, Teddy?"

"Attila the Hun."

She pulled a face of mock horror. "But Roscoe's so cute!"

Truth be told, with his saggy skin, pointed snout, tiny eyes, and crooked teeth, the young honey badger bore a stronger resemblance to Acting Sheriff Elvin Dade than to the Hun, but I answered, "I'm sure Roscoe's mother thinks he's cute."

As if aware he was being talked about, Roscoe flashed his teeth, which didn't look at all cute to me. They didn't look cute to studio staffers, either. With the exception of one camerawoman, the others moved further away from the bright *Good Morning, San Sebastian* set and into the darkness of the big room beyond, where office types were tapping away at computers.

"Is southern Africa the only place where honey badgers are found, Teddy?"

"Oh, no, Ariel," I said to the camera's red light. "They can be found throughout Morocco, Algeria, Iran, Turkmenistan, India, and western Asia, where they spend much of their time raiding chicken coops and small livestock pens. Needless to say, they're not popular with the locals."

Roscoe flashed his teeth again and made a sound like a mewing kitten. Never a good sign.

"Uh, Ariel, not that this hasn't been fun, but…"

Another mew.

I started to rise, but it was too late. With a whip-like motion, Roscoe slipped his collar and jumped to the ground. Accompanied by a chorus of shrieks and a swiveling camera lens, he scurried off the set and into the open office area beyond. Studio staffers climbed aboard their desks, scattering Diet Coke, Fritos, apples, and Whitman's Samplers every which way. A few grabbed Rolodexes for weapons, but fat lot of good those would do against a honey badger. He'd simply eat them.

Ariel sat calmly amidst the chaos. "Quick little bugger, isn't he?"

Roscoe might be an adolescent but his teeth were still large enough to inflict a nasty bite if he got hold of someone. Still, I knew better than to chase him. The exit doors were shut, guaranteeing that the tiny terror wouldn't make it out to the street, so at least he was safe. The staffers' ankles? Not so much.

Fortunately, Roscoe found the Whitman's Sampler box, which slowed his progress. While he chewed his way through cardboard and cream fillings, I dashed into the Green Room, grabbed the raw chicken from Bernice, and ran back onto the set.

"Roscoe! Look what I've got!" I waved the chicken around by its slimy legs to spread its scent through the studio.

Roscoe paused in his gobbling and raised his pointed snout. Chocolates or chicken?

Both, apparently.

With the camera still trained on him, the honey badger gobbled faster, finally finishing up the last piece of cardboard. Then, ignoring the chaos around him, he wheeled around and headed for the chicken.

I dropped the chicken to the floor and Roscoe pounced. Slurp of skin. Juice of meat. Crunch of bones. Two staffers gagged. Honey badger didn't care, merely continued his make-the-chicken-disappear act. By the time he finished, the TV audience had been treated to a full-bore honey badger pig-out.

But I'd managed to slip his collar back on.

As I carted the bloated little furball off the set, I heard Ariel say, "Oh, man, I gotta get me one of those!"

◇◇◇

In a rare fit of mercy, Aster Edwina had given me the afternoon off, so once I returned a snoring Roscoe to his enclosure at the zoo, I headed back to Gunn Landing to talk to some boat people.

As much as I love the Pacific Coast village, it does have a problem. The only actual buildings were old fishermens' cottages, which had all been transformed into antique stores or restaurants, the better to entice tourists, the village's main industry. A few houses lay within the tiny village's limits, but they were the two-million-dollar-plusers up in Old Town, the snobbish enclave which loomed above the village proper on a steep hill. The less financially-flush of us hunkered down on cobbled-together houseboats in the harbor.

Today the village was packed. Several tour buses had pulled into the harbor's parking lot, and a herd of knee-sox-wearing folks were snapping pictures of pelicans, sea lions, and otters. Normally I didn't mind these incursions, but they were blocking the gated entrance to the boat slips. I finally managed to shove the most recalcitrant tourist aside, and made my way to the *My Fancy*, where Howie Fife, who had performed as the Renaissance Faire's leper until he injured his ankle, lived with his mother on the rusty trawler she'd purchased on the cheap after its former owner's untimely death.

"Captain of the *My Fancy*, permission to come aboard?" I called from the dock.

Ada Fife poked her head out of the hatch. "Oh, for Pete's sake, Teddy, we don't stand on ceremony here. Come on in."

A newcomer to the harbor, she had bought the rickety *My Fancy* not so much out of a love for the sea but because she and her son couldn't afford landlubber housing. Fortunately, liveaboarders are a helpful lot, and her neighbors quickly taught her how to vanquish mildew, scrape barnacles, and the premium time to use the laundromat and public showers at the far end of the parking lot.

As further proof of near-penury, Ada had done little in the way of redecorating *My Fancy*. The former owner's sickly green galley table still tilted to starboard and the long dining settee remained covered in disintegrating purple Naugahyde. At least she'd thrown a bright madras scarf over the back of the settee, partially covering the bilious thing. Also new was a series of photographs taped to the cabin walls: Howie as a plump toddler, Howie as a Little Leaguer, Howie sitting on one of the stone lions that guarded the New York Public Library, a gangling Howie in a black robe and mortarboard cap holding his high school diploma. Nowhere did I see a picture of Ada herself or Howie's father, whomever and wherever he was.

"Coffee? Tea?" Ada asked, after I sat down across from the crossword puzzle she had been working.

Ada Fife's voice was as rugged as her face, a low alto perfectly suited to her large, almost masculine features. Her gray-streaked hair hadn't seen a stylist in a long time, if ever, and I suspected that her cheap polyester slacks and blouse came from the San Sebastian Goodwill store. The elderly cockapoo snoring on the settee could have used a professional grooming, too.

Mindful of her tight finances, I turned down refreshments. "I'm fine, thanks. Just dropped by to speak to Howie. Is he here?"

Instantly, her bonhomie disappeared. Instead of joining me on the settee, she leaned against the galley sink, her thin mouth thinning further. "I've heard about you, Teddy, and if you think you're going to give my son the third degree on what happened at the Faire the other night, think again. Besides, Howie's not here."

Her timing could have been better. Uneven footsteps up on deck announced Howie's return. Seconds later, the Faire's one-time leper descended the ladder to the galley, the pain of his sprained ankle apparent on his cherubic face. When he saw me he smiled, revealing teeth that cried out for orthodontia. "Say, aren't you the woman with the llama? Reynaldo? Roberto?"

I smiled back. "Alejandro. And yes I am. Do you like animals?"

Ignoring Ada's frown, he limped over to the settee and plopped himself down next to me. "Like!? Soon as I complete my associate of arts degree, I'm transferring over to Cal State and majoring in marine biology."

"Monterey Bay campus?"

"You betcha. That's why we moved here from..."

"Howie!" Ada's interrupted. "Didn't you tell me you had a paper due, the one on microcystin and its impact on sea otters? Get to it." With an unmanicured finger, she pointed toward the aft cabin.

"Aw, Mom! She's a zookeeper and I wanted to talk..."

The finger remained pointing. "Now!"

With a wounded look on his face, Howie hobbled off.

Hoping to ease the tension, I asked, "His ankle still hurt him?"

"Yes, it does, and that's what I get for letting him take that stupid job at the Faire. Now please leave. I'm very busy." The finger swiveled toward the hatch.

I looked down at the half-worked crossword puzzle. "Stoat," I said.

"What's that supposed to mean?"

I did some finger-pointing of my own at the clue to thirty-one across. "Five letter word for a summer ermine."

With that parting shot, I cleared out.

I was halfway to the *Merilee* when I spotted Dr. Willis Pierce sitting at one of Chowder & Cappuccino's outdoor tables. The drama professor/replacement King Henry was slurping his way through a bread bowl of clam chowder. Since he had also been working the Faire when Victor Emerson was murdered, I decided to take the opportunity to question him. Feigning a casual manner, I bought chowder for myself and walked over to his table.

"May I join you, Dr. Pierce?"

Although several other tables were empty, he graciously pulled out a chair and performed a gallant bow. "Most assuredly, fair maid. Sit thyself down and enjoy thine own hearty repast."

I groaned. "Oh, please. I've had enough Renaissance-speak to last me for the next century."

He chuckled. "That's what you get for volunteering. And since you're not one of my drama students, please call me Willis."

"I didn't volunteer, Willis."

"Ah. I forgot. You're one of Aster Edwina's indentured servants."

"Got it in a nutshell."

His lean, Van Dyke-bearded face assumed a professorial expression. "Know where that saying comes from? The Roman philosopher Marcus Tullius Cicero said that the *Iliad* was written in such a small hand on a single piece of parchment that the entire epic could fit into a walnut shell."

"Really?"

"Really, according to historical record. Nevertheless, the idea of the *Iliad* fitting into any kind of nutshell is preposterous. The classicists used hyperbole to make a point. In Cicero's case, he was probably complaining about his students' sloppy handwriting, which I might add, has changed little in two thousand years. Take my drama students, for instance. Despite the invention of Microsoft Word, I still receive essays on *Richard the Third* that look like they were pecked out by chickens."

"Howie Fife is one of your drama students, isn't he?"

Before answering, he threw a piece of bread to a nearby gull, which only served as a signal to other gulls. Within seconds we were surrounded by the screeching pests, but Willis didn't seem to mind. Another animal lover.

"Howie's one of my better students. Too bad he's so interested in marine biology." As if belatedly remembering my profession, he gave me a sheepish smile. "Since you work with animals I imagine we have a difference of opinion on the subject."

"California already has plenty of actors. Say, weren't you the person who got Howie the paying job at the Faire?"

He sighed. "Fat lot of good it did him since the kid tripped over a pig at Serf City the first day out. You might remember that he still showed up for work the next day, which is when that idiotic Elvin Dade tried to give him the third degree. Thankfully I was there to head the bully off. Considering what Howie and his mother are going through, you would think Elvin would show a little mercy, but no. The quality of mercy *is* strained in Elvin's universe." He sighed. "Poor kid. Given that rust bucket he and his mother live on, they certainly need the money the leper gig paid, although it wasn't much. Ada's a checker at the San Sebastian Ranch Market, but it's only half time work. Being raised by a single mother myself, I know what that little family is going through."

This was the first time I had heard the drama professor mention his childhood. Although always ready to gab, especially about theater, he seldom offered personal details. "My own parents are divorced," I offered.

He gave me a wry smile. "But you and the beautiful Caro weren't quite eating out of dumpsters, were you?"

There being little I could say to that, I moved on. "You know, Willis, considering all the trouble Howie was having with his ankle Saturday, I was surprised to see him back at the Faire the next day."

"No problem there, since his new job is a sitting one. When you see him next, he'll be in the Royal Pavilion pulling duty as one of my courtiers. I'm the new Henry the Eighth, you remember, albeit a much thinner Henry."

The perfect opening. "Terrible about Victor Emerson, isn't it?"

"Dreadful. Someone told me he was killed by a crossbow bolt. Surely that can't be true."

"As the person who discovered the body, I can assure you it is. He died in the llama enclosure, right at Alejandro's feet."

"Poor llama."

Not poor Victor? "How well did you know him? Victor, I mean."

"Since he ran a church and I'm a devout non-believer, I knew him only in passing." At that point, a Pomeranian off its leash scampered up to us. In a flash, Willis rose from his chair and hooked the dog under his arm. "Silly boy," he murmured to it. "Those mean old gulls will peck your eyes out."

After a red-faced woman waving a leash trotted up and claimed the errant Pom, we resumed our conversation.

"Victor ran a wedding chapel, not a church." Why did people keep getting the two mixed up?

"Same thing."

"Not really. A church is…Oh, never mind. Were you there all night? Or did you drive back here after the Faire closed?"

Willis chuckled. "Playing detective, Teddy? Might as well, I guess, since thanks to Homeland Security, Deputy Dawg, er, I mean Deputy Elvin Dade is heading up the official investigation, and good luck there. To answer your question, I much preferred to sleep on the *Caliban* than in a tent or trailer surrounded by drunk monks and jesters. As soon as the Faire shut its gates for the night, I drove home, poured myself a chilled glass of the Gunn Winery's best Chardonnay, and after watching a DVD of Burton and Taylor chewing the scenery in *The Taming of the Shrew*, tottered off to my lonely bed. There's my alibi, poor though it is."

"I wasn't asking…"

"The hell you weren't." But he reached across the table and patted my hand.

Embarrassed by my investigative clumsiness, I changed the subject. "That's nice of you, helping Howie get paying jobs at the Faire. Most of them are volunteer." Like mine.

He waved his good deeds away with a graceful gesture. "We liveaboarders have to stick together."

"How well do you know his mother?"

"Ada? Hardly at all. We only visited once, when I was showing her how to prep for that storm last week."

I scanned the ocean. No storm clouds in sight. No clouds at all, in fact, unless you counted the flock of seagulls following a fishing boat making its way back to the harbor from the open sea. "The weather can be tricky along the coast and if you don't know how to ride it out, you're in trouble. From what I hear, Ada's quite the landlubber." I turned my attention to my lunch. After a few spoonfuls, I said, "Chowder's good, isn't it?"

"Not as good as at Fred's Fish Market. I'm only here because the line over at Fred's was too long. So many tour buses in town."

"But the chowder's only half the price here."

"True. Zookeeping work doesn't pay all that well, does it?"

Only half-kidding, I answered, "Like those dancers in *Chorus Line*, we do it for love."

"Excellent musical. I tried to mount it last year at the college but we didn't have enough good singers who could also dance, so we did *Oedipus Rex* instead. Some of the parents weren't happy."

"Nothing like a little patricide and incest to stir up the locals. Did Howie play Oedipus?"

"I gave him the part of King Laius, Oedipus' unfortunate daddy. Howie transferred here mid-semester, and didn't have enough time to do the main character justice. But even then I could see his level of talent."

This was working like I'd hoped. "Where'd Howie transfer in from?"

Willis shrugged. "I haven't the faintest idea. In California sometimes the less you know about your students, the better off you are. Hell, half the kids have rap sheets these days, and I don't mean that benighted music genre. Howie's a good kid, which is why I helped him. I'd help his mother more if she'd let me, but other than that one time, she's been pretty stand-offish. Some bad history there, I imagine."

"What makes you think that?"

"Bambi told me that Ada once said all men were monsters at heart, but when she asked what she meant, Ada clammed up."

"Do you think that's really her name? Bambi's, I mean."

"Unlikely though it seems," he said, "that's what she insisted during that brief time we two were an item." For a moment he looked sorrowful. But just for a moment. "As the Bard said, 'What's in a name? That which we call a rose by any other name would smell as sweet.' *Romeo and Juliet*, Act II, Scene II."

"How would Bambi know Ada? I mean, Bambi lives in San Sebastian and I imagine she does her grocery shopping there. She doesn't have a boat, either."

He raised in eyebrows. "You're a little behind times. Our beloved Bambi recently inherited the *Runaround*, her aunt's thirty-six foot Pearson. It's berthed next to my *Caliban*. 'If this were play'd upon a stage now, I could condemn it as an improbable fiction.' *Twelfth Night*, Act III, Scene IV."

Which explained why I'd missed the news. Willis' boat was berthed at the pricy northern end of the harbor near the yacht club. Since I wasn't a dues-paying member, Elvis could be living over there scarfing down Krispy Kremes, and I wouldn't know.

"Bambi doesn't seem like the harbor type to me," I said. "Does she even sail?"

"The *Runaround* hasn't left the dock since she inherited it. However, when I walked down here for lunch, I saw her and a few friends partying on deck. Nice little sloop, even though it is fiberglass."

When it came to boats, Willis was a snob. His own wooden, forty-five foot Sparkman and Stephens 708 had once placed second in the Master Mariners Regatta. Although the cabin area seemed cramped for liveaboard life, the *Caliban's* sleek lines had half the harbor drooling. Tight quarters or not, it must have suited him, because unlike most dock-bound harbor residents, he was frequently seen tacking toward Dolphin Island, the *Caliban's* sails eating the wind.

"Where did Bambi say that fascinating conversation with Ada took place?" I asked.

"In the laundromat, where else? They were sitting there watching our washing go round and round. Not that Bambi normally frequents the place, but when she took over the *Runaround*, she had to wash all its linens because the aunt hadn't been aboard her in quite some time. You know what mildew smells like."

Mildew was a constant challenge to harbor life, and it made for frequent visits to the harbor's laundromat. Still, I had trouble envisioning the close-mouthed Ada spilling her guts to a man-magnet like Bambi. Surely she hadn't expected sympathy from that quarter. Or did the two have something in common I didn't know about? Little though I liked the idea, I decided to interview Bambi next.

In the meantime, I had a few more questions for Willis. "Did Howie's mother pick him up right after he hurt his ankle? I don't remember seeing him around until the next morning."

"Ada was working the Faire that day, too, so she brought him home."

"About what time was that?"

"Hmm. Around lunchtime, I think, either before or after. I can't be sure. I was busy walking around quoting the Bard." He gave me a stern look. "Why so curious about the kid's whereabouts? Surely you don't suspect him of offing Victor Emerson."

"Of course not," I said, "but some of the younger people working the Faire bring sleeping bags and make a party of it. Seems like that's the kind of thing kids Howie's age would like, so I imagine he felt bad, missing that."

He gave me a wry grin. "Ada is much too protective to let the kid hang out with them overnight, so it was beddy-bye on their wee little boat for her baby."

"That's a bit of a harsh judgment, don't you think?" Given the problems so many teens had these days, I could understand Ada's concerns, and told Willis so.

He shook his head. "If that was all, you'd be right. But the other day when I was readying the *Caliban* for a sail, I saw Howie talking to Bambi, and from my vantage point, they looked like they were getting along like a house afire. You know how great Bambi looks in a bikini." He looked sorrowful again, but brightened up even quicker this time. "As I was saying, the two were talking quite animatedly, when here came Ada, hurrying down the dock, tripping over her own feet, demanding he get back home. She had a few choice words for Bambi, too, all but called her a Scarlet Woman."

"How strange."

"How astute." He changed the subject so quickly it almost made my head spin. "Speaking of Bambi and Anne Boleyn and that other Renaissance Faire drama, how is your beautiful mother? I hear she's in jail for incitement to riot, of all things. Wouldn't have thought she was the type."

"She's doing as well as can be expected." In between mouthfuls of chowder, I filled him in on Caro's situation, finishing with, "For the first time in her life, she's developed a social conscience."

"Better late than never. Tell you what. I'm teaching an extra-credit summer class tomorrow, and since the jail's so close to the college, I'll drop by and see her. Lift her spirits with chocolate and flowers."

"She's in jail, Willis, not the hospital."

An expression of Shakespearean concern played across his face. "Then 'Come, let's away to prison; we two alone will sing like birds i' th' cage.' *King Lear*, Act V, Scene III."

"Sounds good to me."

Just as long as the song wasn't "Jailhouse Rock."

◇◇◇

Attempting to get information from Bambi would be pointless as long as she was busy with her friends, but it occurred to me as I continued my walk toward the *Merilee* that talking to Deanna and Judd Sazac might be more fruitful. Their *Chugalug* was a thirty-two foot Constellation that had begun its existence as a seafaring party boat, but was now retired to a more sedate life in the harbor. Although the Sazacs had a beautiful Mediterranean-style house perched on a hill above San Sebastian, they spent almost as much time on their boat as they did in their home.

"Ahoy, *Chugalug*! Permission to board?" I called to Deanna, who was up on deck staring out at the Pacific, Judd's Jack Russell terrier at her feet. I didn't see Judd.

Somewhere in her late forties, Deanna could usually pass for thirty but not today. She responded to my voice with a start, and when she turned around, I saw that her eyes were red. She held a half-empty Martini glass in her hand. "Come on up, Teddy. I can't promise to be good company, but at least then I wouldn't be drinking alone."

Ignoring every rule of common decency—after all, my mother's freedom was at stake—I joined her.

"Martini? Chardonnay? Diet Coke?" she asked, when I joined her.

The sun not yet over the yardarm, I accepted the soft drink. As she poured it into a highball glass, I said, "You seem upset. Is there anything I can do?"

"Find me a new husband." From the look on her face, she wasn't kidding.

Deanna's marriage to the two-decades younger Judd had long been the subject of harbor gossip. The fact that they were frequently seen quarreling only added fuel to the fire. I suddenly remembered that they had been going at it at the Faire the night Victor had been killed, too. Ordinarily, I would back away from any hint of marital discord between my friends, but today wasn't ordinary.

"Are you and Judd squabbling again?"

She snorted, making the Jack Russell look up quizzically. "Yes, and before you ask, the 'squabble' as you so delicately word it, was over a woman whose name and description begin with the letter 'B'."

"As in Bambi."

"And as in bitch."

"Surely not." My disclaimer was good manners only, because Judd had a reputation as a skirt-chaser.

"If you don't believe me, Teddy, check out that noisy party on the *Runaround*. When I left, Judd was dancing so close to her I couldn't tell where he left off and she began."

"He's just feeling his oats, Deanna."

"Is that what you'd say if the shoe was on the other foot, and your precious Joe was playing kissy-huggy with her?"

Such was my fury at the thought that I immediately began to compile a list of reasons Bambi might have murdered Victor Emerson, and thus be sentenced to life in prison with no parole. But every time I had seen her and Victor talking together, they'd appeared genial, almost affectionate. And hadn't he officiated at her nuptials? True, her marriage had been short-lived, but I couldn't see why Bambi would blame Victor for that, especially since she had received a large financial settlement after the divorce. No, try as I might, I just couldn't think of any reason the hussy might pick up a conveniently discarded crossbow and shoot the tubby reverend to death.

The crossbow. Maybe I was going at this the wrong way. Instead of trying to pin Victor's murder on anyone other Caro, maybe I should be paying more attention to the unusual murder weapon itself. Who, for instance, had a working knowledge of crossbows?

Then I remembered that crossbow demonstration at the Faire. Deanna had been in the audience, but Judd hadn't been with her.

Before I could stop myself, I asked, "Deanna, did Judd attend one of those crossbow demonstrations?"

"Please tell me you're joking."

"Not really."

Her expression, so anguished earlier, morphed into one of pure rage. "Theodora Iona Esmeralda Bentley, get your nosy ass off my boat."

Realizing that it had worn out its welcome, my nosy ass complied.

◇◇◇

Two hours later I was changing clothes for my visit to the jail when my cellphone came alive. Praying the caller was Joe, I snatched it off the nightstand, only to read the name of my old friend, Deputy Emilio Gutierrez.

Trying not to sound disappointed, I answered. "Hi, Emilio. What's…"

"I'm still on duty so I have to be quick. We received the autopsy report on the man we all knew as Victor Emerson. And you know the ME always checks a deceased fingerprints?"

"Sure, but what does that have to do with anything?"

"Teddy, Victor's real name was Glenn Reynolds Jamison. Eighteen years ago, he escaped from the Ely State Prison in Nevada, where he was doing twenty-five to life for murder. Oops. Elvin's yelling for me. Gotta go."

Thunderbolt duly delivered, Emilio hung up.

Chapter Seven

"How about this fake beard? Not only is it a different color than my own hair, but it changes the shape of my face, too. Bulks it up, don't you think?"

My father and Aster Edwina were standing in Gunn Castle's aptly-named Gold Bedroom, the same bedroom where Wallis Simpson and the Duke of Windsor had once slept. Gold brocade covered the halls, gold silk damask draperies hung from the canopied bed, and gold-themed Aubussons carpeted the oak-planked floor. To keep the room from being too matchy-matchy, several Caneletto landscapes of Venice brightened the walls, their cool blues providing a refreshing contrast. The scent of lilies perfumed the air, much of it emanating from Aster Edwina. She was dressed to kill, too, in a silk shantung dress that perfectly matched the Caneletto skies.

Ignoring her for the moment, I yelled, "Dad? What the hell do you think you're doing?"

After driving my Nissan like a lunatic all the way from Gunn Landing Harbor, I had found my father studying his reflection in an antique cheval glass mirror, the same one in which Wallis Simpson once admired her own thin, rich self.

He turned from the mirror. "Nice to see you, too, Teddy. As for what I'm doing, isn't it obvious? I'm getting ready to visit your mother."

"That beard is black. Your eyebrows and eyelashes are red."

"Maybe I can borrow some black mascara from you girls."

Aster Edwina, who had always had a soft spot for my rapscallion father, giggled. She sounded like an innocent young girl, not the eighty-plus autocrat she really was.

I felt less charmed. "Mascara won't help. Neither will the fact that you're an unforgettable six-foot-four."

"I'll stoop. Lean on a cane."

"No, Dad. Not unless you want me to wind up with two parents in jail."

Aster Edwina cleared her throat and tried to act like an adult again. "As much as I hate to admit it, Danny, Theodora's right. You're still the handsome Daniel St. James Bentley I always knew, and fake beard or no, that vile Elvin Dade will recognize you immediately. If I remember correctly, and I'm certain I do, he used to clean your pool before he signed on to the sheriff's department. You know the idiot would love to add your scalp to his less-than-stellar record, especially since you had to fire him after that dead-rat-in-the-drain incident. He knows how to harbor a grudge."

With a sigh, Dad pulled off the beard. "Caro will be so disappointed."

"She'll live," Aster Edwina snapped.

"But Caro's so sensi…"

Before this could go any further, I interrupted. "Aster Edwina, if you don't mind, there's something I need to discuss with my father. In private."

She threw me a mean look, but for once I didn't back down. "The sooner Dad stops worrying about Caro, the sooner he'll be able to relax and devote his time to you."

My ploy worked, and with a final girlish giggle directed toward my father, Aster Edwina wiggled her bony hips out of the room.

Dad turned back to the mirror. "Maybe a fuller beard? Light brown, perhaps? Or salt and pepper? Then the contrast with my eyebrows wouldn't be so marked."

"Give it up, Dad. You're not going anywhere near that jail."

"Your mother…"

"You. Can. Not. Visit. Mother. Not as long as she's locked up, anyway. But here's how you can help. Turns out you were right about one thing. It takes a crook to catch a crook. I want you to call some of your felonious friends and get insider information on a guy named Glenn Reynolds Jamison who did time for murder in Ely, Nevada. In case I can't find out on my own, I need to know who he murdered and why, who his associates were, and who helped him escape from prison. Find out whether any of his old friends or relatives are still alive. They could be, because he was only around fifty when he got killed."

"Don't want much, do you, Teddy?"

"Nothing you can't take care of. When it comes to sussing out criminal behavior, you and your buddies are the best thing to come along since Google."

A smile. "Now you're flattering me."

"As if you need it, you egotist you. Seriously, can you do that for me?"

He crossed the carpet and kissed me on my nose. "For you, sweetie, anything. As long as it helps your mother."

"Good. Now I'm going to ask you something I've wanted to know for a long time but with one thing or another, never got a chance to ask. Why'd you do it?"

He looked at his fingernails. They were immaculate. "Do what?"

"You know what."

"No, really, I don't."

I bet. "You already had more money than you knew what to do with, were a full partner in a lucrative business, married to a beautiful woman, had a daughter who adored you, owned a gorgeous house, several racehorses, a yacht, a half-dozen Rolexes—you had everything a man could want. Why did you throw it all away by embezzling money you didn't really need?"

He dropped the fascination with his fingernails and looked me in the eye. "It was the challenge, the game. Could I do it? What if I got caught? But what if I didn't get caught? Wouldn't that be fun? It was the adrenaline rush, Teddy. There's nothing like it."

"Not even love?"

He didn't answer right away, but when he did, it appeared to have nothing to do with my question. "Sweetie, you're more like me than you realize."

"I am not!"

"Then convince me you don't get an adrenaline rush from all this detective work."

"I'm doing it to help Mother."

"And the case before this one? And the one before that?"

"I...I..." For some reason, I couldn't finish.

Shaking his head, he left the room.

Unsettled by the conversation, I spent a few minutes tidying my flyaway red hair in front of the cheval glass, then walked down the stone steps to find the housekeeper carrying a silver tray toward the library. It was loaded with a full tea service, including watercress sandwiches and marzipan cakes.

"Miss Theodora, Miss Aster Edwina, and her visitor, whatever his name is, are in the library. Do you wish to join them for tea?"

Mrs. McGinty knew perfectly well who the visitor was, but like the rest of the castle's staff, she pretended she didn't. Before being outed as an embezzler, my father was well-known in San Sebastian County for his numerous charitable activities. Since almost everyone falls upon hard times at least once in their lives, it was a rare family indeed that had never experienced his generosity, castle staff included.

"Tea would be nice," I said, falling into step behind the housekeeper. We clattered along the stone floor like a matched pair of Clydesdales.

In contrast to William Randolph Hearst's light-filled San Simeon a hundred miles to the south, the fourteenth century Gunn Castle was a study in gloom. It had been transported stone by stone from Scotland by Edwin Gunn, Aster Edwina's father, and founder of the massive Gunn fortune, who had been more intent on impressing the neighbors than physical comfort. With six towers, a crenelated roof, and a row of archers' windows, the sun seldom made entrance, and the few sconces lighting the hallway did little to penetrate its perpetual twilight.

"Knowing that you and your fa...ah, the guest prefer non-caffeinated herbals, I've brewed up some chamomile," Mrs. McGinty said.

I was about to thank her when she added, "I'm glad the snake is doing okay."

"Snake?"

She hissed at me. "Ssss-byl."

It took me a moment to realize she was talking about the Gunn Zoo's runaway Mohave rattlesnake.

"Did they find her?"

"No, but she's taking care of herself. Her first tweet yesterday said, 'Mousie was delicious. So was kitty.' Isn't that cute?"

I stopped dead in my tracks, right underneath an Elizabethan pike, which if it fell, would probably behead me. "Are you telling me that Sssbyl's tweeting?"

"Sounds like you haven't been keeping up, Miss Theodora."

Annoyed at being told that for the second time in one day, I said, "Mrs. McGinty, snakes can't tweet. They don't have fingers. Or hands. Or Smart Phones. Or iPads."

The left corner of her mouth tilted up so slightly I couldn't tell for certain if she was smiling. "I imagine Sssbyl's talked someone into tweeting for her. She's quite assertive."

"Next, she'll put together a Facebook page," I snarked.

"She already has one, but tweeting is more immediate. Don't you find that to be so, Miss Theodora?"

"I avoid tweeting whenever possible."

"You're missing a lot, then. Sssbyl's having great adventures out there. Her latest tweet said 'Love is a many-splendored thing.' Isn't that just precious?"

"Not really."

The hinted-at smile fully revealed itself. "You're so much like your fa...like the visitor. He swears he'll get Mrs. Bentley out of jail if he has to tear it down brick by brick." The housekeeper had never stopped calling my mother by her first married name, a habit which hadn't set well with Husband Number Two, Husband Number Three, or Husband Number Four.

"The jail is poured cement, Mrs. McGinty, not brick."

"Slab by slab then."

When we finally reached the library, we found Aster Edwina sitting on my father's lap. The old hussy didn't even attempt to look embarrassed, merely slid off, straightened the skirt of her silk dress and gave me a smug smile.

In contrast to the dim hallway, the library was warm and welcoming. Late afternoon sunlight filtered through stained glass windows, probably looted from some Scottish church, cast jewel-toned reflections around the room. The huge Jacobean chair my father sat on wouldn't have been out of place in a museum.

"Shouldn't you be at work, Theodora?" Aster Edwina asked. After taking the tray from Mrs. McGinty, she dismissed the housekeeper and began to pour.

"You gave me the day off, remember? But you're right, I have places to go and people to see. First, though, there's something I've been meaning to ask you. Why in the world did you let Bambi play Anne Boleyn when you'd already promised the part to Caro?" There was no point in spilling the beans yet on Victor's true identity. She would find out soon enough.

"Promises were made to be broken, Theodora." Without asking if I wanted cream or sugar, she handed me a delicate Crown Staffordshire cup so overfull the hot tea slopped over into its saucer and onto my hand. Accident? I thought not.

But the chamomile tasted delicious. So did the marzipan cake I helped myself to. "Promises shouldn't be broken without a good reason, Aster Edwina."

"Wait a minute, you two," my father interjected. "What's all this about Caro being replaced as Anne Boleyn? That's news to me. When she called me a couple of weeks ago, she sounded very excited about flouncing around as the Queen of England. I told her it wasn't quite the same as being a real queen, but..." He shook his head.

Caro had a rare talent for fantasy, which was why Victor's slight had hurt her so much. Angry all over again, I explained to my father what had happened. "Didn't your girlfriend here tell you that's why Elvin Dade arrested Mom in the first place?"

Aster Edwina ignored his glare. "Yes, I originally told Caroline she could be Anne, but that was before Victor Emerson made what I thought was a very good argument, that she was too old. If my grasp of history is accurate, Anne married Henry when she was either thirty-one or thirty-two, which is pretty much in the same ballpark as Bambi. Ghastly name, by the way. What could her parents have been thinking?" She sniffed. "Whereas your mother must at least be in her late fifties, if not beginning her sixties. Not that anyone can tell, given all those cosmetic procedures she's undergone in her eternal quest of youth. But facts are facts, as Victor so rightly pointed out. Caroline was too old to portray a believable Anne."

On the surface her argument sounded reasonable, but I knew Aster Edwina too well to buy it. For now, I contented myself that the furious expression on my father's face meant the old bat wouldn't be sitting on his lap again anytime soon.

While driving away from Gunn Castle an hour later, I tried to remember where Bambi had been when Victor Emerson—or rather, Glenn Reynolds Jamison—was murdered. Had she spent the night on the Faire's grounds? Although I didn't know her all that well, I couldn't see her bunked down in a tiny tent or sharing an RV with the proletariat. My guess was that she had driven back to her house in San Sebastian when the Faire closed for the evening.

But I would find out.

◇◇◇

Visiting hours had not yet begun when I arrived in San Sebastian, so I decided to spend the remaining minutes sipping decaf at the Uptown Diner across from the jail.

Bad decision.

As I took a seat at the crowded counter, who did I see hogging a booth meant for six but Acting Sheriff Elvin Dade and his insufferable wife Wynona. If Elvin was unpopular, she was doubly so. Self-righteous to a fault, she had even earned the animosity of the parishioners at the strict fundamentalist church the two attended. If the Bible listed ten commandments, she had come up with a dozen more, ranging from forbidding makeup to a fatwa against wearing shorts on the hottest summer day. The Gunn Zoo's summer uniforms—khaki shorts and camp shirt—had so outraged Wynona's puritan sensibilities that she had led a campaign to prohibit schoolchildren from entering the zoo from May through August. Her campaign failed, but not before being rebuked by her zoo-loving pastor for the sin of pride.

Here I sat, in my summer uniform, which I'd dutifully worn to the TV studio earlier than morning. Granted, the shorts weren't all that miniscule, reaching almost to my knees, but they were still shorts, and my camp shirt bared a shocking amount of freckled forearm. By contrast, Wynona wore a print housedress that left everything to the imagination. With her scrawny body covered to her wrists, chin, and ankles, she resembled a plucked chicken stuffed into a flour sack.

I ducked my head and pretended I wasn't there.

That never works, of course. The people you don't want to see you always do, and before I was a third of the way through my decaf, Wynona was breathing down my sunburned neck.

"For decency's sake you should close that zoo down until… until the *season* is over, Teddy."

"Season? What season?" Although I knew perfectly well what had her dander up, it was more fun to play dumb.

"You know. The season where the animals do, uh, what they do."

"Do? What are you talking about, exactly?"

"The…the getting in the family way season."

"Oh, you mean mating!" I purposely said it loud enough that everyone in the diner turned to look. "Why are you so focused on mating behavior, Wynona?" I said that even more loudly.

Her usually pale face turned rosy red, but confident that God had her back, she soldiered on. "What's going on over there is nothing decent God-fearing people should be subjected to, Teddy. Close that dirty place down!"

"Pagans like zoos, too, so that would be religious discrimination, and the Ninth Circuit Court would make us open it right back up."

Her mouth moved a few times, but after no sounds emerged, she scuttled back to her booth, where Elvin Dade sat with his head in his hands. I'll say this for Elvin; he was an idiot but he was no prig.

After that, I was left in peace to finish my decaf. When six o'clock rolled around I ambled across the town square to the jail, where I found my mother in high spirits.

"I'm learning so much from these girls!" she enthused, motioning toward two other inmates visiting with their families. "Now I'm trying to, you know, pay it forward, give of myself."

"By teaching Demonios Femeninos how to do manicures? Why not tell them to go back to school and get a degree? In law, preferably, seeing as they're having so much trouble with it."

"Proper grooming is the pathway to success, Theodora, something it wouldn't hurt you to remember. Just look at you. Baggy shirt, baggy shorts, unbecoming boots, hair a mess. When's the last time you had a mani-pedi?"

"Since I lived with you, probably, which was when? I forget."

"I don't. It was when you came running home with your tail between your legs after Michael left you for another woman."

"Thank you so much for reminding me of that happy time." I took a quick look around to see if other jailhouse visitors were enduring the same humiliations. From their expressions, many were.

"Furthermore, Theodora…"

About five minutes into her recital of my many shortcomings—no one can catalogue them like a mother—I stopped listening. I wanted to tell her Dad was back in town and pining to see her, but I didn't dare on the chance the jail's visiting areas were miked and videotaped. At the slightest hint that San Sebastian County's biggest crook hid out right next door, so to speak, a flotilla of deputies would pile into their cars and tear toward Gunn Castle with sirens a-howl. I was also loathe to tell her that Elvin Dade was still trying to pin Victor's murder on her because it would make her crazier than she already was. Instead, I merely sat there nodding my head like a bobble head doll until she wound down.

"So remember that next time you dare to criticize me!" she finished up.

"Duly noted. To bring up a sore subject again, it might be a good idea to cool it with the social consciousness bit until they cut you loose."

"I'm only exercising my right to free speech, which is guaranteed under the Third Amendment to the United States Constitution."

"It's the First Amendment, actually. The Third is the one that says we don't have to quarter soldiers in our homes if we don't want to."

"There you go again, Theodora, correcting your elders."

Did my youth-obsessed mother just refer to herself as an *elder*? If so, she must have been more upset about being in jail than she'd led me to believe. Maybe all that "Arise and revolt!" stuff was simply a front for her terror.

"I'm sorry, Caro," I said, meaning it. "You're right. Freedom of speech is covered in the Third Amendment." It sort of was, too, since we had the right to yell "Get the hell out of my house!" every time the Marines tried to bunk down in our master bedrooms.

Once I began agreeing with my mother's every pronouncement, the tension between us faded away. Nodding along gave me plenty of time to think about what my father had said to me in the Gold Bedroom: *You're more like me than you realize.*

He was wrong.

He had to be.

◇◇◇

When visiting hours ended, a mollified Caro and I blew goodbye kisses through the Plexiglas barrier. She returned to her social work with Demonios Femeninos while I crossed the street to San Sebastian Liquors to pick up a bottle of Gunn Vineyards' midlist chardonnay. Not for myself, but as an entree to Bambi's cocktail party aboard the *Runaround*. I arrived back in Gunn Landing Harbor a half hour later, fed everyone, then took the dogs for a quick walk.

Due to a southerly wind, the harbor was warm this evening, no jacket required. Hot nights usually didn't roll in until July or August, but the temperature couldn't have been below seventy. The fog held off, too, so as Bonz, Feroz, and I walked along the fence that separated the parking lot from the docks, we passed several boats where liveaboarders sat on deck enjoying this rare respite. Once the dogs did their business I took them back to the Merilee, grabbed the chardonnay, and headed to the north end of the harbor.

Bambi's party was still going strong. The *Runaround*'s deck was packed elbow-to-elbow with liveaboarders, Sunday sailors, and even a few landlubbers. Since the festivities had begun in the morning and it was now well after eight, people who weren't flat-out drunk were at least buzzed, but Bambi acted sober. Odd, given her reputation as a hard-partier. After beckoning me onboard, she accepted my proffered chardonnay with a tight smile. Up close I noticed that her eyes were red. Maybe she'd had more to drink that I thought.

"Considering everything that's happened, I'm surprised to see you, Teddy," she said, over the noise of a boom box blaring a Lady Gaga classic.

My own smile felt as insincere as hers looked. "Despite our differences about a certain sixteenth century queen, neighbors have to get along. So. Welcome to Gunn Landing Harbor, and may all your barnacles be little ones."

"What's a barnacle?"

Another landlubber. "Nothing to worry your pretty little head about since your *Runaround* has a fiberglass hull." But I wasn't fibbing about the "pretty" part. Bambi's body resembled that American icon, the Barbi doll. Her string bikini revealed most of her famous breasts, tiny waist, and impossibly long legs, but the frown lines bracketing her mouth made her look older than the age she admitted to.

She gestured toward an ice-filled cooler. "Help yourself."

"Thanks. Say, Bambi, what do you know about Victor…?" My attempt at quizzing her was cut short by Frank Turnbull, an attorney who specialized in family law. More than a bit overweight, he bore a startling likeness to yet another icon—Santa Claus. With a quick apology to me, he grabbed her around the waist and led her in a creaky fox trot to "Born This Way."

Biding my time, I plopped myself down on a deck chair, only belatedly recognizing the man next to me as Dr. Willis Pierce. "I thought you didn't like noise, Willis."

"My *Caliban*'s berthed right next door and it's not soundproof. The harbormaster came by an hour ago and told everyone to keep it down, but you see how well that's working." He shrugged. "If you can't beat 'em, join 'em. *Macbeth*, Act II, Scene III."

At my expression, he added, "Just kidding. It's from *A Streetcar Named Desire*. Ha ha, kidding again. But how about you? What are you doing here this lovely evening? Don't try to convince me the noise was bothering you, because your *Merilee*'s berthed at the other end of the harbor and you couldn't hear a cannon fired from here." His face assumed a sly look as he lowered his voice to a theatrical whisper. "Oh, I know. You're detecting."

"And here I thought I was being subtle."

"Better leave the detecting to the experts."

"Experts like Elvin Dade?"

He laid a light hand on my shoulder. "Teddy, this is a real, honest-to-God murder case, not *The Mousetrap*. Excellent play that, by the way. We performed it five years ago and sold out every seat. The thing's evergreen, so I'm considering scheduling it next semester. What do you think?" Not waiting for my answer, he hurried on. "As I was saying, you shouldn't do anything re the late lamented Victor Emerson that might put you in the line of fire."

"Given Caro's situation, there's no other choice. Elvin's still determined to pin Victor's murder on her, and with Joe away…"

"Don't say I didn't warn you." He looked glum, but let the subject drop.

We sat in companionable silence, sipping cheap wine, listening to Lady Gaga and watching people who should know better fling their half-naked bodies around the deck. Given the confined space, the amount of liquor flowing, and the number of folks perched precariously on the gunwales, I half-expected someone to be knocked overboard. An hour later, that still hadn't happened. Around the time Gaga was replaced by Usher, we were joined by handsome Yancy Haas, the stuntman who jousted as the Black Knight. A former San Sebastian resident, he had once dated Bambi, too. Come to think of it, who hadn't? He didn't flinch when she returned Frank Turnbull's booze-fuelled attentions, but after remarking on the surprisingly warm night, he managed to get in a dig on Bambi's current choice of suitors.

"She's obviously not into Frank for his looks," Yancy sniped. "Can you believe that whale is wearing a Speedo?"

Willis snickered. "When a whale has money, it wears what it wants."

And they say women are catty.

Sitting on the gunwales were more people I knew including, surprisingly, Deanna and Judd Sazac. When I had talked to Deanna earlier in the day, she accused Bambi of having an affair with her husband, yet here she was, partying on Bambi's boat.

Dancing next to the so-called whale I spotted fellow zookeepers Phil and Deborah Holt, who lived with their five-year-old daughter on the *Flotsam*, a ratty houseboat they had built themselves. The two had been married at Victor's wedding chapel with a Burmese python serving as Best Man and a pygmy goat for Maid of Honor. This set me to thinking about Joe, and our as yet unscheduled wedding. Winter? Next spring? Maybe we should wait until next summer so I could be a June bride. Running off to Vegas like Joe preferred to do sounded tacky to me, but when I had floated the idea of marrying at the zoo he balked.

"Teddy," he'd said, as we snuggled on the *Merilee* the night before he left for Homeland Security, "not that I don't love all those animals, because you know I do, but if we get married within two hundred miles of Gunn Landing, Caro will demand to do all the planning herself. Frankly, the idea terrifies me. Since my father started off as a farm laborer, she's not crazy about having me for a son-in-law, and I'm afraid that given her devious ways, she'll find a way to sabotage the ceremony."

Seeing his point, I had curtailed the wedding discussion to snuggle some more.

Yancy's chuckle startled me out of my mental trip down Lovebird Lane. "Hey, Teddy, who are you thinking about? Moi, perhaps? Willis? Nah, must be your handsome Sheriff Joe. You're positively glowing."

"Wool-gathering, that's all. Say, Yancy, weren't you camping out at the Faire when Victor was killed?"

He nodded. "Me and about a hundred other medieval riff-raff. For the duration of the Faire I'm sharing an RV with Billy Harris, the little guy who plays Sir Bedevere. We trailered our horses over together."

"Did you see anything suspicious that night?"

He glanced at Willis, who merely shrugged. "Why are you asking, Teddy? Oh. This is about your mother, isn't it? Poor woman. That judge is a creep, doing that to her. Sorry, I didn't see or hear anything, and neither did Billy, I expect. We'd invited a couple of wenches over, and as a result were rather, ah, busy."

"Which wenches?"

"I don't wench and tell."

The look in Yancy's eyes told me more questions weren't welcome, so I turned my attention to Bambi, who had finally escaped Frank Turnbull's pudgy clutches, and was headed our way.

After giving me a conspiratorial wink, Willis stood and offered her his seat. "Perhaps the lovely mademoiselle wishes to take a load off."

I smelled expensive perfume, something more overt than my mother's Je Reviens. Bambi still had lots to learn before she matched Caro. Good old Willis, for all his trepidation about my poking into the murder, had delivered her right into my hands. As Usher's sexy baritone stopped in mid-phrase, replaced by tween idol Justin Bieber, Bambi sat down.

"That should cool things off for a while," she said, nodding toward the boombox. "If this thing turns into an orgy, which is the way it seems to be headed, the harbor master'll throw us all in the brig."

"Other than that, how's it going?" I asked.

"Frank Turnbull just asked me out on a date." She wiped at her red eyes. Allegies?

"You go, girl. Not to change the subject, but did you see anything unusual the day Victor Emerson died?"

She sniffed. "You mean like your mother sulking around like a spoiled child? Not that that would be unnatural for her. What a prima donna."

Talk about the pot calling the kettle black. "Besides Caro."

"I dunno. There was a lot of freaky stuff going on. Women with no boobs trying to look busty." She stared hard at my flat chest, then continued. "Makeout sessions between monks and female pirates behind the privies, lepers tripping over pigs…"

"Besides that. Something really unusual, even for a Renaissance fair."

"You mean like Deanna and Judd Sazac screaming at each other near Ded Bob's RV?"

"They're known to argue a lot."

"This was no argument. Deanna hauled off and slapped Judd so hard it knocked his sunglasses off. He was getting ready to hit her back when Ded Bob popped his head out of the RV and told them to put a sock in it."

"Ded Bob's a ventriloquist's puppet."

"He still told them to shut up."

"Could you hear what they were fighting about?"

"Some woman, I think. Not that it had anything to do with me."

Of course not. "Victor Emerson officiated at their marriage, didn't he?"

Another sniff. "He married just about everyone in San Sebastian County."

I pointed to the Judds, who were dancing very, very close. "They look quite the happy couple now."

"Looks can be deceiving." She took a tissue out of her bra and blew her nose.

Once she'd finished, I asked, "Did you hear or see anything else? Other than the Sazac's scream-fest? And the slap?"

"Nosy, aren't you, Teddy. Nah, that's about…No, wait. There was something…Something…" She frowned, trying to concentrate. It looked painful. "I remember now. Before I headed back to San Sebastian after the Faire closed—you won't catch me sleeping anywhere near those nasty RVs, especially not Ded Bob's—I saw poor Victor talking to someone behind the Royal Armory. He looked angry."

"Who was he talking to?"

"I couldn't tell. The guy was in the shadows. I mean, I think it was a man but I can't be sure because it was someone wearing a black cloak with a hood."

"One of the Keegans, perhaps? They both dress like Goths, and they run the Royal Armory."

She shook her head. "Sorry. Look, not that this hasn't been nice and all, chatting like we're old friends when we're really not, but I need to get back and change that tweeny-bop crap for something adult. John Legend or Sinatra, maybe. Can't let anybody get knocked overboard, can I?"

Her hostessy concern arrived too late. I heard a shriek, then a splash. "Man overboard!" someone bawled.

By the time I made it through the crowd to the gunwale, Willis and Yancy were already hauling a waterlogged but smiling Frank Turnbull out of the greasy harbor water.

He'd lost his Speedo.

Chapter Eight

Frank Turnbull's dip into the harbor signaled another visit from the harbor master. This time she brought the Harbor Patrol along with orders to clear the boat, so that was the end of that. At least no one was arrested, just humiliated.

It was after ten when I made it back to the *Merilee*, but from the greeting I received from Bonz, Feroz, and Miss Priss, you'd think I'd been gone a week. After playing with them a while, I fired up my laptop to find out more about Victor Emerson, real name Glenn Reynolds Jamison. Thanks to Google, it was plenty.

On March 5, 1983, a young Jamison robbed a convenience store in Henderson, Nevada. When a customer tried to intervene, what had up until that point been a fairly peaceful armed robbery—if there is such a thing—went fatal. The customer, one Nicholas French, swung a six-pack of Diet Coke into Jamison's cheek. Jamison's .45 automatic went off, striking the customer in the mouth. The doctor who performed the autopsy said the man was dead before he hit the ground.

Jamison ran outside where a dark-colored car waited with its engine running, but before he could climb in, a nearby group of teenagers tackled him. The getaway car drove off, leaving Jamison behind. He eventually took a plea deal to escape the death penalty, but steadfastly refused to name his accomplice. Twelve years later he escaped from Ely State Prison by hiding in a laundry truck. A nationwide manhunt ensued, but although he was said to have been spotted in states as far-flung as Pennsylvania, Florida, and Missouri, he was never captured.

Now Jamison—a.k.a. Victor Emerson—lay dead on a slab, some other murderer's victim.

After learning all this, I might not have cared who killed Victor because his victim had been only twenty-four when he died. Nicholas French had only been picking up Lay's Sour Cream and Onion Potato Chips and Diet Coke for his pregnant wife. As far as I was concerned, Victor reaped what he had sown, albeit belatedly.

I stared at the image on my laptop. A young, clean-shaven man stared back from his booking photo. Other than the reddish-blond hair, the photograph looked nothing like the Victor Emerson I knew, but thirty years will make a big difference in a person's appearance. Victor's face rounded out when he packed on the pounds, and his hairline receded. When I squinted my eyes and paid attention to only the features, the resemblance became apparent. In Glenn Reynolds Jamison's mug shot I could see Victor Emerson's piggy eyes and his almost-feminine cupid's bow mouth.

Same man, different lives.

"Who killed you, Victor?" I whispered. "Whoever was driving that getaway car? A relative of your victim?"

I wasn't yet ready to believe his killer might be someone close to me.

◇◇◇

During my lunch break the next day I drove over to Gunn Castle to share what I had discovered about Victor Emerson with my father, and find out whether he'd learned anything not covered by Google.

"Miss Aster Edwina is in the library conversing with our houseguest," Mrs. McGinty said as we clattered down the hall. "How pleasant it is to have him here."

"Yeah, he's quite the charmer."

Upon entering the library, I saw the old rogue relaxing in a wingback chair while the aristocratic doyenne of the great Gunn family massaged some sort of cream onto his hands. When she looked up and saw me, she didn't even have the decency to look embarrassed.

"Oh, it's only you, Teddy. Shouldn't you be at work?" Rub. Rub.

Dad, recognizing that massage time had ended, withdrew his hands. "Hi, Teddy. I have some information for you."

"And I for you. Could we have a word in private?"

Aster Edwina glared, but at a reproving look from my father, she suggested Mrs. McGinty take us into the drawing room. She herself had business to take care of in the library. Reading up on the Marquis de Sade, probably.

As a child, I had always found the drawing room intimidating with its multiple fireplaces, paired Gainsboroughs, scary suits of armor, and wall-mounted displays of vicious-looking medieval weapons. Now I merely found it drafty. After Mrs. McGinty backed out of the room, Dad and I sat on facing Victorian settees more attractive than comfortable.

I told him what I'd already learned about Victor. "Now it's your turn," I finished.

"May the Gods of Google continue to smile on you. As for my paltry offerings, what do you want first, the good news or the bad?"

"Lump it together."

"You're no fun."

"Said the felon to the abettor."

"Manners, Teddy, manners." He fetched a cell phone from his pocket and poked it a couple of times. A screen lit up, full of data. "Here's what I've learned. It may not sound like much, but I'm certain more information is yet to come. First of all, the man you knew as Victor Emerson most definitely did have an accomplice in that convenience store heist, a gal named Kate Garrick. She was his main squeeze and was pregnant, to boot. If the robbery had been successful, they were going to stay with one of Kate's cousins until the baby was born, then move to Florida."

Ironic, considering that the victim's wife had been pregnant, too.

"What happened to the girlfriend? And the baby?"

"After the killing, Kate dropped out of sight for a few months, not even her parents knew where she was. When she turned up again, there was no baby in sight."

"Adoption?"

"Always a possibility, among other things."

I didn't want to think about the "other things."

"What else did your source tell you?"

He poked the cell phone again. "She wound up marrying a blackjack dealer at one of the Vegas casinos and after a few years, they moved to Jersey. That's all I've got on her. So far, anyway. I have more feelers out. As to Glenn Jamison's…"

"Call him Victor or I'll get confused."

"Whatever you wish. Anyway, as to your Victor's prison career, word going around is that he was a snitch. That's someone who…"

"I know what a snitch is, Dad."

"Yes, every high school has one. Zoos, too, I expect. Like I was saying, Glenn…ah, Victor wound up in the prison infirmary on more than one occasion. One time he had a broken finger, the other time he'd been shanked." He looked up. "A shank is…"

"I know what a shank is, too."

"Been watching prison movies, have you?"

"My all-time fav is *Busty Blond Bombshells in Big Chains*."

His face took on a disapproving expression. "You weren't raised to be so snotty, Teddy."

"No, I was raised to be my felon father's co-conspirator. But don't mind me, just go ahead and tell me the rest of what your criminal friends found out, probably by twisting arms and pulling out fingernails and such."

The disapproving expression deepened. "My friends are white collar criminals. Good people. Never violent."

"And the Yeti eloped with Big Foot."

"Do you want to know what I know or do you want to just sit there cracking wise?"

I tried to look contrite. "Sorry, Dad."

"You should be, you ungrateful brat. Anyway, the people I spoke with say that escaping was the only thing that kept Victor alive. Up until now, that is. He made a lot of enemies during his sojourn in Ely, and those people aren't the forgiving kind. Especially when it comes to snitches."

"Were you been able to come up with the names of people he snitched on?"

"Not yet, but I will. My sources are still working on it. Oh, and here's another tidbit I picked up. Know what Victor was called in prison? You'll love it."

"Enlighten me."

"The Preacher. Seems his father was a Pentecostal minister and our boy had been well-drilled in Scripture, not that it seems to have worked out very well in the behavior department, which seems to be true of so many preachers these days. On Sundays, when the prison chaplain wasn't available, probably escorting some poor wretch to the electric chair or gas chamber or whatever death device they use in Nevada, Victor would lead the services, hallelujah, brothers and sisters!"

During his pause for breath, I was able to put two and two together. "Dad, preachers marry people."

"Why state the obvious?"

"Don't you get it? While growing up, Victor must have seen his father perform hundreds of marriage ceremonies, so setting himself up as a phony chaplain was easy. Ergo, the wedding chapel."

The playfulness left his voice. "There's one little problem that doesn't seem to have crossed your mind yet, and it's not good news for your mother."

"Which is?"

"Your Victor Emerson was a convicted felon living under an assumed name, which means he was legally ineligible to officiate over state functions. I happen to know from my own matrimonial adventure with your mother that in order to perform a binding marriage ceremony, the reverend or rabbi or justice of the peace or whatever must have an up-to-date, state-approved license to do so. The license must be issued in the person's legal name, otherwise, any marriage he or she performs could be considered null and void."

I looked down at my arms and saw goose bumps. "Victor performed marriage ceremonies for Mother twice."

"Yes he did, Teddy, both times to multi-millionaires. Thanks to Facebook and Twitter and the like, Gunn Landing gossip makes it all the way to Costa Rica, so I happen to know that when those marriages ended, Caro received large spousal support settlements, making it possible for her—and you—to continue living in the luxury to which I'd accustomed her. What do you think both of those exes are going to do now, hmm? Shrug and let the spousal support issue slide? Knowing the filthy rich as well as I do, when the news about Victor's falsified license comes out those men's attorneys will rush to civil court and demand Caro pay back every penny of their clients' money."

"But she married them in good faith!"

He put the cell phone back in his pocket. "Where money's concerned, there's no such thing as good faith."

◇◇◇

Feeling sick, I drove back to the zoo. After parking my Nissan in the employee's lot, I sat there for a while, just thinking. When the truth came out, even someone as dense as Acting Sheriff Elvin Dade would understand he had been handed the Mother Lode of motives. He no longer had to convince the county attorney that Caro killed Victor in a passing snit over the Anne Boleyn snub. Instead, he could argue that somehow she'd found out the phony reverend's true identity and realized her ride on the Money Train was about to end. Faced with the prospect of a financial apocalypse, calmer souls than my mother might respond with rage.

But a murderous rage?

I didn't think so. Caro might be greedy but I couldn't see her killing someone over money. She would simply marry another multi-millionaire after ensuring that the selected reverend or justice of the peace was on the up-and-up.

As I headed across the zoo parking lot to the employee's entrance, it occurred to me that Caro's was not the only person whose marriage—or marriages, plural—now existed in legal limbo. Off the top of my head, I could name several couples Victor had married, many of them friends of mine. Zookeepers Deborah and Phil Holt. The battling Sazacs. Bambi O'Dair and her ex. Medieval weapons retailers Melissa and Cary Keegan. Maybe even Caro's maid and her unemployed ex-con husband. Some of the couples had children, with complicated their situations. Once a judge ruled on the status of their marriages, would their children be labeled illegitimate? Illegitimacy might not be the social disgrace it had once been, but it could play havoc in certain legal cases. Inheritance, for instance.

What a legal quagmire Victor Emerson/Glenn Jamison had created!

Would all his former clients have to re-marry to be considered on the up-and-up? Would fathers be forced to adopt their own children?

I didn't know enough about the law to guess how it would play out in the end, but it was a good bet that when the family law attorneys of San Sebastian County found out about the sham marriages, they would lift a chorus of hosannas to the heavens. This thought immediately brought back the image of Frank Turnbull minus his Speedo, so I forced myself to stop thinking about such things.

Thus it was only hours later, when I was in the midst of shoveling anteater dung into a wheelbarrow, that the names of another not-really-married couple occurred to me.

Acting Sheriff Elvin Dade and his holier-than-thou wife, Wynona.

Chapter Nine

If Wynona had discovered her marriage was invalid and her children's legitimacy thrown into question, the shame and embarrassment might have sent her off her head. Maybe enough to commit murder. If so, it would explain Acting Sheriff Elvin Dade's odd behavior in the llama enclosure. Elvin's brain operated on low wattage, but even someone as dim as he knew better than to stomp back and forth across a crime scene, obliterating the killer's tracks—not to mention pulling out the crossbow bolt and wiping it down, destroying any remaining fingerprints.

My shock segued into anger. No wonder he had been so quick to accuse Caro. He was sacrificing my mother to keep his wife out of jail!

Hands shaking, I resumed shoveling anteater dung until the enclosure was spotless. Hard physical work has its perks, and one of them was burning off the adrenaline that accompanied a full-out rage attack. By the time I trundled the loaded wheelbarrow over to the recycling area for local gardeners to pick up, I had calmed enough to use my brain again. An officer of the law, Elvin Dade would never frame an innocent woman, not even to save his own wife. *Oh, yes, he would,* a little imp whispered into my ear. I tried to ignore it. As for Wynona, I'd never liked the self-righteous prig, but imagining her as a cold-blooded killer proved impossible. It was also inconceivable that she had seen a crossbow before working the Renaissance Faire, let alone had the skill to murder someone with it. The imp whispered again, reminding me that she might have attended one of the Faire's medieval weapons demonstrations. As for skill, Victor might have been shot close up—something we would never know because of Elvin's clue-destroying behavior.

The imp went on to remind me of an observation by Sherlock Holmes crime writers loved to quote: *Once you eliminate the impossible, whatever remains, no matter how improbable, must be the truth.*

How much did I really know about Wynona?

Not much, I realized. Unlike me, she wasn't a lifelong San Sebastian County resident. I'd once heard that Wynona's family moved to San Sebastian when she was a teen, and that her parents had been killed in a car wreck around the time of her marriage to Elvin. Soon afterwards, she and her new husband had immediately decamped from a shabby rented bungalow into her parents' much nicer house.

The imp whispered into my ear again: *Convenient car wreck, wasn't it?*

Disgusted with my suspicions about an innocent, however obnoxious, woman I sent the imp packing. One thing was for certain. A trip to the county clerk's office was in order. I needed to find out how many other marriages Victor had officiated over, but to do that I needed to take some time off. Rather than beg Aster Edwina, I would ask the zoo director.

Zorah Vega was in her office when I stopped by the zoo's administration building after clocking out. On a bulletin board she had pinned a colorful blowup of Sssybil's Facebook page, on which the snake had described her adventures.

Without looking up from a huge pile of papers, Zorah okayed my request. "Phil and Deborah Holt came in this morning asking for extra hours, something about dental bills, so that'll work out nicely for all of you. Apparently that weird boat they live on needs major repair work, and given your recent problems with the *Merilee*, you know all about liveaboarder expenses."

Months earlier I had been driven to near-financial ruin buying a new motor for the *Merilee*, but the Holt's appropriately named *Flotsam* was another matter entirely. Built out of mismatched remnants from various salvaged vessels, the houseboat was in constant peril of being declared unseaworthy.

"And by the way, Teddy, you're the lion this year."

"Huh?"

"You know, for the Great Escape."

With everything else on my mind, I had forgotten about The Great Escape, the yearly drill that honed the zoo's Code Red skills. Heaven forbid a lion escaped its enclosure, but if one did, we would be ready.

"Zorah, I don't think…"

She looked up from her papers for the first time. "It's next Friday at six-thirty, which'll give you time to get into your lion costume after the zoo closes for the day. I've already plotted your escape route. This time the media will be following part way, so make sure Ariel Gonzales' crew gets good coverage. Girlfriend's all pumped about it."

"But…"

"It's obvious that our capture skills need honing. Take Sssybil's escape, for instance. It could have been handled better, which is probably why she's still not back. Good thing she's not loose in a heavily populated area, huh?" Her face twisted into a half-grin. "And at least she's tweeting regularly and keeping her Facebook page up to date. Ha! I hope the next time we hear from her, or about her, it's not because somebody got fanged or a farm worker went after her with a hoe. In the meantime, I'm holding Phil Holt personally responsible. He should have notified me earlier there was termite damage to the reptile house. I can't imagine why he didn't. Something else on his mind, maybe? Probably that damned houseboat. Money troubles are the worst, aren't they? Oh, well. Come to think of it, the same warning goes for you, too. If you see a problem or something that could eventually become a problem, notify me immediately."

"Of course I will, but about the Great Escape. I can't…"

"Here's the way it's gonna work." She stood up and walked over to the big mural of the Gunn Zoo on the wall behind her. Tracing her finger along the trails, she said, "You, in your lion costume, will 'escape' from the night house behind the big cat enclosure. You'll run down the hill along Africa Trail toward California Habitat with park rangers, zookeepers, and the media hot on your furry little heels. Make sure you growl a lot. And take swipes at them with your paws every now and then. Be the lion!"

"But…"

She shushed me with a wave. "Save your breath, Teddy. Aster Edwina personally chose you for this. She says you really know how to play to the camera."

I groaned.

Continuing to trace the Great Escape route on the map, she said, "On Africa Trail, you'll run past the zebras, giraffes, Watusi cattle, rhinos, and elands. Very camera-friendly stuff. From California Habitat you'll cut across that little valley to Down Under, maybe slow a bit so the cameras can get the koalas and wallabies, they're so cute and the children love them. You'll have about ten minutes to take a breather there, because everyone will stop following you. They'll be coming back up here to do other things. But after your break, you'll run up the Tropics Trail hill to Monkey Mania, where the chasers will pick you up again."

"Wait a minute, what 'other things' will they do?"

"That's where I come in. Aster Edwina wants me to demonstrate how the zoo puts together diets that range all the way from termites to cow carcasses, so I'll lead the media and anyone else who wants to come along on a tour through the animals' cafeteria."

"Maybe you should skip the termite barrel. And the worm trays. For non-zookeepers they can be sickening."

"Aster Edwina's orders," Zorah replied, shaking her head. "She wants people to realize it's not all glamour and glitz around here."

Since I could still smell the anteater dung on my shoes, I had to agree.

"Anyway, while we're doing that, " she continued, "you'll still be hanging out in the bushes near Down Under, getting all rested up. When we're through with the animal cafeteria tour, I'll radio you that it's time to start toward Monkey Mania. The media will be there by then, so make sure you're running flat out, okay? They'll chase you all the way back to the lion house and then net you. Try not to fall too hard, okay? Once, the guy who played the lion broke his wrist. All in all, it'll be about a two-mile run, but you're in good shape so you shouldn't have any trouble, especially with that ten minute rest stop near Down Under. And the day should be cooling down by then, so it shouldn't be too hot in that lion suit."

Resistance being futile, I nodded glumly.

Zorah beamed. "I appreciate your enthusiasm, Teddy."

On the way back to my car I checked my cellphone. Still no calls from Joe, not that I'd expected one, but I had received a tweet from Sssybil.

"Open up that Golden Gate, Sssan Francisssco here I come!"

◇◇◇

The county clerk's office didn't open until ten, so I decided to spend Thursday morning cruising the Internet, looking for information on the people working the Faire the night Victor was killed. Deciding it would be best to get the easiest out of the way first, I started with zookeeper Deborah Holt. We'd been good friends for a couple of years now, and I was certain she had no guilty secrets.

Which showed me how wrong you can be about your friends.

The first hint Deborah had a less-than-pristine past came from her Facebook page, where one of her posts raised my eyebrows. "Deer Woman better watch her step around my husband. I've got a Black Belt in karate and know how to use it."

It didn't take a rocket scientist to know who Deer Woman was, but Bambi and the reptile keeper? On second thought, why not? Deer Woman had bedded just about every other male in San Sebastian County, and Phil Holt was good looking in a string-bean sort of way. After a few more minutes of looking into

Deborah's background, I found something even more startling. Twice during her college years at San Francisco State, she had been arrested for attacks on other women, each time for the same reason: jealousy over a man. In both cases the criminal charges were dropped, but her second victim took her to civil court and was awarded twelve hundred dollars in damages.

The information so startled me that I decided to postpone snooping on my other friends. Besides, Bambi remained alive and well. Victor Emerson was the victim, not San Sebastian's blond husband-snatcher.

◇◇◇

As it turned out, getting a complete list of Victor's sham marriages at the county clerk's offices was much harder than cruising the Internet. The stern-looking woman at the Information Desk told me in no uncertain terms that if I had a name she could help me, but that I would need a warrant to get a comprehensive list of all the marriages Victor had performed. Since I wasn't an officer of the law, she added maliciously, I wouldn't be able to get said warrant. My appeal to her better nature fell on deaf ears, possibly because she had no better nature. I left the San Sebastian County complex disappointed.

Working with dangerous animals had taught me to always have a backup plan, so after visiting Caro at the jail—she was impossible as ever—I headed north to Victor's wedding chapel. Located on a county road a couple of miles outside San Sebastian city limits, it sat well back from the highway. The chapel was so surrounded by trees and high shrubbery that an elephant could be standing on its porch and no one passing by on the highway would notice. Perfect.

I rolled my Nissan to a stop between two flowering rhododendron bushes, which made the little truck effectively disappear from the highway. After slipping on a pair of latex gloves, I walked over to the chapel, which was little more than a white wooden rectangle with a steeple stuck on top. It wasn't as tacky as I had imagined. The paint was sparkling and the deep green shutters flanking the flower-boxed windows gave the plain building the countrified charm that had appealed to so many San Sebastian County couples.

The trailer behind it, half-hidden by more rhododendrons, was a different story.

When I parted the bushes and stepped closer, I saw that the single-wide displayed rust along its seams, and the cement pad underneath was crumbling. The tatty curtains in the windows looked like they hadn't been washed in years. The trailer's small yard, surrounded on all sides by brush and rhododendrons, fared somewhat better, leading me to believe that Victor had spent most of his time outside, where two Walmart lawn chairs nestled together behind a small barbeque pit. Growing closer, I could smell the remains of past fires.

But I wasn't here to snoop into Victor's domesticity or lack thereof. What I was after would be found in the chapel. Accordingly, I turned my back on Life With Victor and approached the chapel again. Its front and back doors were sealed by police stickers, but after a quick walk-around, I found an unlocked window. After dragging one of the lawn chairs underneath it, access proved easy.

Victor had only been dead for five days but the chapel's interior already signaled neglect. A cobweb stretched across a latticed arbor and dead flowers drooped from two dusty vases. I had last been here to perform maid-of-honor duties at Caro's latest wedding, and remembered that Victor had brought the wedding registry down from the pulpit. The registry was still there, which I guess must have been its usual spot, but a quick flip through the pages revealed marriages only as far back as April.

After a brief search in the office, which was much less sparkling than the chapel's public area—I found several more registries in a battered file cabinet. They were big fat books, the oldest stretching back to the time the chapel had opened for business. I dropped them carefully out of the window, then followed. I closed the window behind me, and carted the lawn chair back to where I'd found it. No point in advertising my presence.

Once the marriage registries were safe in the Nissan, I turned my attention to Victor's rusting trailer again. It would be a shame to have driven all the way out here without at least taking a peek, so I walked over and tried the door. Yellow-taped and locked. I had no luck with the windows, either, so I gave up and drove home, content I had already found what I needed.

◇◇◇

Back at the *Merilee*, Miss Priss hissed a complaint while the Chihuahua joined DJ Bonz in a loud welcome home chorus.

"I'm glad to see you guys, too," I said. "Want walkies now or later?"

Not waiting for an answer—dogs never say "later" to walkies—I snapped on their leashes and we set off, the tiny Feroz easily keeping up with my terrier's three-legged hops. Because the evening fog hadn't yet rolled in, Gunn Landing Park was more crowded than usual and not only dog owners were availing themselves of its amenities. Some liveaboarders were cooking dinner on the charcoal grills. Others had formed a pickup basketball game on the small asphalt court. Among the ball players I recognized reptile keeper Phil Holt and Judd Sazac, one half of the battling Sazacs. Howie Fife cheered them on from the sidelines, his over-protective mother nowhere in sight. After the dogs had done their business, I walked over to join him.

"How's the ankle, Howie?"

"Still sore, but I'll be okay by the weekend. Enough to play the court minstrel, anyway. All I have to do is sit on a cushion at the Royal Pavilion and sing 'Greensleeves' and stuff like that."

That surprised me. "You sing?"

"Sure. And play the lute. Dr. Pierce made me learn last semester so I could play Feste in *Twelfth Night*. I liked it so much I learned a bunch of other Renaissance-type songs. Want to hear one?"

Without waiting for my answer, he sang in a surprisingly sweet counter-tenor, *"O mistress mine, where are you roaming? O stay and hear! Your true-love's coming, that can sing both high and low."* Then he stopped, blushing.

I was stunned. "Why, Howie, that was beautiful! You sound like you've been singing all your life."

The blushed deepened. "I have, actually. My dad taught me."

"He's a singer?"

"More of a producer, but he…"

"Howie!" Ada Fife's sharp voice cut across the park. She was standing by the first row of picnic tables. "Dinner's ready!"

Howie's face turned from red to white. "Oh, God, forget what I just said, okay? I'm not supposed to…Uh, gotta go!"

As he started away from me I could see that his limp was almost gone, but by the time he reached his mother it had returned full force.

Interesting.

A tug on the leash reminded me I had not come to the park alone. Feroz was scrambling his little legs in a vain attempt to reach a piece of blackened hamburger held out by a woman at a sizzling charcoal grill, swigging something red from a wineglass. Bambi, looking considerably less frenetic than at her party. Not only less frenetic, but even glum.

"Behave!" I told the Chihuahua. "That's not on your diet."

Bambi—I almost smiled when I remembered she'd been dubbed Deer Woman by my friend Deborah—gave me a half-hearted smile. "A little Kobe beef never hurt anyone, especially a dog."

Thus speaketh a non-dog-owner. "You baste it with anything?"

"Tequila. Some tabasco."

"Like I said, not on his diet. Feroz's digestion tends to be iffy, if you know what I mean, and that can be a real problem on a boat. By the way, why are you cooking out here? Having problems with the *Runaround*'s galley stove?"

She took another sip of wine. "I just didn't want the boat smelling like grease for the next month, because I'm putting it up for sale."

"Why? The *Runaround* is such a lovely craft."

"If you're not the seasick type. Frank Turnbull was going to take me out for a sail on the thing this morning but I lost my breakfast before we made it out of the harbor, so I'm sticking to dry land from now on. This'll be the first thing I've eaten all day."

She gestured at the picnic table heaped with lettuce leaves, sliced tomatoes, mayonnaise, catsup, pickles, onions, an open bottle of Gunn Vineyards 2006 Merlot, and several Dixie cups, the better with which to drink a six-pack of Diet Coke. Quite a spread for a dinner-for-one.

"Why don't you join me?" she asked. "Willis Pierce was supposed to stop by but I just got a call from him saying that something came up at the college and he can't make it, so I've got more than enough here. And I'd kind of like the company. I'm feeling lonely."

That a woman like Bambi could be lonely surprised me, but I guess it happens to all of us at one time or another. I had felt unsettled myself since Joe had left for Virginia. Still…I declined a burger, but having an ulterior motive, sat down at the picnic table anyway, the dogs settling themselves at my feet.

"You might talk me into some of that merlot," I said.

"That's fine, but on the way here, I managed to break the other wineglass."

"A Dixie cup'll do."

"Talk about a waste of good wine," she grumbled, taking a swig from her glass.

I could have said the same thing about the expensive Kobe beef she had cremated, but only watched while she slapped a thick black patty on a plain white bun and slathered it with condiments. When she sat across from me, I noticed something else. She wore as much makeup as usual, but the thick coating of Erase couldn't hide the dark circles under her eyes, and the whites around her eyes were veiny and pink. Allergies can be hell.

Testing the waters, I said, "Shame about Victor, isn't it?"

"Yeah."

"He performed your marriage ceremony to Max Giffords, didn't he?"

"Fat lot of good that did."

Did she mean because the marriage had so quickly ended in divorce, or had she somehow learned that her marriage was a sham and that she might now be called upon to return the hefty settlement she'd received? I decided not to ask. "You two were pretty close. Bet you miss him."

She put her burned burger down before tasting it and took a deep drink of merlot. "Why would I miss Max? He was such a troll."

"I meant Victor Emerson."

Another gulp of merlot. "Oh. Victor. He was a close friend so of course I feel bad." She actually looked it, too.

"You two dated for a while, right?"

She slammed her wineglass down so hard the stem snapped off. "You're disgusting, Teddy!" To my astonishment, she reached across the table, snatched the Dixie cup from my hand, and tossed it to the ground, splattering poor Bonz with red wine.

I know when I'm not wanted, so I escorted the dogs back to the *Merilee*.

Once the animals were fed and I had washed the merlot off Bonz's white and brown coat, I put Adele on the CD player and began looking through Victor's marriage logs. In the first book, besides the couples I already knew about, I recognized the names of the mayor, two sheriff's deputies, several members of the San Sebastian City Council, various workers at the Faire, Caro's new maid, a few zookeepers, and a large chunk of the harbor's liveaboarders.

How many of them had attended one of the medieval weapons demonstrations? Maybe all of them. I closed the book and started on the second.

Halfway through I found two names that made me gasp in disbelief.

Chapter Ten

Friday at the zoo was relatively uneventful. No more animals escaped and the elusive Sssbyl still hadn't bitten anyone. She was stirring up trouble, though, because she bragged in her morning tweet that she'd breakfasted on a litter of baby rabbits. This outraged a local member of PETA, who sent out an answering tweet of her own, "@PetaGrrl—Sssbyl shld remember some folks eat snakes. Vegans rule!" Not missing a trick, Sssybl tweeted back, "@Sssbyl—Vegansss R yummy 2!"

While working with the animals during the day, I tried to keep my mind focused on them, but it was hard. Victor Emerson had been dead for less than a week and the inept Elvin had done little to solve the case. Granted, the names I found in Victor's marriage registers opened up a new area for investigation, but would it be enough? If only Joe were here! He would know what to do. But he was still somewhere in the wilds of Virginia with Homeland Security, unreachable by phone or by Internet.

I spent the rest of the day feeling lost and lonely, and by the time I clocked out I had made myself thoroughly miserable.

Determined to fight my way out of bleak mood, I filled the evening with a longer-than-usual visit to the San Sebastian County Jail, where I discovered that Caro had a new manicure. This time the couleur de jour was Starstruck Orange Glitter.

"Isn't that a bit gaudy for you?" I asked.

She sniffed. "It's from a line called Prison Chic, which is highly appropriate considering my situation. But let's not waste our time discussing something as trivial as color. The jailhouse grapevine says Elvin Dade is trying to frame me for Victor's murder. Is that true? If so, why didn't you tell me?"

"I didn't want you to worry." No point in telling her yet that half the people in San Sebastian County, including Wynona Dade, had motives to kill Victor, too. For my own reasons, I wanted to wait until the media broke the story.

"I'm already worried, Teddy. You don't think I killed him over that stupid Anne Boleyn thing, do you?"

"Of course not. You wouldn't hurt a fly." Unless the fly hurt me. "Not to change the subject or anything, but does Soledad Rodriguez get many visitors?"

"Why do you care? It's not like you're friends or anything."

"I thought it would be a nice gesture to get to know my mother's cell mate, so I brought this." I held up the box of Whitman's Sampler the guards had allowed in.

"You're giving chocolates to Soledad instead to me?"

I flashed the other box. "For you, Caro, nothing but Godiva."

The cranky tone disappeared. "In that case, I find your gesture toward Soledad very kind."

"It is, isn't it?"

Bribes work. A half-hour later I was facing the leader of Demonios Femeninos through the Plexiglas partition while she eyed the Whitman's Sampler. Soledad Rodriguez wasn't as young as I'd expected, probably her late twenties. Maybe her hard life aged her early. Like many gang-affiliated women, she had shaved her eyebrows and drawn them back with thin black lines. Her full mouth wore no lipstick, just a brown penciled outline that mirrored her stark brows. The overall effect was more than a little frightening, which was probably why she'd adopted it.

She pointed a long black nail toward the candy and in a thick Spanglish accent said, "'Bout how many pieces of chocolate are in there? I can't have some and not share with my *chicas.*"

I looked at the Sampler, which the guard had promised to lift over the barrier at the end of our visit. "It's the forty-ounce box so I'd guess seventy? Eighty?"

"And you just giving them to me?"

"That's right."

"Even when I don't know you?"

"You've been nice to my mother."

"But you still want something. What?"

"Huh?"

She crossed her arms and the sleeves of her orange jump suit slipped up, revealing a tattooed female devil. "You heard me, Rojo."

"Rojo?"

"Red. What you want from me?"

Maybe it was my imagination but it seemed like the longer we sat there, the thicker her accent became. With her fierce appearance and defiant manner, she reminded me of Del Malinga, the zoo's Brazilian jaguar no one could get near. Not that anyone wanted to.

"I need information, Soledad."

"You want me rat out one a my *chicas*, Rojo, get your skinny ass gone before I come over this screen and whop it."

"I wouldn't dream of asking you to rat out one of your *chicas*, Soledad. And my ass isn't skinny, but thanks anyway for the compliment. Now let's look at the situation. You're in here awaiting trial for murdering Duane Langer, right?"

"So?"

"What I want to know is, did you really murder your husband?"

For a very brief moment shock erased the ferocity on her face. Then she recovered. "You crazy! That white Viking Vengeance dude not my husband."

"*Au contraire*. A little bird told me Victor Emerson married you and Duane six years ago at that chapel outside of town. Given the state of war that exists between your associates, I understand wanting to keep it secret, but I need to know if you two ever got divorced, and if so, when and why? He rough you up or something?"

She leaned back in her chair and sat there in silence, her face blank. When she finally spoke again, the Spanglish was gone.

"Why do you need to know and why should I tell you? What goes on in my life is none of your business."

We were finally getting somewhere. "In a way it is. You've been accused of killing someone, and so has my mother. Unless I'm wrong, you're both innocent. To get right down to it, your marriage to Duane is on file at the county clerk's office, and your divorce will be, too—if you got one. It would be the easiest thing in the world for me to walk over there and request those records, so why don't you save me the walk? My feet hurt."

Curiosity replaced some of the hostility. "What makes you think I'm innocent? Sure, your mother doesn't have death in her, a slap or two maybe if someone does something bad to someone she loves, but nothing more."

"Don't sell Caro short. She once almost broke a woman's nose."

As I recounted my childhood run-in with Aster Edwina and my mother's subsequent response, the hint of a smile softened Soledad's face. "Props to Caro. That Aster Edwina is one tough broad."

"Not that day."

"Tell me, Rojo, what brought about your fine and generous opinion of me?"

"I've heard a lot about you, and shooting someone six times in the back isn't your style."

White teeth flashed. "I lean more toward a knife in the gut, Rojo."

"So you say."

She shrugged. "Believing that kind of thing keeps the *chicas* in line."

"Back to Duane, then. Did you two ever get divorced?"

"No."

"Why not?"

"Are you going to laugh if I tell you it's because I'm Catholic?"

"Some people take that kind of thing more seriously than others."

"I'm one of them."

"Then you're Duane's widow. Will you inherit anything? Money? House? Car?"

"When we got married I didn't take anything from him and he didn't take anything from me. And for your information, he never hurt me. Never. And I never hurt him. Regardless of the the color of our skins, we loved each other." Tears threatened those hard eyes.

I let her recover before asking, "You kept the marriage secret because?"

"Because those racist dudes in Viking Vengeance would have killed us both if they found out. The *chicas* wouldn't have been thrilled, either."

I thought about that for a moment. "Soledad, have you thought about how lucky you are to be in jail right now? Where you're protected from the Vikings?"

The eyes softened even more. "Teddy, I thank the Virgin every night."

◇◇◇

At first, Saturday seemed even more uneventful than Friday. I awoke on a gently rocking *Merilee*, fed my appreciative furballs, and as I walked the dogs through the dewy park, saw the disappearing fog uncover a sun-spackled Pacific. Ah, Paradise.

Then I bought the newspaper.

"MURDERED MINISTER WAS ESCAPED KILLER!" screamed the headline on the *San Sebastian Gazette*.

The article got most of it right, referring to Elvin Dade as "acting sheriff" not capping the title. The reporting team had even printed the names of Victor Emerson's later customers. Bev Martin, the editor of the *Gazette*'s Op Ed page, and who had been married by the phony minister with the groom's pet pig in attendance, summed up her column with the following paragraph:

> "This morning some San Sebastian Countyites will
> be re-examining their marriages, wondering whether
> to get hitched all over again or say sayonara forever.

Since I'm six months pregnant and Gordon's old-fashioned parents would frown at being the grandparents of an illegitimate child, my maybe-not-legal hubby and I will immediately hie ourselves hither to the nearest real minister to legalize our sinful union, but only *after* we double-check his credentials."

When Alejandro and I arrived at the Renaissance Faire, a bevy of fair maids, monks, jesters, and vendors were huddled near Llama Rides reading the newspaper together. Most thought the situation hilarious, especially since Elvin Dade and Wynona were mentioned twice on the front page.

Cary Keegan, a grim vision in his usual black, didn't find it so funny. "What the hell are we supposed to do?"

"Get married again. If Melissa is willing, that is," a monk quipped.

"What do you mean by that?"

"You're not exactly Prince Charming, you know."

Before Cary took a fist to the monk, I told the crowd their noise was upsetting the llama. Since several had been the victims of earlier spit bombs, they dispersed.

All except Speaks-To-Souls. The animal psychic stood there with two new greyhounds, the earlier two already adopted. "Poor Cary," she said, as she watched him walk away.

"Poor Cary, my foot. The man's a thug."

"And poor, pitiful Melissa is an innocent victim?"

Her attitude took me aback. "Please tell me you don't believe there's ever an excuse for domestic abuse."

"There are no bruises in that relationship, just manipulation."

"Well, yeah, I guess he does plenty of that, too."

"Teddy, I was talking about Melissa."

She and her greyhounds strolled away.

Unsettled by her comment, I fitted out Alejandro for the day, making certain his saddle's cinch was tight enough not to slip, loose enough not to pinch. Having learned that saddles forecast the advent of children, he stood patiently.

The Faire opened promptly at eight. For this second weekend, more fair-goers had opted for costumes and soon the High Street swarmed with scores of sexy wenches, monks, jesters, and pirates. Llama Rides did a booming business. Throughout the morning child after child lined up to ride the serene Alejandro. The children behaved well enough, but the parents were another story. In their eagerness to get photographs of their precious darlings on Alejandro, several moms and dads tried to slip around the gate for a closer shot, although I had posted a sign telling them to stay well back. Fortunately, I was always able to stop them before they made it through.

At ten, Deborah Holt came by to spell me for thirty minutes. The fact that she was no longer legally married to the reptile keeper didn't seem to bother her.

"Guess Phil and I'll have to get married all over again," she said, chuckling. "Good thing we still like each other, unlike a few couples I know. Several of us zookeepers are going to use Pastor Smithfield, in Monterey. He's around seventy and has lived there since he was a baby, so his life's an open book. No trouble with the law, either, other than that pot bust back in the Seventies. But how about our old Victor, huh? Robbery. Murder. Escape from prison. Who'd have thought the tubby little guy had it in him."

"His killer, probably."

"Guess you've got a point there. I'll feel better once he's caught."

I couldn't resist a grin, myself. "*He*? Tut tut, oh sexist one. Most women could use a crossbow if the occasion called for it. Didn't you see Melissa shoot it at the demonstration?"

"That was just a target. In real life a woman wouldn't do something like that."

"Didn't you hear about that woman over in Castroville last week? Fed her boyfriend rat poison and sang *Rolling in the Deep* while he flopped around on the floor."

"Poison's more of a woman's weapon," she said, disapprovingly.

"We've come a long way, baby."

She gave me a look. "Teddy, sometimes you plain creep me out."

I spent the rest of my break seeing the sights. This was Willis Pierce's first full day as King Henry the Eighth. For the occasion, he had dyed his black hair and beard red, and put enough padding around himself to resemble the much-married Tudor king. Although he nodded regally when his courtiers bowed and scraped, it was easy to see he didn't enjoy his new role as much as the old one—roaming the Faire quoting Shakespearean sonnets. Bambi didn't look happy either; so much for her winning the battle over Anne Boleyn. I smiled to show I bore no grudges over her behavior the other day, but she looked right through me with reddened eyes.

Remembering Speaks-To-Souls strange comment about Melissa and Cary Keegan's marriage, I drifted by the Royal Armory. The crossbow display was gone, replaced by two long claymores and a goofy Goth-style sword that appeared more decorative than deadly. For once, Melissa looked happy. She was showing one of the claymores to Yancy Haas, who was wearing full Black Knight armor. According to the Faire's schedule, he had already fought one joust today and would fight three more before the day was over. He seemed spry for a man who was repeatedly knocked from his horse by the actor playing Sir Galahad, then I reminded myself that as a professional stuntman he knew how to fall. Melissa's glowing beauty might have had something to do with his cheery demeanor, too.

"This claymore is as pretty as you, Melissa," I heard him tell her.

Looking thunderous, Cary interrupted their conversation. "That's enough, Yancy. You gonna buy that claymore or not? Put up or shut up."

Melissa cringed as if expecting a blow, but Yancy merely said, "Shut up, I guess. Since I'm not playing a Highlander, I'll pass on the claymore, although I'll admit it's a fine piece of workmanship. Have a nice day, you two."

Nodding to Melissa, Yancy headed back to the jousting arena.

Cary scowled at his wife. Recalling what Speaks-To-Souls had said about her, I wondered if her expression of abject terror might be a little too practiced.

Continuing along the High Street I was surprised to see Wynona Dade assisting the high school principal acting the part of the Lord High Torturer as he pretend-flogged a shrieking peasant. I had taken it for granted that after discovering the legality of her marriage was questionable, the holier-than-thou woman would be in seclusion somewhere, mourning her common law wife status in sackcloth and ashes. Yet there she stood, dressed in prim gray Puritan garb, laying out torture implements. Talk about type casting.

I resolved to be pleasant. "How doeth thou today, Maid Wynona?"

She gave me a mean smile. "Passably well, Maid Theodora. And how doeth *thou*, now that your aged mother rotteth in jail, as well she shouldest?"

You can insult me, but don't insult my mother. "Dame Caro's sorrowful habitat is only temporary, Maid Wynona, and I wouldst charge ye to remember that mine so-called 'aged mother' looks a hundred fortnights younger than thyself."

The Lord High Torturer stopped flogging and the peasant stopped shrieking. Behind me, two monks sniggered. Having scored a good one, I flounced off.

But Wynona had put a damper on my break, so after purchasing a large root beer from the Drunkard's Den I hurried back to Llama Rides, where Alejandro's deep-throated welcome took the sting out of Wynona's words.

"No wonder I like animals so much, Alejandro," I said, scratching him behind his ears. "They can't talk."

"Maaaa?"

"Present company excepted, of course."

"Maaaa."

It was back-to-back llama rides for the rest of the morning. Watching Alejandro enjoy his tiny admirers kept my spirits from flagging. One nine-year-old boy, already too large for a ride—forty pounds was tops and the kid was built like a linebacker—questioned me about my job as a zookeeper. His parents, dressed as Robin Hood and Maid Marian, looked on fondly as I gave him a rundown on my less than glamorous daily chores.

"Sometimes it's a lot like construction work, but you'll need at least a bachelor's degree to get your foot in the door, preferably a master's. A major in zoology helps, but any of the sciences are important."

He frowned. "I don't like school. Especially science."

Before I could respond, Robin Hood asked, "Is there a lot of money in being a zookeeper?"

"Not really."

"We'll just buy him a llama then. How would you like that, Jimmy?"

Jimmy liked it.

"How many acres does your house sit on?" I asked Maid Marian.

"It's just a tract house with no yard to speak of," she answered. "But we have a nice little patio. He'd fit there."

"Then please don't…"

Too late. They were already headed for the Swan Boat Rides.

When one o'clock approached, my grumbling stomach reminded me I had skipped breakfast. As soon as Deborah Holt arrived I tied the CLOSED sign to the gate.

"I've already given Alejandro some timothy hay sprinkled with chopped carrots, so all he needs now is some rest," I said. "Don't let him give any rides until I get back. He's been working all morning and needs some time off. We still have tomorrow to go, and I don't want him worn out."

Knowing Alejandro would be well taken care of, I set off for lunch.

The food tent at Peasant's Retreat was so packed with hungry Faire workers that I had trouble finding a seat where I could gnaw on my huge turkey drumstick. A place finally opened up next to a smiling Jane Olson, who was sitting at a crowded table next to Deanna Sazac and Yancy Haas. A member of the Royal Court, Jane was resplendent in a deep burgundy gown, a color that almost matched her long hair. Yancy Haas didn't look as spiffy. From the size of the large scrape on his forehead, he'd been whacked in the last joust.

"Teddy, I'm worried about Caro," Jane said, after we'd exchanged the usual pleasantries. "When I visited her at the jail yesterday, she didn't seem to understand the gravity of her situation. All she wanted to talk about was 'fighting the power.' You simply must do something to help that woman."

Jane was a close friend of Caro's and had been married almost as many times as my mother. I remembered seeing Jane's name in one of Victor's marriage ledgers. Unlike Caro's here-today-gone-tomorrow spouses, Jane's current husband looked like a keeper. The mega-rich L.G. Olson, known locally as "The Gold King," had descended from a prospector who struck it rich during the California Gold Rush. As genial as he was generous, L.G. had not only founded an orphanage in Uganda, but was a long-time member of the Gunn Zoo Guild. His latest act of charity was in donating a new Chevy Camaro ZL1 for the zoo's fund-raising raffle.

Watching Jane carefully for any sign of evasion, I said, "I'm doing all I can to help Caro, but you've known her long enough to realize how difficult that can be. Especially now. Victor performed two of her four marriages, which puts her spousal support payments in financial limbo. Say, didn't Victor marry you to L.G.?"

Not a flicker from those blue eyes. "Yes."

"What do you plan to do about it?"

"Get remarried as soon as possible. I'm sure the children would appreciate it."

I smiled. "Especially since two of them are attending St. Xavier's. Religious school, and all that. The nuns might have trouble with your peculiar, ah, marriage status."

"I wouldn't doubt it." She didn't sound like she cared.

Deanna Sazac spoke up. "A lot of us are in the same boat as Jane."

"Will you remarry Judd?" I asked, but once the question was out of my mouth, I wanted to bite my tongue.

A hush fell over the table. After what seemed like an eternity but was probably only a few seconds, Deanna said, "Maybe. Maybe not. I don't know whether to be grateful to Victor for giving me this out, or to hate him for marrying me and Judd in the first place."

No one seemed to know what to say about that. Mortified, I made an even bigger blunder. "Jane, didn't you attend the weapons demonstration last weekend?"

Before she could answer, Yancy said. "Good God, Teddy! Next thing, you'll be asking her where she was when Victor was killed."

I felt my face and ears turn red. "Sorry, Jane. Seems like lately every time I open my mouth I insert my foot." Playing detective was hell on a person's manners.

Jane returned my rudeness with a faint smile. "Being questioned like a murder suspect would make anyone uncomfortable."

"I wasn't trying to…"

"Teddy, for the record, I did not kill Victor Emerson and neither did dear L.G., so please let me finish my lunch in peace. This apple dumpling is quite delicious. I suggest you try it."

"Maybe after I finish my turkey leg." Put firmly in my place, I changed the subject. "The zoo's annual Great Escape is next Friday, and I've been tagged as the lion."

Jane smiled again, this time more genuinely. "Will it be televised? After the grilling you just gave me, I'll enjoy seeing you hunted down like a wild animal."

Yancy Haas laughed along with the rest of everyone else the table. "She got you there, Teddy. What is this Great Escape thing, anyway? Since I spend most of my time on one film location after another, I miss a lot of local events but that one sounds like fun. Can anyone go?"

From the table in back of us, a jester piped up, "Friday? But what time? I might even take off work to see that!"

"It starts at six." I went on to explain that because of possible legal complications, only zoo staff and the media would be allowed in. Even they had to sign waivers. "A posse of zookeepers and park rangers running through the zoo with nets can get pretty hairy, and there have been casualties. But, yes, you can watch the chase on the news because Ariel Gonzales will be covering it."

They all looked disappointed at not being able to see the carnage firsthand, but Yancy asked, "Ariel's the new anchor on that morning program, right? The ex-Marine?"

I nodded. "Good thing she'll be reporting, not chasing. The Great Escape is supposed to loop around the entire zoo, but she'd have me netted before I made it out of Africa Trail."

"What happens once they net you?" Jane asked.

"They 'sedate' me, then carry me off to Quarantine on a stretcher. A real animal who'd escaped would stay in Quarantine for several days, or at least until the tranquilizer was entirely gone from its system and it was settled down enough to go back to its enclosure. What most people don't understand is that escapes scare the animal as much as it does humans because the poor thing's out of its environment. People are running around screaming, and there's a rifle-waving mob chasing it. While the animal is still in Quarantine, its habitat is checked to see if there was a system failure—like a bad lock—or a human one. Whatever caused the escape must be corrected before the animal is returned."

Yancy looked wistful. "I worked with a lion once on some sword-and-sandal flick with Dwayne Johnson, you know, the Rock. Friendly animal—the lion, I mean. His trainer walked him around on a leash."

Others at the table jumped to share warm and fuzzy stories about the pet lions, tigers, and leopards they had either encountered or read about, which had me shaking my head. Too many people believed that once a wild animal grew accustomed to their presence, it would behave the same way as their pet cat or dog. A lot of those folks wound up dead. I tried to interject some common sense into the discussion, but no one wanted to hear it. Common sense isn't romantic.

Admitting defeat, I picked up my half-eaten turkey leg and exited the tent.

Before making it back to Llama Rides I encountered Willis Pierce headed toward Peasant's Retreat with a drumstick twice the size of mine. The former Shakespeare looked no happier than earlier.

"Miss your old job?" I asked, sympathetically.

He flicked a fly off his drumstick. "You think? Oh, gee, what could possibly be more fun than sitting on my butt all day in a small tent, listening to the Royal Court mangle Elizabethan speech. The Duke of Norfolk has a Brooklyn accent, for Pete's sake! At least young Howie always gets it right. My influence, I dare to believe. His singing voice approaches the professional, too. If this were New York, I'd steer him toward Broadway, but sadly, it's not. He prefers fish."

"Marine life."

He pulled a face. "Fish."

With that, he waved farewell with his drumstick and continued on to Peasant's Retreat.

A little further along I ran into Bambi, who had opted for a Castle Burger instead of turkey. She was walking arm in arm with Judd Sazac, and from the moony look on his face, they weren't discussing the weather. The two were also headed toward Peasant's Retreat, unaware that his wife would spot them the moment they walked in. For a brief moment I thought about issuing a warning, then decided not to. The Sazac's troubled marriage was none of my business.

Neither was the marriage of Melissa and Cary Keegan, but when I passed the Royal Armory, I was surprised to see black-clad Cary looking stricken as his wife exited the stall with a triumphant expression. Had Melissa finally had enough? When she caught sight of me, she immediately contorted her beautiful face into one of anguish and dabbed a lace-trimmed handkerchief at a dry eye.

"Don't ever get married, Teddy. Men are brutes." Voice trembling, she threw a glance over her shoulder at Cary. She cringed, dabbed her dry eyes again, then hurried away.

Unbidden, an image of Joe flashed across my mind. His kind brown eyes. His soft lips. His gentle hands.

She was wrong. Not all men were brutes.

Maybe not even Cary.

Although I was still gun-shy after discovering my friend Deborah's troubled past, I decided it was only fair to check out the Keegans and the Sazacs. And Bambi, of course. Just because her husband-stealing behavior was overt didn't mean she wasn't covering up even worse crimes.

I spent the rest of my break wandering along the High Street, watching acrobats and jesters, listening to troubadours, and admiring the Green Man as he pretended to be a tree. Maybe it's just me, but I'd always found the Green Man, a figure from English folklore, to be sinister. Tolkien's "ents" aside, there's something unnerving about a walking, talking tree. The Faire's wasn't too creepy, though, and as the actor stretched out his arms and rustled his cloth "leaves," I saw the wisp of a smile on his green-painted face.

At the north end of the street the Silly Slatterns had just left the Middleshire Stage, replaced by Ded Bob, the ventriloquist act. After a few ribald jokes, the wise-cracking skeleton dummy asked for volunteers. Hands shot into the air. Although I enjoyed Ded Bob's wickedly humorous one-liners, I didn't have enough time left to see the show, so I started back to Llama Rides.

As I drew abreast of the Royal Pavilion a knight in full armor stepped out of the gaily-bedecked tent and hailed me.

"Good morrow, fair damsel!"

Even through the metallic echo, I recognized his voice only too well.

My father.

"Are you nuts?" I hissed. "What if someone recognizes you?"

He didn't trouble to lower his voice. "In case you haven't noticed, daughter mine, I'm covered head to toe in this very hot, very heavy, very authentic relic from days of yore that Aster Edwina was gracious enough to loan me. The legs were too short, but I was able to cannibalize another set to add to them. Bet you can't even see the patches. Didn't know I could do metalwork, did you? Oh, I've learned so many useful things from my years on the run. Now, since we need privacy for the very important thing I'm about to tell you, whither us away to that wee alley behind the Viking Encampment. Forsooth, et cetera."

"Forsooth, yourself," I muttered, but followed dutifully on his heels as he clanked along.

Once we were out of sight of the main thoroughfare, he asked, "How's your mother?"

"Doing as well as can be expected."

"Is she still beautiful?" He sounded wistful. Despite their mutual problems, I'd always suspected my mother and father still loved each other.

"Caro wouldn't allow herself to be anything other than beautiful, Dad. Didn't you have 'a very important thing' to tell me?"

"Oh, that. I received an interesting phone call last night from one of my informants. Remember Victor's girlfriend and getaway driver? Named Kate Garrick? Seems that a cousin of hers lived, and maybe still lives, in San Sebastian County."

"Are you sure?"

"Yes, indeedy, which might be why Victor settled here after his escape. Remember my telling you that he and Kate had been planning to stay with some cousin until the baby was born? From my own experience on the lam I know it's never easy starting a new life among strangers, so if you have a connection someplace, that's where you head. Unfortunately, my informant isn't certain about the cousin's name. He thinks it's Suzanna or Cheryl or Sharon or something else that starts with an 'S'."

"Cheryl is usually spelled with a 'C'."

"Maybe they were into funky spelling, this being California. As I was saying…"

"Cousin on Kate's father's side or mother's side?"

"I didn't ask for a genealogy chart!"

"Dad, if she was a maternal cousin, she would have been born with a different last name, but if the relation was on her father's side, the cousin would share Kate's surname of Garrick. That would make hunting her down relatively easy, even if she eventually married."

Low muttering behind the armor. "Well, I don't know, and I doubt if my informant knows, but I'll ask the next time he calls. One more thing. A few years after Kate married that blackjack dealer, she died."

Before I could ask, he added, "Of natural causes."

"What happened to Victor's kid? Did her husband raise it?"

"My informant had no clue."

"Boy or girl?"

An exasperated sigh. "No clue there, either. And that's all I have for you now, but listen, is that turkey leg any good? I've worked up quite the appetite lugging around all this armor."

"Delicious. But since you'd have to remove your visor to eat, I don't advise it."

"I'll order one to go, then. And maybe a couple more for Aster Edwina and Mrs. McGinty. That housekeeper used to be quite the looker, you know."

With that, he clanked off.

Although irritated with my father for venturing out in public, however disguised, I found his information intriguing. If Victor's girlfriend had lived, she would now be in her fifties. There was no guarantee her cousin was close to her age, but allowing for a ten year span either way the cousin could be anywhere from her forties to sixties. Vague, yes, but if I could somehow come up with her name…

Thinking furiously, I headed back to Llama Rides.

"Thanks for watching him," I told Deborah, who had been talking with an entire family dressed as peasants. In the far corner, Alejandro stood with his back to us, munching on chopped carrots.

"No problem. Hey, I just heard you're going to be the star of the Great Escape this year. That should be fun."

News traveled fast in the Renaissance. "That's what Aster Edwina keeps saying."

"Don't worry about it. Phil was the lion once. That's before we got married, and I think you were still living up in San Francisco. He had a great time."

"Then Phil's not the guy who fell and broke his wrist."

She grinned. "As a matter of fact, he was. Since it was his right wrist and he's right-handed, he was pretty much helpless, so I started taking casseroles and whatnot over to his apartment, and helped him with the housework. One thing led to another."

"'Another' meaning you two wound up married."

The grin faded. "Yeah. By Victor Emerson. The creep. Good thing someone killed him before I got to him."

Face flushed with anger, she walked away.

"Hey, Alejandro!" I called. "Ready to go back to work?"

At the sound of my voice, Alejandro deserted what was left of his lunch and trotted across the enclosure toward me.

"Maaa!"

I started to tell him I was happy to see him again, too, but he moved right past me and headed for the little peasant girl standing by the gate, her tiny hand stretched. Upon reaching her, he lowered his head and gave her a slobbery kiss. The fact that he dribbled soggy hay all over the child's carefully ripped dress didn't bother her parents at all; they beamed.

"What a sweet llama!" the mother said. Perfect orthodontia shone through her artistically begrimed face.

"With children, yes, not so much with adults, so make certain you stay behind the fence while your daughter takes her ride."

"We have a dog like that," the father said, knowingly. His teeth were as perfect as his wife's. "Bess tolerates us but she adores Stacey and any other child within licking distance."

Whenever I heard a story like that, I could guess its history. "Is Bess a rescue dog?"

A nod. "We figure that in the past some adult must have treated her badly, but whatever child she lived with, probably a little girl, was more gentle."

"That's Alejandro's story, too." Looking down at the girl, I said, "You ready for your llama ride, Stacey?"

She was.

I picked up the little peasant and sat her down on Alejandro's saddle. "You can talk to him as you ride. He likes that."

She complied, and by the time her ride was over, Alejandro had heard all about Goldilocks and the Three Bears. He looked disappointed when I handed her back to her parents, but when he spotted a boy her age waiting by the gate he cheered right up.

Alejandro had a happy afternoon.

For a while.

The next couple of hours passed similarly, with scores of adoring children lining up for a chance to ride the llama. At one point a tour group comprised of kids too big to ride but not too old to admire him stood and watched as he toted around a kindergartener. Alejandro was enjoying his popularity so much that I didn't at first notice when his body language changed. But as I led another little girl toward him for a ride, I saw his ears go back and his entire body get stiff.

"Alejandro?"

He made a noise that sounded almost like a dog's growl.

"What's wrong, boy?"

From behind me, I heard a man say, "I'm tellin' you, Marge, thash Alejandro!" His speech was slurred, as if he'd downed too many ales.

"Let's just go," a woman said. She sounded irritated.

Then thudding feet made me turn from the child to see a heavy man with a flushed face cut away from the crowds and tear toward the gate, his arms flapping like an ostrich trying to take flight. One of his hands held a beverage cup. Liquid sloshed as he ran.

"He wansh a beer!"

"Ernest! Stop!" the woman yelled.

Ernest kept coming.

I lifted the little girl away and told her to run to her parents. Then I grabbed the llama's lead rope and held on tight.

Too late.

With a nimble move for a man in his condition, Ernest vaulted the fence with one hand, and continued running toward Alejandro, his cup-holding arm outstretched. So intent was he on reaching the llama that he didn't see the child. He ran right over her, sending her sprawling into the dirt.

Ever hear a llama scream? It's a horrible noise, somewhere between a shriek and a cough.

Wheeck! Wheeck! Wheeck!

Alejandro jerked the lead rope from my hand. With teeth bared and ears flat against his head, he dashed forward to insert himself between Ernest and the shocked child. His herd guard instinct had taken over, and he was going to protect that tiny creature no matter what.

Wheeck! Wheeck! Wheeck! he screamed at Ernest. *Get the hell away from her!*

With an insensitivity born of inebriation, the fool just kept coming.

"Hey, Al, yoush…"

Alejandro didn't let him finish. He hit Ernest with his shoulder, knocking the man away from the child. The beverage cup flew in the other direction, spraying beer into the air.

Ernest squalled in protest.

Then Alejandro began stomping him.

Ernest's squalls turned into screams that almost matched the llama's as those clawed feet pounded him again and again while the little girl picked herself up off the ground and made a beeline for Mommy and Daddy.

The second she reached them, Alejandro ceased his attack.

It wasn't over yet. As I snatched back his lead rope, Alejandro hocked up a big green-tinged ball of phlegm and spit it into Ernest's face.

Chapter Eleven

Whenever there's an animal attack, no matter how insignificant, bureaucracy grinds into gear. In this case, the first step was to alert First Aid, then Security. As Ernest's wife muttered darkly about lawsuits, an EMT attended to his wounds. Security, late on the scene because of a fistfight between a minstrel and a monk on High Street, took the drunk into custody until two San Sebastian County deputies arrived and whisked him away.

The second step in the bureaucratic mill was less pleasant: informing Aster Edwina.

The old woman was not pleased. "You say you actually heard the word 'lawsuit?'"

"His wife was pretty upset."

"Besides you, who saw the attack?"

"Numerous people, but I was too preoccupied to take witness statements."

"You could at least have gotten their names."

"Well, I didn't."

"He'll have to be put into Quarantine."

"Who? Ernest?"

"Don't get smart with me, Theodora. Get that llama into the Quarantine barn before he causes more trouble."

She rang off.

The little girl and her family, as well other witnesses to the attack, having been dispersed by Security, Alejandro now stood alone in the far corner of Llama Rides. Head down, ears flopped sideways, he looked the very picture of a depressed animal.

"I'm so sorry, sweetie," I told him, as I led him toward the horse trailer. "You didn't do anything wrong but you're going to be punished anyway."

Cursing Ernest-whoever-he-was, I loaded Alejandro into the trailer and drove him back to the zoo.

◇◇◇

Given everything that had happened, I expected Aster Edwina to release me from working the Faire, but she didn't. Sunday morning found me attempting to milk a goat at the Village Idiots Encampment. The goat didn't like it and neither did I. When she kicked over the pail a second time I threw my hands up in defeat.

"Taking a break," I called to a nearby peasant, who in civilian life was the chief neurologist at San Sebastian County Hospital.

"Lazy trollop!" After theatrically scratching himself, Dr. Arnold Steinmetz scratched the ears of the piglet he was holding.

"Back at ya, Arnie. Want me to bring you anything from Dowager's Dumplings?"

"Spotted Dick would be nice. Forsooth."

"A la mode?"

"In for a farthing, in for a pound, trollop."

"See you in fifteen, then."

The Faire was even more crowded than yesterday, but my heart gave a sad little twist as I passed the empty Llama Rides enclosure. The fact that Camel Rides was doing big business with a new camel didn't make me feel any better. I kept seeing Alejandro's sad face when I left him in Quarantine.

People who think animals don't have feelings have never known any animals.

On my way to Dowager's Dumplings I noticed that Ded Bob was just finishing his act on the Middleshire Stage, and it occurred to me that I had not yet talked to him. The ventriloquist had been resting in his trailer when Deanna and Judd Sazac were brawling, and although I could guess the nature of their argument, it wouldn't hurt to have my suspicions confirmed.

The skeleton puppet and his burlap-clad peasant handler were still in costume when they arrived at the trailer. Since past experience had taught me that the actor who performed the Ded Bob routine liked to stay in character, I addressed the puppet. "Well met, skeleton sir."

"Likewise, fair hussy," Ded Bob cracked back, ogling my low cut gown. "Wanna see my etchings?"

"Sorry, although I'm certain they're a delight. As is your own fair, if skeletal, self. Could I speak to your human, please?"

"You mean Smuj, here?" He pointed a bony finger to the gauze-veiled man holding him. "He's *non compos mentis*, so anything you have to say you can say to me. Sure you don't wanna see my etchings? They're anatomically correct." Another ogle at my breasts.

"Absolutely sure. All right, Bob, I hear that on the day Victor Emerson was killed, you heard the Sazacs arguing outside your trailer."

"Maybe I did and maybe I didn't."

"Let's say you did."

"Hmmm. Let me think back. Ooops. Can't. Brain's all rotted away." He waggled his skull. "See? No rattle! Nothing but empty air."

Maybe banter wasn't the right approach. "Elvin Dade's trying to frame my mother for Victor's murder."

"My etchings are framed, too. Wanna come in and see?"

"Please, Ded Bob!" I sniffled, not entirely for effect.

The skeleton drooped his head. Smuj, who had a softer side than his alter ego, spoke up from underneath his face veil. "Oh, all right. I never could say no to a lady. You are one, aren't you, Teddy? Okay, okay! Stop with the dirty looks already! And for God's sake, don't cry! I don't see what this has to do with your mother's unfortunate situation, but from what I could hear, Deanna Sazac was accusing Judd of being a little too friendly, if you know what I mean, with that Bambi woman. He denied it, but Deanna ripped him up one side and down the other, all at the top of her voice. He had to shout over her just to be heard. I'd already done three shows that day and had two more to go, and there went my plans for a nap. Once I realized someone was getting roughed up, I had Bob here yell for them to stop."

"That's all?"

"What'd you expect me to do, shoot them? Oops. Bad joke, considering."

"Did either of the Sazacs mention Victor?"

"Once. Judd said something about Victor pushing things too far, whatever that meant."

"Those were his exact words, 'pushing things too far?'"

"Yeah."

"And you say you have no idea what that meant?"

At this, Ded Bob snapped back to attention and craned his skeletal head toward my bodice. "The peasant's too dumb to lie, hussy. Now, about those etchings…"

◇◇◇

By the end of the day, I'd made up my mind that no matter what Aster Edwina threatened, I wasn't going to pull another shift at the Renaissance Faire. I missed the zoo. I missed my fellow zookeepers, I missed the zoo's visitors. More importantly, I missed the animals, especially poor Alejandro, now isolated in Quarantine.

I was determined to do something about that.

So focused was I on Alejandro's misery that I forgot to change out of my wench outfit before visiting Caro, and my entrance to the jail was accompanied by wolf whistles all around.

"You look like a tart," my mother said when she saw me.

"That's the whole idea."

"I could kill Aster Edwina for this."

"Uh, Mother? You're in jail. Do you really think it's a good idea to be talking about killing people?"

"How many times do I have to tell you not to call me 'Mother'!"

"Caro, you do get my point, don't you?"

"What point?"

"Never mind. How's your day been?"

"It's been a living hell, Teddy. As if you care."

"I care, Mo…Caro. I know this has been terribly difficult for you, but maybe I can help talk you through it. So c'mon, what's been happening?"

She sniffed. "Not much, really."

"Tell me about the 'not much,' then. As your daughter, I need to know what you're going through."

Mollified, Caro treated me to a summation of the horrors of her day. They included a morning consult with her attorney, group manicures with Demonios Femeninos, yoga with her friend Giselle Coventry (serving thirty days for her second DUI), flower arranging lessons in the rec room, and scrapbooking sessions with a visiting social worker.

The San Sebastian County Jail was a living hell, all right.

◇◇◇

When I finally dragged myself home to the *Merilee*, it was after eight. I expected my animals to greet me with glee, but none of them came to see me when I stepped below decks. All three—Miss Priss, DJ Bonz, and Feroz Guerro—were huddled together in a shivering heap of fur in the corner of the galley's banquette.

"Hey, guys, aren't you hungry?"

Nothing but whimpers and a mew.

"Don't want walkies?"

More whimpers.

A brief sniff told me why the dogs didn't need walkies. After I'd spent the next few minutes cleaning up the mess, they remained huddled together. The evening was still warm, so it wasn't as if they were cold.

"People, show some consideration. Mama's home and all's right with the world."

I kneeled down and held out my hand, expecting at least one of them to jump off the banquette and come visit, but not one of them budged.

"Bonz!" I commanded. "Here!" For emphasis, I slapped my thigh.

The usually obedient Bonz didn't move. He just looked at Feroz, who looked at Priss. Priss closed her eyes and pretended to be somewhere else.

Something was wrong. Very wrong.

I looked around. All appeared normal at first, but then I noticed that the door to the aft bedroom was shut. Knowing how much the animals liked to curl up on my bed, I always left it open in my absence.

Someone had been on my boat.

Maybe still was.

I kept up a running commentary about my day while I very quietly tiptoed to the galley counter and pulled out a knife from the knife rack. Then just as quietly I tiptoed to the aft bedroom door and yanked it open.

No intruder lurked there.

Just a dead rat on my bed with a crossbow dart through its heart. Hanging from the protruding end of the dart was a note.

"STOP AKSNG QESTONS OR YOUL B NXT"

Chapter Twelve

I ran down the dock to Linda Cushing's *Tea 4 Two* and interrupted her in the midst of feeding her cats.

"Did you see anyone hanging around the *Merilee*?" I asked, trying to look calm. Like me, Linda lived alone, and there was no point in scaring her.

She shook her head. "Sorry. I spent the day with a friend in Monterey. Did someone break in?"

"Yes, but nothing was taken." I didn't mention Mr. Rat.

Under ordinary circumstances I would report my grisly find to Joe, but since Homeland Security had rendered him unavailable, I called my old friend Deputy Emilio Gutierrez as soon as I returned to the *Merilee*. No point contacting that fool Elvin Dade.

"Can you talk, Emilio?" I asked as soon as he answered.

"Just for a minute. I'm standing in line at the San Sebastian Cinema. Elena will kill me if we miss *The Muppets Go to Mars*, so make it snappy."

As succinctly as possible, I told him about the rat and the note, adding, "The spelling was too bad to be authentic. Someone with an education trying to act the opposite."

He lowered his voice. "How much blood was there?"

"Almost none, come to think of it. The rat could have already been dead when it got shot by the crossbow."

"Hmm. And you say your animals weren't hurt?"

"Just scared."

"Teddy, you won't like hearing this, but it sounds to me that the intruder might have a soft spot for animals."

He was right. I didn't like hearing it. "You mean someone like a zookeeper, don't you?"

"Someone like that, yes."

"None of my friends would do something like this!"

"If I remember correctly, Emerson officiated at some of your zoo friends' weddings."

There was nothing to say to that.

"Teddy?"

"What?"

"Want some advice?"

"Let me guess. It's 'Stop poking around and mind your own business.'"

"Quite the mind-reader, you are. That's exactly what I was going to say. Leave the detective work to the professionals."

"Professionals like Elvin Dade? Not while my mother is rotting away in jail."

A long sigh. "Your family and mine go way back so I've checked on Caro every day. I can assure you she is not rotting away. If anything, she's having the time of her life. Look, as frustrating as all this has been, Sheriff Joe will be back soon and the Victor Emerson case will be turned over to him. He won't be able to get your mother out before her thirty days are up—I'm sure you remember that riot she started in the courtroom—but all this nonsense about linking her to the Emerson murder will disappear like the hot air it is."

"I hope you're right."

"Bank on it. Now here's some advice you can accept. Take a sheet of plastic, wrap up the rat, the dart, the note, the whole mess, and stick it in your freezer. As soon as this blasted Muppet film's over I'll drop by to collect the evidence and drive it to the lab to see if whoever did it got sloppy and left fingerprints. But for now, please, please, please don't do any more detecting. I'll…"

I heard a woman's voice. "Two adults?"

"Yep," Emilio answered. Then to me, he said, "Gotta go. But remember what I said. Stay safe. Mind your own business."

Click.

Emilio had been right about one thing. Before I put the "evidence" in a plastic garbage bag, I slipped on a pair of rubber gloves, flipped the animal over, and looked at its underside. Tire tracks ran the length of its body, proving that the animal had met its maker not via crossbow, but by car. So, yeah, maybe Emilio was right about the other thing, too.

But not the zookeeper part. Zookeepers revere life.

Especially my friend, Deborah.

A galley refrigerator is small, its freezer microscopic. To make Mr. Rat and his accessories fit, I removed my ice cube tray and two frozen dinners. No big deal. They were long past their expiration date anyway.

Evidence on ice, I stripped the bed and headed for the laundromat.

◇◇◇

Two hours later, laundry finished and folded, I went onto the Internet, looking for animal lovers with shady pasts. I found no more negative postings about Deborah, thank goodness, but when it came to someone else, Google hit the jackpot.

Judd Sazac, the doting owner of the harbor's most loveable Jack Russell terrier, had once made the *Los Angeles Times* during a homicide investigation. Five years earlier, he had been a person of interest in the murder of Sandi Birutta, the Beverly Hills socialite he was dating. The authorities' interest in him dropped when Birutta's gardener was caught trying to pawn some of her jewelry. Although the gardener maintained his innocence in Sandi Birutta's murder, he did plead guilty to theft. His current address was Folsom State Prison, but for robbery, not murder. That part of the crime was never solved.

Did Deanna Sazac know about this?

For her own safety, I decided the news couldn't wait until tomorrow, so as late as it was, I called her and told her what I'd discovered. Yes, she said, she knew all about Judd's past; he'd told her everything. And she'd appreciate it if from here on out I minded my own bleeping business. She didn't say bleeping.

"Poking around in other peoples' lives can get you hurt," she spat, before hanging up on me.

Cursing myself for ruining another woman's evening, I went to bed.

◇◇◇

When I awoke the next morning, I suffered a brief moment of displacement. Yes, my pets were still curled up at the foot of the bed, and I could hear Maureen, the harbor otter, bumping against the hull to beg for her morning sardine, but everything looked different. Why in the world was I in the forward bunk space, which was usually reserved for visitors? Then I saw the stack of strongly bleached laundry sitting on the galley table next to a carbon copy of a police report. It all came flooding back. Dead rat. Threatening note. Two uncomfortable conversations with Emilio, one on the phone, one when he stopped by to pick up Mr. Rat.

My first emotion wasn't fear, it was anger. How dare someone defile my *Merilee*!

Happy animals recover fast, so when I grabbed their leashes, Bonz and Feroz danced matching jigs. As we headed out to the park, we left a complaining Priss behind. From her plaintive cries, you'd think she hadn't been fed in a year.

I would like to say I didn't look at my animal-loving neighbors any differently this morning, but I did. Last night's events had left me so paranoid that I didn't say a word to any of them. When Linda Cushing, sitting on the deck of *Tea 4 Two* cradling one of her many cats, waved a cheery good morning, I had to force myself to wave back. In the park I eyed my fellow dog-walkers with suspicion: Deborah's husband Phil Holt and the couple's rescued Heinz 57; Judd Sazac and his Jack Russell terrier; even poor Howie Fife, hobbling along with his mother's elderly cockapoo. Could any of them have left that note?

By the time I returned to the *Merilee*, I despised myself.

"Not one of my friends," I muttered, dishing out Miss Priss' Fancy Feast. "Not one of my friends."

While feeding Bonz and Feroz their separate diets in separate bowls, I changed my mantra to, "Not an animal lover."

I kept it up all the way to the zoo. After clocking in, I headed straight for Quarantine.

Quarantine isn't just one barn; it is a series of large, airy sheds at the back of the zoo. Whenever a new animal is brought in, it stays here until one of the zoo's veterinarians certifies it healthy enough to go on exhibit. Sometimes, if an animal is suspected of having a contagious disease or is badly injured, it stays in an isolated shed near the clinic, where it can be checked on every hour. Alejandro, not meeting either designation, was being kept in the main barn, along with a zebra about to give birth, an Arapawa goat with its newborn, and an eland with a sore leg.

I found Alejandro lying in a back stall. Some other animal keeper had obviously been there earlier, because his stall was clean, and he had been supplied with fresh water and plenty of llama pellets mashed with sweet horse feed. But he still looked miserable.

When I unlatched the stall gate and walked in, he didn't even get up, just looked at me with those sad llama eyes.

I knelt down beside him. "Oh, sweetie, I'm so sorry."

He looked away.

"Would you like some chopped carrots?"

Silence.

"Want your ears scratched?"

Continued silence.

"Or I could shanghai a couple of children and drag them down here to keep you company."

Maybe it was my imagination, but I thought one ear flickered slightly at the word "children."

"I'll do what I can to spring you, sweetie."

I waited for an answer. None.

Since he wouldn't speak to me, I took the initiative and began scratching his ears. He shut his eyes in pleasure, but remained silent. Knowing how lonely he was, I spent a few minutes keeping him company, but eventually, other duties called. As I let myself out of his stall, he called…

"Maaam!"

Come back.

◇◇◇

At the zoo's Friendly Farm enclosure, deep shadows marred Deborah Holt's usually brilliant blue eyes, probably out of concern for Alejandro. She walked over to me, trailed by a flock of chickens.

"Were you the one who freshened up Alejandro's stall this morning?" I asked.

"Of course. The poor thing looks so depressed. What happened yesterday? I heard he attacked someone, but that's about it."

After I gave her the sordid details, her tired-looking eyes lit up. "You say the drunk's name was Ernest. Would that be Ernest Dalrymple, by any chance?"

"I was too busy keeping him from being killed to ask his last name. Is it important?"

"Could be. Ernest Dalrymple was Alejandro's former owner. From what I hear, he knocked out one of Alejandro's teeth trying to get the poor thing to suck from a bottle of beer. Fortunately, his neighbors saw the whole thing and called the Humane Society. When they couldn't find a proper home for him they contacted the zoo. I went and picked him up myself."

A quick call to a sleepy Emilio Gutierrez revealed that, yes, a man by the name of Ernest Dalrymple had been arrested for Drunk and Disorderly at the Faire yesterday and had already bonded out. Not only was Dalrymple screaming about filing a lawsuit for wrongful arrest, but he appeared bound and determined to get Alejandro put down.

"Put down!?" I screamed into the phone. "But he's the idiot who caused the entire incident!"

Emilio tut-tutted. "With an animal that size, an attack is a serious thing. If you want to save Alejandro's life, you'd better come up with some witnesses who'll swear the man provoked the incident. In the meantime, don't you know what time it is? Seven! I worked late last night and was looking forward to sleeping in."

Before I could apologize, he rang off.

"Deputy Gutierrez says we need witnesses," I told Deborah.

"I don't... Wait a minute. When I was working the admission booth, I remember seeing a group of kids from San Xavier Prep. One of the girls mentioned wanting to see Alejandro. I told her she was too big to ride, but she didn't care. She just wanted to see him 'cause she'd fallen for him in a big way when her parents brought her to the zoo."

"A school tour? I remember a big group of kids, but I thought they were from that Monterey summer camp. Isn't school supposed to be out for the summer?"

She shook her head. "My nephew goes there, and last time I saw him, he mentioned that one of the classes was doing an extra-credit report on the Elizabethan Era, so that probably accounted for the tour."

"But the schools all let out in May."

"Not San Xavier. They were shut down for three whole weeks last month and had to make up for lost time. Listen, I'll see what I can do to track down one of the chaperones, but right now I have to feed these chickens. They're starting to peck at one another, and you know what that can lead to."

Pushing aside the vision of chicken cannibalism, I felt a glimmer of hope. The age range at Xavier Prep, where I'd once taught before following my then-husband to San Francisco, was between twelve and fourteen. Maybe one of them, or even a tour escort, had witnessed Alejandro's attack. If enough people swore the llama had been provoked, Dalrymple's mean-spirited attempt at having his former pet put down would fail.

Ciara Pawling, a zoo volunteer and an old friend of mine, taught eighth grade English at Xavier and her cell phone number was on my cell. Taking a chance, I punched it in and was pleased when she immediately answered.

"You'd better not be calling me about Victor Emerson's murder, Teddy," she said, only half-jokingly. "Just because Victor married me to a piece of slime doesn't mean I'd kill him because of it."

"How is Brad these days?"

"You haven't heard? After I caught him with that Bambi woman, I threw him out."

"Sorry."

"He is, too. So what's the reason for this call so bright and early in the morning?"

"I heard some of the Xavier kids were at the Renaissance Faire yesterday. Why aren't you out for the summer?"

A snort. "We should be, but you know what they say about these old dumps with National Register of Historic Places name-plates—it's just another way of saying it should be put out of its misery. We developed plumbing problems in late May. Sewers backed up, no running water, you name it, it went wrong. What else can you expect from a two-hundred-year-old building that wasn't all that great to begin with?"

When I explained Alejandro's situation, she said that although she wasn't one of the chaperones, she knew who they were. "I'll call you as soon as I find out if they saw anything."

Feeling somewhat better, I rang off and started on my regular zoo duties.

Carlos, the magpie jay who last year won my heart by his romantic offering of twigs with which to build our bridal nest, had been given a mate. Now he didn't know me from Adam.

"Unfaithful cur!" I called.

Magpie jays will mimic any noise that strikes their fancy. Carlos' attempt at returning my call came across as "Uh-aikle-er!" When I laughed, he mimicked that, too.

I continued my rounds, visiting Wanchu the koala, who was asleep, and Lucy the giant anteater, who also paid no attention to me because she was busy suckling her baby. While I was clean-ing out the anteaters' night house, my cell rang. Ciara Pawling, with good news.

"Brian Chesney and Yvette Allred both saw what happened yesterday," she said. "That guy, whoever he was, knocked down a little girl when he ran at the llama. They say the llama was only protecting her."

I would have clicked my heels in glee but they had too much manure on them. "Do you think their parents would allow them to testify at a board of inquiry?"

"No doubt about it. Don't their last names mean anything to you, Teddy? Chesney. Allred."

"Would their respective mothers be Mrs. Timothy Chesney III and Mrs. George Hampton-Allred?" Close friends of my mother.

"Got it in one, kiddo."

This was excellent news. Both women were long-time members of the Gunn Zoo Guild and were deeply dedicated to the welfare of all animals.

"I don't have their phone numbers on..."

She didn't wait for me to finish, just reeled off the numbers. I thanked her and called the first one. Yes, Mrs. Chesney said, she'd certainly allow Brian to testify if it came to that. Damn right, Mrs. Allred followed up. She'd drive Yvette to the hearing herself, and what in the world did that man think he was doing, knocking down some little kid, and did I know—according to Yvette—that the man was raving drunk? In a further bit of good news, I learned that, yes, her daughter had recognized the man as Ernest Dalrymple, who at one time owned Dalrymple's Scuba and Dive, where she had once taken lessons. The dive school failed when Dalrymple started showing up drunk.

I reported the conversations to Deborah. After she finished cheering, I added, "I'm going to call Aster Edwina right now. On second thought, I'll drive up there and tell her in person." Actually, I had another reason for going to the castle. I wanted to see my father.

Since the castle was more or less next door to the zoo, Mrs. McGinty was soon ushering me into the cavernous hallway.

Upon entering the library, I found Aster Edwina reading to my father from a leather-bound book. It was a bedtime story of sorts, but definitely not the kind meant to be read to children.

"Why aren't you at work, Teddy?" she said, putting the X-rated book down.

"Two witnesses have come forth to say they say the entire incident with Alejandro. They'll both testify that the man leaped over the fence, knocked down the little girl, then—and only then—the llama rush to the rescue. Furthermore, I also found out that the guy, Ernest Dalrymple, was his former owner."

She looked pleased, a rare sight. "The same man who once knocked out the poor creature's tooth?"

"The very same. Alejandro knew firsthand how rough Dalrymple could be, so he was defending the kid."

"I knew none of this when I ordered the animal into Quarantine, but I'm afraid it makes no difference. Until Dalrymple retracts his story it's better to keep the llama out of the public eye."

"But..."

"No 'but's, Teddy. I'm thinking about the liability issues. Anyway, you could have told me all this by phone, so why are you here when you're supposed to be at work?"

"I wanted to talk to Dad."

Aster Edwina sniffed. "Not about the zoo, I take it. Family matters? That fraudulent reverend person?"

"Both."

"Then expect your pay to be docked." Nose in the air, she sailed grandly out of the room, followed by Mrs. McGinty.

"How'd you know I have more information for you?" my father asked.

"I didn't. I wanted you to promise not to leave the castle. Showing up at the Faire yesterday was outrageous."

He turned his back and studied the big stained glass window. "Lovely, isn't it? Did you know that old Edwin Gunn had it imported from Scotland?"

"Of course I do. Promise me."

"Men don't like bossy women, Theodora."

"Right. Some of them prefer manipulative sneaks. Where's that promise?"

He kept looking at the window. "Who is that getting beheaded?"

"Charles the First. He pissed off Cromwell. Now quit trying to change the subject and promise me you'll stay here in the castle. If Elvin Dade gets his hands on you, you're toast."

He finally turned around to face me. "Why bother to make a promise I know I'll break? Now about that information I have. Sit down and make yourself comfortable. You're going to love this."

Grumbling, I sat down on a chair so old that Cromwell himself might have sat in it.

"My source called me back late last night and gave me the name of the late Victor Emerson's child." He paused, a sly smile on his face. "Bet you can't guess who."

Dad did like his little games, which is why he embezzled all that money in the first place. Years of experience had taught me it was easier to just play along. I started the guessing game with the person I considered least likely. "Wynona Dade, Elvin's wife?"

"Nope."

"Elvin himself?"

"No again. Please put a little more work into this, Teddy. You know Elvin's too old to be Victor Emerson's child."

I narrowed my guesses to people more or less my age. "Yancy Haas, the stunt man. He's playing the Black Knight at the Faire."

"Lovely guess, and I do laud you for it, but sadly, not Mr. Haas. In case you didn't know it, I once met his father—a brute of a man, by the way—and the two look just alike."

My patience was running thin. "Are you going to make me get out the San Sebastian County phone book and guess by alphabetical order?"

"You're no fun. Your mother, now, there's a woman who knows how to play games."

"Fat lot of good that did. You left her."

"Only because the Feds were hot on my heels. If she'd move down to Costa Rica with me I'd re-marry her in a heartbeat."

"Which I don't have to answer." Ever notice how ugly an overly made-up woman can look when she scowls?

Before she had a chance to slam the door in my face, I pushed it open and walked in. Her house was as gaudy as she was. Maroon carpet. Plastic plants. Matching lavender-and-pink paisley sofas. Except for the sofas, every other piece of wood or metal was covered in gilt, including the frame of the crystal chandelier overhead, which was so massive that if it dropped on you, death would be the only possible result. Brothels had better taste, not that I'd ever been in one.

"You sure don't hold back, do you," I said, surveying the décor.

She huffed up next to me and snatched a Hollywood-style white and gilt phone off a glass topped table. "Get out before I call the police."

"Acting Sheriff Elvin Dade? Go ahead and call, because I'm sure he'd love to hear about your relationship to Victor Emerson."

"You're disgusting, Teddy. I've already told you that, but you're even more so today. You stink of manure."

Without being invited, I sat my dirty self down on one of the sofas. "Sorry about that. I was so anxious to see you that I didn't bother showering after work, and yes, I'll admit that I've waded through a lot of crap today." In more ways than one.

"Please leave."

"Once we're through. For now, sit down and get comfortable, because we're going to have a long chat. About Victor."

"Why? I didn't kill him." For the first time I noticed that underneath all that makeup, her eyes were still red. She was attempting to hide the grief I had mistaken for allergies.

I softened my tone. "Crime statistics prove that when women kill, their victims are rarely their fathers."

The hand that held the telephone receiver began to tremble. "Wha…what do you mean?"

"Hang up the phone, Bambi. You're not going to call anyone and we both know it. And for Pete's sake, sit down before you fall down. "

She plunked the phone into its cradle, then sat down on the sofa across from mine. Her knees were trembling, too. After taking a few deep breaths, she said, "How much do you want?"

"Huh?"

"That's why you're here, isn't it? To blackmail me?"

It was my turn to be shocked.

"I'll pay you whatever you want, Teddy. But just once. You can't keep coming back or I'll...I'll..." She started to cry.

I'd never liked Bambi, but I could understand any woman's love for her father, regardless of his criminality, so I went over and put a comforting arm around her shoulders. When her sobs subsided, I asked, "Who's been blackmailing you?"

"No one's been blackmailing me, they were blackmailing Victor." From long habit, she still called him by his phony name. "Someone..." She stopped, pulled a tissue out of a gilt-trimmed dispenser, and blew her nose. "Oh, don't act dumb, Teddy. You know all about that, because it was you, wasn't it? Now that he's dead you're going after me."

"Wait a minute. You say your father was being blackmailed? Over what?"

"Don't pretend you don't know." More nose-blowing.

"Somebody found out who he really was?"

"Of course. You found out about him and threatened to tell the cops unless he gave you money. But he didn't have any money, he was just getting by. Why'd you have to pick on him?"

"Listen to me, Bambi. Why in the world would I need to blackmail Victor? If I wanted money, all I'd have to do is hit my mother up for a loan, and she'd give it to me in a heartbeat. Well, she'd probably charge interest. Besides, blackmailers don't kill their victims. It's usually the other way around."

The minute the words left my mouth, it occurred to me that Bambi, who wasn't all that bright, might have turned the story around. I had seen the tatty trailer Victor lived in, and doubted that anyone would be crazy enough to try and get blood from that stone. "Did your father come right out and tell you he was being blackmailed?"

"Kinda."

"Just kinda? Give me his exact words."

She jerked her head away and thrust out her chin in an attempt to look tough. "You always need to know everything, don't you?"

"Only when my mother's in jail." And my father faced a long prison term if Elvin Dade got wind of his whereabouts. I knew better than to tell her that part.

The doorbell rang. Before she could jump up to answer it, I grabbed her again, not so gently this time. "Tell whoever it is to go away. If you don't, we'll wind up having a three-way conversation about your father."

"You bitch."

"Sticks and stones."

She smoothed her dress and tottered to the door on those too-tall stilettoes. After a murmured conversation, her visitor went away, but not before I recognized the voice of Judd Sazac.

I was tempted to say nothing when Bambi tottered back because her fling with a married man was none of my business. Still, I couldn't help myself. "It's her money, not his."

"What are you talking about?"

"The Sazacs. They're living off the trust fund Deanna's grand-father set up. If Judd leaves her, he gets nothing."

She frowned. "Are you sure?"

"My grandfather, who was one of the savviest trust attorneys on the Central California coast, set it up so I can assure you that it's unbreakable. If something happens to Deanna, the money will be held in trust for her children. They won't have access to it until they turn thirty, so even then Judd won't get a dime. Since he's perennially unemployed, his financial future isn't good, either. Certainly not enough to keep you in the lifestyle to which you've become accustomed."

"But he said…"

"Infatuated men can tell convincing lies, Bambi."

She looked up at the gaudy chandelier, as if imploring it to drop on her. It didn't.

"Now tell me why you think someone was blackmailing your father. And I repeat, it wasn't me."

Everything about her began to droop. Her face. Her shoulders. Even those fabulous doctor-supplied breasts appeared to droop a few inches. "Oh, all right. It doesn't matter now anyway, does it? I stopped in to visit Victor one day and found him in his trailer, counting out money on the table. A big stack of fifty-dollar bills, a few hundreds. When I asked him what it was for he told me it was 'secret-keeping money' and that the less I knew about it, the better."

"From that you inferred someone was blackmailing him?"

"That's what it looked like to me."

"You didn't stop to think he might be the blackmailer, counting his payoff?"

"Don't be ridiculous. He was the one who had plenty to hide. If the law found out about him, they'd send him back to prison, so he was really, really secretive. About everything. Why, for years he never once said anything to me about who he really was. I just thought he was an old family friend who every now and then looked at me funny. Aunt Edna, my mom's sister, was close-mouthed about everything, too. I didn't find out Victor was my father or anything about that stupid robbery until she developed multiple sclerosis and decided it was time to tell me everything. She told me he'd kept in contact with Mom until she died. He…he really cared about her."

Emotion overtook her again. I gave her time to recover, then urged her to continue.

"About a year after Mom died—heart attack, in case you care, which you probably don't—he escaped from prison. He made his way to Los Angeles and lived on the street for a while until he decided to get in touch with Aunt Edna. She told him she'd help him if he moved up here, so he did. She financed his trailer and even the chapel. He paid her back but it took a long time. He never had much money."

"Which is another reason he made an unlikely blackmail victim, Bambi." Despite my disapproval over her dalliance with

Judd Sazac, I'd begun to feel sorry for her. Mother dead, aunt dead, father murdered. Her life hadn't been easy.

But it didn't excuse her home-wrecking habits.

"Did Victor ever say anything about knowing somebody's secret?"

"Not that I can remember," she said. "We mainly talked about Mom and stuff that went on in New Jersey while I was living there. You know, school friends and things. He was disappointed when I decided not to go to college, but I told him there was no reason to, I was doing okay, that I got a nice settlement from Max Giffords. I thought I'd be able to get one from Judd once we got married and then divorced, but now that I know the money's all hers, he's not worth the effort, is he?"

"Probably not." I wasn't interested in Bambi's financial schemes so I steered her back to her conversations with Victor. "Tell me more about your dad, what you two used to talk about."

"Oh, his chapel business, who was marrying who, what kind of wedding they wanted, stuff like that. His favorite weddings were when they wanted him dressed like Elvis. He didn't like the animal ones so much because half the time the animals crapped all over the chapel before the ceremony was finished, and guess who had to clean it up. At least he got to charge extra for that."

"You did know those marriages weren't exactly legal, didn't you?"

She gave me a blank look. "Why wouldn't they be?"

Didn't the woman read the papers? Or had she been so overwhelmed by a combination of grief and greed that she'd not understood the fake reverend part?

"Victor received his mail-order divinity degree and notary license under an assumed name, which means by fraud. Therefore, he had no legal authority to perform marriage ceremonies. Or witness any other legally binding contract, for that matter."

Her face, already pale under the heavy makeup, paled further. "Victor married me and Max. Are you telling me our marriage wasn't legal?"

"Probably not." I could guess what she would ask next.

She didn't disappoint. "But my divorce settlement! What happens with that?"

"I'm no lawyer but I think there's a good chance you'll have to give it back. If Max comes after it, get yourself a good family law attorney."

When I left the house, she was still cursing.

◇◇◇

On my way to see Caro, I thought about everything I had learned. No wonder half the people in San Sebastian, including myself, assumed Victor and Bambi were having a May-December love affair. Whenever the two were seen together, there had been obvious warmth between them. The real truth gave credence to the old saw, "Appearances can be deceiving." Bambi was hardly an admirable woman, but after our conversation I was certain of two things.

She loved her father.

And she had not killed him.

◇◇◇

Mother was more agitated than usual when I arrived at the jail.

"What's that smell, Theodora?" she snapped. "Don't tell me you didn't shower before you came here!"

"I was in a hurry. How are you doing?"

She waved a freshly-manicured hand. "Oh, I'm doing fine, just fine. Food's lovely, bedding's sublime." She leaned forward until her nose was almost touching the Plexiglas barrier. "*Of course I'm not doing well! I'm in jail, you hear, jail! And now my only child, from whom I've expected so much, visits me reeking of cattle dung!*"

There was a collective wince from the other jail visitors. Caro isn't much for screaming, but when she does indulge, there's not a soprano at the Met who can match her lung power.

"It's llama dung, actually. With a soupçon of wallaby and a dash of anteater. Would you like me to leave?"

"Do what you want to do."

If I walked out on her I would never hear the end of it, so I stayed. Since she had not yet accepted the fact that Elvin Dade was still looking at her for the Victor Emerson murder, I decided not to bring up Bambi's disclosures. I saved that information for her attorney.

I also didn't mention Mr. Rat.

Given so much withholding, our time together was strained and it was with great relief on both our parts when visiting hours ended. On my way out, I noticed Acting Sheriff Elvin Dade talking to a deputy near the corridor that led to the office suites. Apparently worried that the exiting visitors might hear him, he held his hand to the side of his face, shielding his mouth. He didn't see me and I stayed well away to make certain he didn't smell me, either.

Observing Elvin's secretive behavior made me wonder if he himself was the open book he appeared to be. Yes, he had contaminated the crime scene by wiping any surviving fingerprints off the crossbow dart—which everyone present, including myself—viewed as proof of his incompetence. He had intentionally tried to cover up the killer's identity because he suspected his own wife of killing Victor Emerson.

But why? The timing was wrong.

My old truck ate up the miles toward home, the surrounding darkness providing little distraction as I tried to make sense of things. Victor's true identity had not been revealed to the public until the *San Sebastian Gazette* ran its article six days after his death. True, Elvin could have alerted Wynona as soon as the fingerprint match came in, but that was *after* Victor's cooling body lay in the morgue for several hours. At the time of the murder, no one, including Elvin and his wife, knew who Victor really was.

Or was I wrong about that, too?

Not necessarily. If Elvin had discovered before the night of the murder that an escaped convict was living in San Sebastian, he wouldn't have given a thought to the possible marital consequences. He and his minions, along with all the media he could muster, would have descended upon Victor's trailer and taken him into custody with a slam, bam, thank you ma'am. But if Wynona had found out the truth before her husband did, she might have been panicked enough to make a pre-emptive strike. Which posed yet another question.

When, exactly, did Elvin discover his wife had a motive for murder? A week before the killing? Days? Just hours?

As the hills of inland Gunn Landing rolled silently by in the indigo night, I wondered how Wynona could have blundered onto Victor's guilty secret. To my knowledge, Bambi was the only other person in the county who had known the truth about him, and I doubted she and Wynona were confidants. Or did the two women share a connection I didn't know about? I was tempted to take out my cell and call her, but decided not to. Given the rage Bambi had been in when I left her house, letting her cool off until morning would be wiser. Besides, Tuesday was my half day. After my appearance on *Anteaters to Zebras*, I would drop by her house for another talk, whether she welcomed it or not.

In the meantime, there was someone else I'd grown more curious about: Ada Fife.

Howie's mother was hiding something, that was certain, but whether it had to do with her own past or some minor crime that Howie had committed, I needed to find out, so I opened my laptop and signed onto Google.

As far as the Internet was concerned, no Ada Fife matching her description had ever existed, same for her son Howie. Neither appeared on Facebook, LinkedIn, YouTube or any other social media, which in this day and age was distinctly unusual. One possible explanation was that she and Howie were living under assumed names.

"Ada, who are you?" I whispered to my laptop screen.

Never one to leave a puzzle unfinished, I thought back on what I had observed about the two first hand. From my visit to their boat, I'd seen a photograph of Howie as a Little Leaguer and another one of him perched on one of the New York Public Library's stone lions. Maybe he and his mother were from New

York? There was no discernible accent in Ada's voice, but that didn't necessarily mean anything.

I remembered Howie once saying something about his father's occupation. A musician? No, he'd said, "more of a producer." Maybe that was enough to go on.

One more thing. "Howie" was probably short for "Howard," so in Google's search area, I typed Howard+New York+producer.

And received thousands of hits, too many to go through individually.

I tried again, this time typing "Howard+Ada+music producer+New York," putting quotation marks around the whole mess.

That reduced the hits to two hundred and fifty-one. I resigned myself to scrolling through the entire list, but stopped at entrant number eighty-three, where I saw a headline in the *New York Tattler*, a Westchester County newspaper.

OPERA PRODUCER'S WIFE AND SON DISAPPEAR

After finishing the article, I understood why Ada kept such a low profile at the harbor.

The abuse of money and power. The abuse of children by their parents. Just thinking about the misery inflicted upon the innocent made me forget all about Bambi.

And Mr. Rat.

Chapter Fourteen

Alejandro was still depressed when I stopped by to see him the next morning but he cheered up somewhat during our one-sided conversation.

"People are complicated, aren't they, Alejandro?"

"Onnn."

"You would know, I guess, given what that nasty Dalrymple did. Knocking out your front tooth. Hurting that little girl."

"Maaa!"

"Why did he buy you from that llama farm in the first place if he couldn't take care of you?"

"Mph."

"Maybe he thought it was a good idea at the time, but then the 'new' wore off and he got bored. That often happens with people who buy exotic animals for pets. Once they discover how much work it entails, they either start abusing the animal or dump it in some zoo's parking lot. I'd like to give Dalrymple the benefit of the doubt and say that he probably didn't mean to hurt you. But then again, maybe he did, 'cause he's sure mean enough to sue the zoo for something that was his own fault in the first place."

"Aiiiii!" Maybe it was my imagination, but he sounded angry.

Better change the subject. "Are you making friends?" I waved toward the other animals—the zebra, the goat, the eland. They had their ears pricked forward, watching us. Although the barn was a safe and comfortable temporary home for quarantined animals, there was little entertainment, and they appeared to appreciate this interruption of their dull routine.

So did Alejandro, whose expression became placid again. He stepped forward and nuzzled my ear with his soft lips.

"Mmmm."

"I love you, too, sweetie, but you know what? I need to pick up some animals and drive them over to the TV station for their fifteen minutes of fame. Maybe someday I'll take you. Would you like that?"

"Maaa!"

"Then that's what we'll do."

I gave him a goodbye scratch behind the ears and set off for the animal clinic, where the day's charges would be waiting for me.

Bernice Unser, the zoo volunteer who always accompanied me on these trips, was waiting by the cages. She looked nervous. "I'm not that comfortable with snakes," she admitted.

"You'll like Lillian, though." I squatted down and peered into the albino boa constrictor's cage. After pigging out on breakfast, Lillian appeared relaxed and happy. "Lillian's friendly, which is why we chose her for the program. Ever since Sssbyl started tweeting, snakes are rising in popularity."

Bernice brightened. Despite her fear of snakes, she'd become a Sssbyl fan, too. "Did you see this morning's tweet yet?" She held out her phone so I could see the screen.

At 5:46 a.m. Sssbyl tweeted how much she was enjoying her visit to San Francisco. "Sssigned Bridal Regissstry at Gump'sss, ate mousssie on wharf, usssed wi-fi at Ssstarbucksss. Good timesss!"

"Bridal registry?" I asked. "Sssbyl's getting married?"

"Remember, last week she tweeted 'Love isss a many sssplendored thing.' Apparently it's serious."

I wanted to be happy for Sssbyl, but my own love was somewhere in the woods of Virginia and I missed him like crazy.

◇◇◇

During the live program of *Good Morning, San Sebastian*, Ariel welcomed Pooh Bear the bearcat with open arms. Literally.

The minute I took the two-foot long juvenile bearcat out of his cage he leapt on her, licked her neck a couple of times, then snuggled up in her lap. As she stared down at him in amazement, he began to chuckle.

"He sounds like he's laughing!" The tough ex-Marine was obviously charmed.

"That's how bearcats sound when they're happy. He's sure taken a shine to you, hasn't he? With your black hair, I'll bet you remind him of Elysa, the keeper who hand-raised him. Like many of the zoo's animals that have to be bottle-fed for whatever reason, he's grown into a real snuggle-puss."

While Pooh Bear chuckled away, I explained that bearcats, who lived mainly in the Middle East, India, and Southeast Asia, were classified as binturongs. They had received their nicknames because their faces and extraordinarily long whiskers resembled a cat's, and their bulky bodies, a bear's.

"He looks like something Dr. Seuss might have dreamed up," Ariel said, stroking the Pooh Bear. "And he smells like buttered popcorn."

"That scent, their cute appearance, and their sweet personalities are just some of the reasons why they're so frequently turned into pets. That, plus, the fact that they're murder on cockroaches and rats."

Pooh Bear stood on his hind legs and began snuffling through her hair with his pointy snout.

"What's he doing now?"

"Looking for bugs. But I've got something better." I reached behind me and pulled out a paper bag. "Watch what happens now."

Bearcats love grapes, and the minute I pulled a fat concord out of the sack, he emitted a squeak and beat feet to my own lap, where he clasped my wrist with his little paws and lowered the grape to his mouth. Munch. Gulp. He squeaked again. *More, more.*

It didn't take him long to get through the entire bag of grapes, which was just as well, because Bernice was waiting backstage with more animals. This time a stage hand named Jeff helped her lug out a large cage. The stage hand remained as Bernice moved away with a still-chuckling Pooh Bear.

"Remember my saying that some people keep bearcats to help control the rat population?" I said to the camera. "Here's a South American animal that's often domesticated for the same reason."

With Jeff standing beside me, I opened the cage door and dragged Lillian out—coil after coil after coil. Although she had not yet reached her full maturity, she was six feet long and weighed around forty pounds. With Jeff holding one end and me the other, we looped the snake around my shoulders. Lillian enjoyed the heat of a human's body so she didn't try to get away, just lay there, tongue darting, head bobbing gently.

"Pretty, isn't she?" I asked Ariel, scratching the boa under the chin while trying not to stoop under her weight. "As you can see, she's an albino. She has pink eyes and her skin is a lovely cream color with yellow and gold markings. Unfortunately, this pretty skin has caused these animals to be hunted into endangered status, so if you see a woman walking around in boa-skin shoes or carrying a boa-skin handbag, you might want to say something about her fashion choices."

Sermon over, I launched into some of the lesser known facts about boa constrictors: they were non-poisonous; after incubating the eggs in their bodies, females gave live birth to up to sixty young; some species grew as large as thirteen feet; many could stretch their jaws wide enough to swallow a wild pig whole after they'd constricted it to death in their muscular coils.

"If you want to have a boa constrictor for a pet, make sure you don't already have a dog or a cat. Uh, and make sure your children have grown up and left home."

Ariel laughed, but Jeff looked stricken.

"Thinking about buying a constrictor?" I asked.

He nodded. "I was."

"Have kids?"

He nodded again.

"Young ones?"

"Two and four."

"Then you'll be glad to know that the San Sebastian County No Kill Animal Shelter has a wonderful assortment of dogs and cats waiting to be adopted. Thanks to the financial success of the Renaissance Faire—huzzah!—this week the shelter is skipping the usual fee for vaccinations." I pushed Lillian's bobbing head away and reached into my chest pocket. "Here's a coupon. After you've chosen your new family member, present the coupon and you'll get fifty percent off neutering."

With that, we stuffed Lillian back into her carrier and Jeff took her away.

I turned to Ariel. "And now I have a surprise for you. A little bird told me it's your birthday. Am I right?"

Bemused, she nodded.

At my signal, Bernice stepped back on set carrying a birthday cake. A sulphur-crested cockatoo was perched on her shoulder, humming softly.

"Ariel, meet Chico. He's almost eighty years old, but he can sing like a chick half his age. Chico, strut your stuff!" I cued him with a snap of my fingers.

When he launched into the "Happy Birthday Song" in Spanish I could swear I saw tears in the ex-Marine's eyes.

◇◇◇

For once the segment of *Anteaters to Zebras* had gone off without a hitch. No one escaped, no one got bit. Giddy with success, Bernice and I sang chorus after chorus of "The Bear Went over the Mountain" as we drove our charges to the zoo. Once we delivered them back to the clinic we went our separate ways, Bernice to Monkey Mania where she was currently volunteering, me to Quarantine.

On my way to the barn, I looked at my watch. Almost noon. Even Bambi would surely be out of bed by now. I took my cell out of my pocket and began to punch in her number, then changed my mind. She bore no love toward me and would surely tell me to get lost. Dropping in, like I'd done yesterday, might work better. It was important to find out how well she knew Wynona Dade and if Bambi ever let slip her father's real identity.

My visit with Alejandro took mere minutes. Deborah Holt was already there, accompanied by zoo director Zorah Vega. They were making a big fuss over him and it was a relief to see him looking happy again. He seemed to perk up even more when I renewed my promise that one day he'd have his own fifteen minutes of fame on "Anteaters to Zebras."

"That animal's got star written all over him," Deborah said.

"Don't rush it," Zorah cautioned. "Because of the mess with Dalrymple, I want this llama to keep a low profile for a while."

After agreeing that caution was the best policy, I gave Alejandro a few scratches behind his ears, then left.

◇◇◇

When I arrived in San Sebastian, I parked my truck down the street from Bambi's house in order not to give her advance warning of another unwelcome visit. As I approached, I noticed how little the outside of her house matched the gaudiness within. A neat hedgerow separated the yard from its neighbors. Lining the cobbled path up to the house were lovely plantings of blue hyacinth and pale pink tulips. White and lavender gladioli softened the rectangular sweep of the long porch, which was in turn livened by multiple hanging baskets of ferns.

In the light of such tasteful elegance, I doubted Bambi did her own gardening.

Smiling, I raised my hand to knock, then noticed that the door stood slightly ajar.

"Bambi!" I called.

No answer.

San Sebastian isn't a particularly dangerous town, but like every other small city, it experienced its share of burglaries and break-ins. A woman like Bambi, living in an upscale neighborhood like this, would surely know to keep her doors locked. I looked up and down the street to see if she had simply stepped out to visit with a neighbor but saw no one.

I called out again. Still no answer.

Worried, I pushed the door open. "Bambi? It's Teddy. Are you all right?"

I stepped into the hall. Nothing. There was no sign of her in the gilt-and-purple living room, either. Nor the kitchen.

But when I walked into the master bedroom and saw what I saw, I knew Bambi would never be all right again.

Chapter Fifteen

"Tell me again what you were doing in Bambi O'Dair's house."

For what had to be the tenth time I told Acting Sheriff Elvin Dade that I had merely dropped by for a visit, but upon finding her front door open, walked inside and found her body.

He narrowed his mean little eyes. "I happen to know you two weren't friends, so why would you 'drop by for a visit.'"

Of all the times Elvin had to pick to ask an intelligent question, it had to be while I was standing in front of a murder scene as cop car after cop car sirened toward us. Eight were already parked at the curb, and two more blocked off both ends of the street. The only good thing about the situation was that one of the deputies on the scene was Emilio Gutierrez.

Bambi's neighbors were out in full force, too. A herd of Looky Loos stood on the sidewalk, whispering and pointing.

At me.

"Okay, Elvin, so I dropped by. What of it? Bambi and I talked from time to time." No lie there.

"That's 'Acting Sheriff Dade' to you. What were you talking about last night?"

"Who says I was here last night?"

He jerked a beefy thumb toward an elderly woman talking earnestly to a plainclothes detective. "Mrs. Scarborough said you came by just as *Dancing with the Stars* was coming on and that you left before it was over. She also said she heard a big ruckus like furniture being thrown around and Miss O'Dair screaming her head off."

"Then why didn't she call the police?"

"I'm asking the questions here!"

"So you are." I gave Mrs. Scarborough a dirty look. She dirty-looked back. "Please, El…uh, Acting Sheriff Dade, can I go home now? I've told you everything I know, multiple times. The minute I realized Bambi was dead I backed out of the house and called you guys."

"How could you tell she was dead?"

"The nylon stocking tied around her neck. Her bulging eyes and tongue. The fact that she was cold when I checked her carotid for a pulse." Somehow I was able to keep my voice from cracking.

"What do you know about carotids?"

"Zookeepers sometimes have to check to see if an animal's dead or alive. Fortunately, that doesn't happen often."

Because of the nature of his questions, concern over my own legal situation eclipsed my horror over finding Bambi murdered. Wasn't having one member of my family in jail satisfaction enough for him?

"You know, Acting Sheriff Dade, on second thought, I'd better call an attorney."

When I reached for my pocket he grabbed my wrist. "Deputy Gutierrez!" he bawled. "Frisk her!"

Emilio followed orders but I could tell he wasn't happy about it. Me neither. I was naïve enough to believe that when my only weapon turned out to be a cellphone that would be the end of it, but I was wrong.

The next thing I knew, I was sitting in a patrol car, my hands handcuffed behind me.

◇◇◇

The interview room at the station smelled like dirty sneakers, and having a sweaty Elvin Dade sitting across the table from me didn't help.

"Why'd you do it, Teddy?"

I am not my father's daughter for nothing. "I want a lawyer," I repeated for around the one hundredth time since those cold handcuffs clamped around my wrists.

Elvin waved my request away. "Hey, now, Teddy. We've known each other all our lives, and if there's one thing I've learned about you Bentleys is that you people never do anything without a reason. What did Miss O'Dair do to provoke the attack? C'mon, tell old Elvin. He'll understand."

There's not much worse than having a total fool condescend toward you, so I repeated those magic words, "I want a lawyer."

"Did she attack you first? And you simply defended yourself? That bedroom was wrecked. Chair turned over, nightstand drawer pulled out and papers all over the floor…"

"I want a lawyer."

"And I want a million dollars. From the state of Miss O'Dair's body, she died sometime last night. Did you strangle her before you left, when Mrs. Scarborough heard all that noise, or did you come back later and do it?"

"I want a lawyer." Having never been in trouble or purchased a large piece of property, I didn't really have an attorney, but I knew who to call. Albert Grissom, my mother's defense attorney. He might give us group rates.

Elvin narrowed his eyes in an attempt to scare intimidate me. "Hey! Stop being so stubborn and tell the truth for once!"

"I want a lawyer."

"No, you can't have…"

The door behind him opened and to my surprise, Grissom strutted through the door carrying a briefcase thick enough to smuggle bootleg copies of the Encyclopedia Britannica. When he plopped it down on the table, the table groaned.

He pinned Elvin with a stern look. "My name is Albert Grissom, sir, and my client isn't saying anything. Unless you have enough evidence to charge her, you must release her."

After recovering himself, Elvin snarled, "You're not the one in charge here. I am!"

"Oh, really? Something tells me you're going to learn different when Sheriff Rejas gets back. As I said earlier, but apparently must say again, if you don't have enough evidence to charge my client, you have to let her go."

"I can keep her in custody as long as I want!"

Grissom give him a thin smile. "The U.S. Constitution and the laws of the Great State of California say you can't."

The defense attorney waited for an answer. When none came, he said, "Fine. My client and I are leaving right now. Come on Teddy, we're out of here."

Not waiting for me to say anything, he grabbed me by the arm and hauled me out of the chair. Only then did he notice that I was still cuffed.

"Oh, for God's sake, Elvin, take these off her!"

Grumbling, Elvin did, whereupon my attorney and I hit the road.

On the way out to the parking lot, Grissom said, "That's the first time an officer of the law ever called me to come down and represent a client."

I couldn't have been more shocked. "Elvin Dade did that?"

"Don't make me laugh. It was your old buddy Emilio Gutierrez. Good man, there. He also said to give you a message. 'No fingerprints on Mr. Rat or anything else.' Do you know what that means?" When I nodded, he continued. "I do have a bit of bad news for you, Teddy. It seems your truck has been impounded and you probably won't get it back for several days, if then. The techies are crawling all over it hoping to find hair, blood, DNA, or whatever. But don't worry, I'll drop you off at San Sebastian Motor Rentals."

"I shouldn't have to rent a car because Bambi was strangled. And I didn't see any blood."

"There's always something, Teddy. Death's messy."

I wished he hadn't said that because I couldn't get Bambi's contorted face out of my mind, let alone the smell of the body fluids that had leaked out of her during the night. "Uh, wait a minute."

Stepping away from him, I leaned over the curb and vomited into the gutter. It took a while, but when I was through, Grissom handed me a handkerchief and a breath mint.

"Good defense attorneys are never without them," he said.

◇◇◇

LOCAL SOCIALITE MURDERED! screamed the evening edition of *The San Sebastian Gazette*.

Still shaken from the morning's events, I was sitting at the *Merilee*'s galley table reading the paper in disbelief. After giving a summation of the ersatz socialite Bambi O'Dair's life, minus her connection to Victor Emerson, the reporter called me "a person of interest." To close his article, he wrote, "At present, Miss Bentley's mother, the much-married Caroline Piper Bentley Hufgraff O'Brien Petersen, is incarcerated in the San Sebastian County Jail on charges stemming from her arrest on Sunday for the murder of Victor Emerson, a.k.a. Glenn Jamison. Miss Bentley's father, Daniel St. James Bentley IV, scion of one of the oldest families in California, is accused of embezzling millions of dollars from his grandfather's firm of Bentley, Haight & Busby. He has been on the run for twenty-five years."

The reporter all but wrote, "Like mother and father, like daughter."

The thinly veiled allegations were upsetting, but I knew better than to call and complain. Past experience with the press had taught me that my every outraged word would be repeated in tomorrow's morning edition. At least the reporter hadn't referred to me as a "socialite."

I was still upset when my cell phone rang. It was the producer of *Good Morning, San Sebastian*, informing me that "Anteaters to Zebras" was on hiatus until my legal situation resolved itself. Almost as soon as he rang off, Ariel Gonzales called to say she'd done everything possible to keep the segment on the air but the suits were worried about their ratings as long as I remained a murder suspect.

"I can't believe it," she growled. "Have you seen those characters on reality TV these days? Talk about a bunch of trolls!

You could be a mass murderer and still come across as a nicer person. Whatever happened to the concept of innocent until proven guilty?"

Her ire on my behalf made me smile. "Thanks, Ariel. It's comforting to know I've got a Marine on my side."

"The stagehands are pulling for you, too. Stay strong, girlfriend. And keep your doors locked. I've got a bad feeling about this."

She hung up, leaving me thinking about Mr. Rat.

Bonz, curled up in my lap, whined then nuzzled my hand. Ever since I had arrived home he'd not left my side. Animals can sense emotion, and although I tried to contain my horror over the morning's events he picked up on it.

"It's okay, Bonz. We'll protect each other."

When you've been all but accused of murder in the local newspaper, you find out who your friends are. In the next couple of hours I received calls from just about everyone I knew, including Yancy Haas, Deborah Holt, and young Howie. Strangely enough, I hadn't yet heard from my father. He was probably out robbing banks somewhere.

Even Frank Turnbull, the plump Speedo-wearing attorney I'd met at Bambi's boat party, called to offer his support.

"Since Victor Emerson was revealed as a fraudulent marriage provider, among other things, I've been swamped with people, including your own dear mother, enquiring about their marital and parental status. I want you to know, Teddy, that no matter how busy I am, I'll always be here for you. Ah, by any chance did Victor marry you to that Michael fellow?"

"Fortunately not," I said, amused by the blatant ambulance-chasing. "It wouldn't have mattered anyway since I didn't ask for anything in the divorce settlement and Michael didn't offer."

"Oh." He sounded disappointed. "Well, take care of yourself, kid. Gotta go."

I was trying to decide what to do about dinner when I heard Linda Cushing call, "Ahoy the *Merilee*! Permission to come aboard!"

I opened the hatch to see Linda, firefighter Walt McAdams, Dr. Willis Pierce, and—surprisingly—Deanna Sazac standing on the dock, their arms filled with casseroles and assorted six-packs. Even the formerly hostile Ada Fife had come calling, but protective as ever, she'd left Howie behind. As I waved them aboard, Willis brandished two bottles of Moet and quoted, "'Do you think because you are virtuous, that there shall be no more cakes and ale?' *Twelfth Night*, Act II, Scene III."

Walt, more down-to-earth, said, "Here, have a Bud."

Misery shared is misery halved. For the next couple of hours we partied like only liveaborders can. Willis quoted more booze-related Shakespeare, Linda presented a shoulder to cry on, Walt did his impression of Britney Spears (always a hit), and once Deanna Sazac had downed enough Moet to loosen up, she intimated that whoever strangled Bambi had done a solid for every married woman in San Sebastian County.

"Now that Bambi's out of the running, what's going to happen with you and Judd?" I asked.

"Nothing, since we're not legally bound. I've already told him I was taking back my maiden name. Along with his Porsche."

My wince must have been visible, because she added, "I also said that if he's a good little boy, I'll give it back."

I was saved from giving her unsolicited relationship advice when Willis, somewhat tipsy by then, interjected, "'O, beware, my lady of jealousy; it is the green-eyed monster which doth mock the meat it feeds on.' *Othello*, Act III, Scene III."

"I'm not jealous!" Deanna lied.

He gave her a hard look. "The sooner you admit it the sooner you can deal with it. Me, no play, no act, no scene. I've lived in the harbor long enough to watch you talk to Judd like you're talking to some servant. Bambi wasn't that hot—I've seen her undressed..." Everyone's eyebrows raised, including mine, but he continued, "...and her surgeon wasn't all that good. Guess that's what happens when you go bargain-hunting; you wind up with keloid scars where you'd rather not have them. But back to you, Queen Deanna. Why don't you try treating the guy like an equal for once? Judd wasn't into Bambi as much for her looks as he was for the ego boo."

"What's an ego boo?" Walt asked, while Deanna sat there speechless.

Willis made a face. "You don't read *Entertainment Weekly*? It's short for 'ego boost.' Bambi made Judd feel like a big man. Not that he is, but sometimes to keep the peace we have to pretend our partners are more than they really are."

"Speaking from experience, Willis?" I asked.

"Let's just say that I once suffered through a relationship similar to Judd's." He raised his hands as if to stave off Deanna's growing wrath. "It was long before I moved here and the less said about my late unlamented marriage the better. Serena Sue, my clumsily named ex-missus, was almost as bossy as you, Deanna dear, so sheath those wicked talons. I'm just sharing my own experience so that you might show more compassion to Judd. He may be an unfaithful jerk but he loves you."

"Thank you, Dear Abby," Deanna snapped, but from the look on her face, I suspected she was giving his advice some thought.

Deanna's attack of jealousy reminded me of another woman—my friend Deborah Holt. Remembering her "Deer Woman" threat on Facebook, and the newspaper articles about her violent behavior in college, I had to face facts: Deborah had to be considered a suspect, at least in Bambi's death.

But I certainly wasn't going to tell Elvin Dade.

Later, during a lull in the festivities, I sidled up to Willis. "I didn't know you were married before."

His rant must have sobered him because he had switched from champagne to Pepsi. "Correct, Teddy. And never again. Once bitten, twice shy, as they say. I went the limit to win Serena Sue's admiration, and it didn't do any good. She just kept nagging me about my flaws. But to paraphrase Kit Marlowe, that was in another country, and although the wench isn't dead, I certainly learned my lesson."

I was about to ask if he still kept in touch with Serena Sue—every now and then I received a remorseful phone call from my own unfaithful ex—but Walt leaped into the conversation.

"Women will bleed you dry if you let them." *In vino veritas,* apparently.

Willis gave him a wry grin. "Another veteran of the divorce courts?"

"Yeah, too bad it wasn't Victor who married us. Then I could go after the money I wound up paying the witch to get rid of her."

Willis laughed. I didn't. I'd known Walt's ex-wife for years and liked her. "Walt, I know we're friends and all that, but I seem to remember the divorce somewhat differently. Didn't she catch you with that topless dancer over at the Pretty Pink Pussycat?"

He shrugged. "A one-off, big deal. It didn't mean anything."

"It did to your wife."

Walt took another swig of his Budweiser. "You women all stick together."

Before I could reply, my cell phone rang. The display showed it was a Gunn Castle number. My father?

"Let me take this," I told everyone, stepping out onto the dock. The air was cool, the stars were out, and so was the tide. The *Merilee* creaked and rocked at her slip, creating music that landlubbers, poor things, never get to hear.

But the call wasn't from my father. It was Aster Edwina.

"Teddy, get up here right now. I did my best to hide the newspaper from your father but somehow he managed to find a copy and now he's talking about turning himself in. He's going to tell that fool Elvin he killed Victor and Bambi both."

Chapter Sixteen

If I didn't love my parents so much I'd hate them.

"This has gone on long enough!" my father yelled, waving the *San Sebastian Gazette* around as he paced around Gunn Castle's elegant drawing room. "I can't let my only child go to prison!"

Usually debonair, Dad looked like a wild man. His hair was uncombed, his eyes staring. He had even incorrectly buttoned his double-breasted sports coat and one side hung lower than the other.

Aster Edwina didn't look much better. Neither did Mrs. McGinty.

The room crackled with tension.

"Calm down, Dad," I said, struggling to remain calm. "I'm not going to prison. I wasn't even officially arrested. None of that 'person of interest' stuff is true."

"Don't tell me what's true! I know the way the law operates! Look what happened to your mother, for God's sake! That beautiful woman is sitting in a jail cell as we speak! None of this would have happened if it weren't for me! The least I can do is take the fall!"

When I was nine years old my father's embezzlement scheme was outed by his partners' newly acquired anal-compulsive accountant. The gig being up, as the saying goes, Dad flew the coop. Since he'd committed a federal crime, the Feds attached all our assets, and within weeks my mother and I lost everything. We were out on the street. Only the charity of a distant relative saved us from relocating to the homeless encampment under Gunn Narrows Bridge. Our situation would have been hopeless without my mother's resolve. She might have lost her home, her jewels, and her furs, but she still had her looks. After several successful campaigns to marry the richest men possible, she reclaimed her former financial glory. The crimes, the deceit, and the blatant fortune-hunting had been hell on me, but I got over it.

Now this.

"Dad, there is nothing, I repeat, nothing tying me to Bambi's murder. Elvin Dade is just a tiny little man grasping at this one last chance to throw his weight around. Once Joe gets back from Virginia and finds the real killer, all this nonsense will go away, but if you turn yourself in now, you're screwed. You'll wind up in Leavenworth or San Quentin, depending on who gets a piece of you first—the Feds or the great state of California."

He hung his head. "It's what I deserve."

Yes, it is, I thought, but didn't say. "If you go to prison, how do you think Mother will feel? Or me?"

"Or me!" Aster Edwina cried. "Daniel, you simply cannot do this to the people who love you!" She immediately clapped her hands over her mouth as if she'd just revealed a state secret.

Big woop.

But she had given me an idea to press my case on a different level. "Dad, if you're in prison, what'll happen to Dominga?"

His expression turned into one of horror, but being the sly fox that he is, he immediately covered it to one of pure innocence. "I don't know anyone named Dominga."

"How strange, considering she's been your mistress for three years."

Aster Edwina glared at him. "Daniel, is that true?"

He fixed his eyes on a thirteenth century battle axe hanging on the wall. "Of course not."

"Oh, Dad. You forget I met her the last time I visited your place in Costa Rica. You introduced her to me as your maid but I've known very few maids who wear four-carat diamond solitaires. Not only that, I heard you tiptoeing down the hall to her room one night. Without your financial support, which you can only furnish if you're un-incarcerated, Dominga will have to return to her former, er, profession. Is that what you want?"

"That wasn't a diamond. It was a zirconia."

"No it wasn't."

"Her father bought it for her."

"A stable hand?"

"You're such a snoop."

"Guilty as charged, but I hope you see my point. Confessing to a crime you didn't commit isn't going to help anyone, especially her." Or me. Or Caro.

With a sigh, Dad eased himself onto a Louis XIV sofa rumored to have once cushioned the tush of the Sun King himself. "I don't know what else to do, Teddy."

Sensing a slight decrease in the room's tension—even the overdressed dandy in the Gainsborough portrait hanging above the fireplace appeared to breathe a sigh of relief—I went in for the kill. I sat down beside Dad and patted his liver-spotted hand. With a pang I realized my rascally father was getting old.

"Stay here with your good friend Aster Edwina. Continue doing what you've been doing, which is to stay in contact with your crim…ah, business associates. Learn what you can from the safety of the telephone. Remember how much valuable information you've already given me."

"But it's not enough!"

"I'll be the judge of that."

Dad was right, though. His information, although good, had not yet supplied me with what I really needed to know: who had Victor Emerson been blackmailing?

◇◇◇

Crisis averted, I returned to the *Merilee* and cleaned up the remnants of my friends' impromptu party. I swept, scrubbed, and took out trash. Then I polished the silverware, rearranged the dishes in my galley cabinets, organized the junk drawer, and changed the bedding in the fore and aft bedrooms. I cleaned out my tiny closet, shined several pairs of shoes, and made up a garbage bag full of donations for Goodwill. That accomplished, I brushed Priss, Feroz, and Bonz, rubbed Neatsfoot Oil into their collars, and scoured and disinfected their respective bowls. Then I started polishing the *Merilee*'s brass fittings.

Halfway through, I stopped.

What was I doing? Keeping the *Merilee* tidy was a good idea, but not at one in the morning when I had to be at work at six.

Exhausted, I collapsed on the aft bunk.

No fingerprints on Mr. Rat.

Bodies and minds don't always agree on the best recipe for optimum health, so three hours later I was still awake. My aching body cried out for rest, but my mind refused to let go of the night-long mantra: *No fingerprints on Mr. Rat.*

I looked at the clock. Four a.m., which meant it was seven in Virginia. I shrugged the animals off me and picked my cell phone off the nightstand.

No answer, but the sound of Joe's baritone telling me to leave a message was somehow comforting. "As soon as Homeland Security gives your phone back, call me," I told him. "Bambi O'Dair was murdered, Mom's still in jail, Elvin arrested me, and I've been 'hiatused' from *Anteaters to Zebras*. Love you!" After making a few kissy noises, I hung up. Rethinking the message I had just left, I realized no man in his right mind would return that call.

Sleep being a no-hoper, I got out of bed and fired up my laptop. Might as well use my insomnia in a more constructive manner, such as running a check on the owners of the crossbow that had killed Victor: Cary and Melissa Keegan.

Their web site revealed little about their personal lives; it only touted their medieval wares. Same for their Facebook page, although it had drawn some interesting posts from Medievalists throughout the country. I hadn't realized there were so many.

Googling them individually proved more productive.

Cary, thuggish though he appeared, had a clean record. More than clean, actually. His name was mentioned as a volunteer for various charitable groups, including Habitat for Humanity, Special Olympics, and the Piper Center for Special Needs Children. In the article about the Piper Center, he was quoted, saying, "Before he passed, my brother Jimmy was a special child, so organizations like this really strike home. Whatever I do, I do in his memory."

Google wasn't as kind to sweet, cowering Melissa Keegan. During her first marriage—I hadn't known she'd been married before—Melissa Mackey Keegan had twice been arrested for domestic violence. The first time, after hitting Mr. Mackey over the head with a hot iron skillet when he complained about burned pork chops, she was let off with a warning. But when a month later she poured scalding water on her unfortunate spouse, who had been doing nothing more violent than playing a video game, she spent two months in jail. Five months after Mackey divorced her—he apparently drew the line at scalding water—she married Cary.

Somehow Speaks-To-Souls had seen through her. I hadn't.

I was about to Google stuntman Yancy Hass when a wet nose nudged my bare foot. Bonz had finally woken up.

"Don't tell me you want walkies already," I told him.

I'm telling you, telling you, he barked. *Go get that leash, already.*

The sound of my voice woke Feroz, and within seconds, both dogs were dancing anxiously around my feet.

Bowing to the inevitable, I logged off the Internet.

There's something magical about being alone with dogs so early in the morning. Even the birds are still asleep. The only sounds I could hear, besides the grunts and snuffles of Bonz and Feroz, were the wind's whispers through the Monterey pines and the incoming tide as it kissed along the shore.

Those truly relaxing minutes clarified my mind enough that when we returned to the *Merilee*, I knew exactly what to do.

It was time for some breaking and entering.

Chapter Seventeen

It was still dark when I pulled my rented econo-compact in front of Victor's trailer. The police tape was still up, but we scofflaws pay no attention to such things. After pulling on a pair of latex gloves and smashing a rear window with my heavy flashlight, I slithered through and landed on Victor's unmade bed.

In a way, trailers are like boats. Neither has much square footage, and what little space exists is used wisely, with closets and cupboards built into every possible nook and cranny. Within minutes I had searched them all without finding what I was looking for. No problem. Victors' marriage logbooks proved him to be an assiduous bookkeeper, and I was certain that a record of his blackmailing enterprise was somewhere in this trailer. All I had to do was find it.

If I were a wily ex-con who wanted to hide a written account of criminal behavior, where would I hide it? I sat down on the ragtag sofa and switched off the flashlight. With the sense of vision out of action, other senses rushed in to fill its place. For the first time I noticed the musty smell of a closed-in room, the chirp of a sleepy bird waking in the woods behind the trailer, the drip-drip-drip of a loose faucet.

Victor would not have hidden anything under the mattress; it was such a common hiding place even the dense Elvin Dade would look there. In the freezer? Also common. Behind the toilet? Same old same old. As I sat there thinking, a faint glimmer of pale morning light leaked into the trailer, but only enough to provide contrast to the complete darkness that had been there before. The sun would be up soon, and with it, an increased chance of getting caught.

"C'mon, Victor. Where'd you hide your blackmail ledger?"

Sitting in the dark not having worked, I flicked my flashlight back on and skittered the beam around the trailer's tiny living room. I saw ragged drapes covering the kitchen window, dirty tube socks lying between the sagging sofa, a tilting magazine rack/lampstand combination, flies enjoying breakfast on a moldy slice of bread, a crumpled tee shirt hanging…

Wait.

Magazine rack?

Taking a cue from Edgar Allan Poe's "The Purloined Letter," where a major clue was hidden in plain sight with similar items, I stepped over to the rack and pulled out a stack of *Hustlers*. Not a tasteful find so early in the morning but a fortuitous one. In the November issue, nestled between facing pages showcasing the rosy rumps of two well-developed women, lay a small account book.

I opened it and struck blackmail gold.

The same code names appeared on every page. Flipping through the book to the final entry, I found…

    05/15—r'cd Taxi—$250
    05/16—r'cd Scarlet—$125
    05/18—r'cd Woodstock—$125
    05/25—r'cd Aloha—$100
    05/29—r'cd Taxi—$250

Whoever Taxi was, he—or she—was really being squeezed.

But the day was getting lighter by the minute, and hanging around while I puzzled out the ledger was not a good idea, so I shoved it into my pocket and exited the trailer through the front door. Traveling via window hadn't been fun.

I was about to enter my econo-compact when I heard another car's engine coming along the lane that led to the trailer.

For a second I stood frozen, but the engine sounds cut off a short distance behind the trees. A car door opened, then slammed. Whoever the person was, he wasn't worried about being caught.

Then I heard a woman's voice. Singing.

"Gathering flowers for the Master's bouquet,
Beautiful flowers that will never decay.
Gathered by angels and carried away
Forever to bloom in the Master's bouquet."

Wynona Dade wasn't a half bad alto.

As I listened, Wynona continued to warble the hymn, but when her voice slowly faded I realized she was walking away from the trailer, not approaching it. Despite my situation, her presence made me curious, so I walked down the lane until her voice became louder. She had parked her creaky Ford Focus next to a narrow path leading into the woods, where I could see the flicker of her blue print dress weaving between the trees. I shadowed her quietly as the path looped away to the north for a few yards, then back south toward the trailer. After a few minutes the trees thinned and I could see her more clearly.

Wynona carried a bucket, but for what? Collecting magic mushrooms, perhaps? The thought of stodgy Wynona getting religiously lit on sh'rooms amused me until I realized that with the path so close to Victor's trailer, he might have discovered her guilty pleasure. Maybe her name was in his blackmail ledger, her code name "Scarlet," his twisted version of a joke.

Just before the path had circled around all the way back to the trailer, the trees dwindled to nothing, revealing a sunlit opening in the woods. The only reason I hadn't noticed it before was because the pines and undergrowth began again at the far side, completely hiding the trailer from view. When I drew closer, the scene took my breath away. A flower-strewn meadow dazzled my eyes with the blooms of gold California poppy, red and yellow columbine, deep purple redmaids, and lavender lupine.

Still singing, Wynona stopped in the middle of the clearing, put the bucket down, and bent over.

Hymns. Wildflowers.

Wynona was gathering flowers for a church altar.

Well, good for her, but her devotions were none of my business. I turned to go, then stopped. I looked back at her, then at the far side of the meadow, then again at Wynona. I had originally thought Victor might have caught her doing something naughty, but it could have worked the other way around. If the trailer wasn't visible from here, she wasn't visible from the trailer, either.

What if Wynona had overheard Victor in the act of shaking down one of his blackmail victims?

Before I could talk myself out of it, I stepped into the meadow and said, "Lovely morning, isn't it Wynona?"

With a shriek she dropped a handful of yellow primrose. "What the hell are you doing here?"

"Tut tut. The upright Wynona Dade swearing like a sailor."

"Hell's where sinners go, which I'm sure you'll find out in due course." She pursed her prissy mouth.

Although her irritation at seeing me was obvious, what I had expected to see wasn't there: guilt. Being caught hanging out a few feet from the back of Victor's trailer did not bother her, which made me certain I was right. She had something on the dead man, not the other way around.

"You discovered who Victor really was before he was murdered, didn't you, Wynona?"

"You're crazy. Now please go away and let me do what I came here to do—the Lord's work." She picked the primrose up from where they had fallen.

"Yellow primrose and golden poppies will make a nice altar centerpiece."

Despite her irritation, she preened. "I'm known county-wide for my skill in flower arranging."

"I'm sure you are, but back to my question. When you were out here last week, did you overhear Victor in the process of blackmailing someone?"

She turned, a puzzled look on her face. It wasn't faked. "Are you drunk?"

Strike one. I pitched another fast ball. "Sorry. If mere blackmail had been the subject of the conversation you overheard you would have run straight to your husband and told him all about it, wouldn't you? There would have been an investigation, followed by an arrest, and we'd have read all about it in the *Gazette*. It would have been quite a feather in Elvin's cap, putting the collar on an escaped murderer. But of course that's not what happened, is it? Here's what I think really went down. You came out here early one morning to do your churchly duty, but while you were picking flowers near the trailer, you heard Bambi's voice. Along with everyone else in San Sebastian County, including me, you suspected the two of having an affair. So you snooped."

"I don't snoop." There was the guilt-ridden expression I had been looking for. Her unlovely face became even more unlovely, and she clutched the primrose blooms so tight it's a wonder they didn't scream for the police.

"You heard enough to realize that Victor and Bambi were father and daughter, not lovers, didn't you?" I continued. "You also learned something that upset you more than a mere bout of heavy breathing would have—that Victor wasn't really a minister or notary public. Not being unintelligent, you realized it meant that you and Elvin might not be legally married. Quite a blow for the moral overseer of San Sebastian County, wasn't it? That was something you never wanted made public."

She glanced toward the trailer. With the light as strong as it now was, the trailer remained invisible.

"Like I said, Teddy, you don't know what you're talking about." But her voice quavered.

"Your church holds services on Wednesday, Saturday, and Sunday, so I'm guessing that you were picking flowers just before the Faire opened on Saturday moring. That's probably when you overheard them. Did you rush straight home to tell Elvin?"

She swallowed.

"You did, didn't you? The fact that he didn't come over here and arrest him right away means you convinced him to hold off, that the shame would be too great unless you two could rectify your marital situation before the ugly truth became public. That's why, when Victor was found murdered, Elvin believed you did it. He thought you were under the impression that with Victor dead, no one would ever know you two had been 'living in sin' for more than a decade."

She shook her head so hard and fast it looked more like a spasm than denial. "I didn't kill him. I…didn't kill anybody. I…I couldn't. Even though Elvin said…said he'd have to arrest him and who cared what everyone thought about…about… Oh, what will my chi…children think of…of me?" Her broken whisper sounded almost like a prayer.

I didn't like Wynona but at the sight of that prissy lower lip all a-tremble, harder hearts than mine would break. I shoved my way through the waist-high flowers toward her.

"I know you didn't kill anyone, Wynona," I said, hugging her to me. "But your husband doesn't know that. You'd better tell him before he arrests more people to cover up the murder he thinks you committed."

She looked at me for a moment with eyes as big and sad as Alejandro's, then wept on my shoulder.

◇◇◇

By the time I arrived at the zoo I was covered in tears, snot, and primrose pollen. Fortunately there was a shower in the women's locker room, so after a good scrub-down I put on my spare uniform and set off for the quarantine barn. Leaving Victor's blackmail book in my locker was worrisome, but the choice had been between that or the glove compartment in my tiny econo-compact. At least the locker was can opener-proof.

In Quarantine I found Alejandro rocking back and forth on his legs, a classic sign of animal stress. His stall was large as stalls go, but not large enough to give him the exercise he needed. At the Faire I had made a point of telling people it was cruel to keep large animals in small spaces, yet here he was, confined in a stall. Knowing the situation was only temporary made it no better.

Risking Aster Edwina's wrath I punched in her private number on my cell and told her what I thought.

She let me finish, something rare for her. At the end of my rant she said, "I agree."

"You do?"

"Yes, I've always been uncomfortable with the whole quarantine process, necessary though it is. Tell you what. We need to keep Alejandro away from the public during the day until the zoo's attorneys convince that drunken Dalrymple person to go fly a kite, but starting this evening we'll let him spend the night in the Friendly Farm barnyard. It's quite large and he'll have the other animals for company. He likes the chickens, I've heard. It will be your job to return him to his stall in Quarantine before the zoo opens, so you'll have to get here earlier. You'll also need to transfer him to the barnyard after the last visitor leaves in the evening. This means you'll have to work late."

"That's very kind of you, Aster Edwina. I don't mind the extra work."

"At the Gunn Zoo, our animals come first. Now get back to work. Be aware that I'm docking your paycheck for the length of this conversation. You could have waited until your lunch hour to talk about this."

"But…"

Too late. She'd already rung off.

◇◇◇

I spent the early part of the morning being fitted for the costume I would wear as a runaway lion during the Great Escape. It was only two days away, and if the costume's legs were too long, I wouldn't be able to run fast enough to make the assembled media happy. The suit was hot, and the bulky head partially obscured my sight line. Once Zorah noted my measurements, I scouted out the escape route. I jogged from the big cats' night house at the top of Africa Trail, down the hill to California Habitat, then south toward Down Under, where I took a short breather.

On the big day, I would lurk in the nearby brush for ten minutes while the TV cameras filmed the wallabies, then toured the animal cafeteria. Once Zorah messaged me on the radio, I'd head east toward Tropics Trail, then make a beeline north to Monkey Mania where my chasers would spot me again. The chase would pick up speed until they finally netted me in front of the cameras.

It seemed simple enough. At a slow jog, the entire route took less than thirty minutes. Maybe I could even stretch that rest break.

During lunch I stopped by Quarantine to see Alejandro and found four young children visiting him. He appeared happy for the first time in days.

"What's going on?" I asked keeper Deborah Holt, who appeared to be in charge of the kids. I tried to keep my voice casual, but ever since I had learned about her background, being around her made me nervous. "The public's not allowed in Quarantine."

She shrugged. "They're my nephews and nieces, and they've promised to behave. Other keepers have been sneaking their own younger relatives up here. I'm surprised you didn't catch on earlier."

"I've been busy."

Something flickered in her eyes. "Trying to figure out who killed Victor Emerson? Stop the detecting, Teddy."

"If I don't do it, who will?"

"Your boyfriend, when he gets back."

"But in the meantime, Elvin's trying to pin the murder on my mother. Don't forget, she's sitting in jail as we speak."

The grim look on her face lifted. "From what I hear, she's making friends and influencing people."

"What do you mean, from what you hear? You have contacts at the jail?"

"Soledad Rodriguez is my cousin."

I hid my shock. "Small world."

"Definitely. And with a murderer on the loose, you're better off not drawing attention to yourself, especially when it comes to amateur detecting. What if Victor's and Bambi's killer finds out you're snooping around?"

"I'm being careful." No point in bringing up Mr. Rat.

One of the children called to Deborah, a little girl who had just snagged her pretty pink dress on a ragged board.

"Looks like I'm needed," Deborah said, "but remember— keep your head down and leave the crime-solving to the police."

I left the barn feeling uneasy.

Had Deborah been threatening me?

◇◇◇

Wednesday tends to be a slow day for the zoo, but this one turned out to be an exception. Although the presence of Victor's blackmail ledger in my locker remained at the back of my mind, I was too busy to do anything about it. Soon after I arrived at the giant anteater enclosure with a pooper scooper and wheelbarrow, a group of Girl Scouts from Monterey approached. Their troop leader said they were working on their Naturalist badges, and it would be helpful if I could lead them in a short discussion about the animals. Lucy made it easy for me since she was playing Chase with six-month-old Little Ricky. When Little Ricky grew tired, he flopped down on his side. Mama Lucy flopped down next to him, tenderly grooming his dense fur with her long talons.

"See Lucy's talons?" I asked the scouts, who were busily writing into their notebooks. "They're four inches long. She uses them to tear apart rotten logs to get at termites, her favorite food."

A freckle-faced redhead of about twelve who looked enough like me to be a distant relation, asked, "Does she just slurp them down or chew them for a while? I've seen termites and the queen can be an inch long."

"The average termite is nowhere near that big but it wouldn't matter if they were twice their size. Anteaters have no teeth.

When they lap up termites with their yard-long tongue, they simply swallow them."

"Are you kidding me? Her tongue is three feet long?"

"And blue."

Another scout asked, "Do anteaters make good pets?"

I smiled. That was one of the first questions most children asked about any zoo animal that caught their fancy. "Absolutely not. Lucy looks tame and loveable playing with Little Ricky, but giant anteaters are the only animal in Central America that can take down a jaguar. Remember those four inch talons? When they're attacked, they rear up on their hind legs, brace against their big, thick tails, and rip out the jaguar's stomach. Believe me, you don't want an animal like that around the house."

The little redhead spoke up again. "But if it could be tamed?"

"Lucy has been around people almost all her life, and she's still wild. I've been taking care of her for several years and to a certain extent, I've earned her trust. But I would never turn my back on her. She's what zoos call a Code Red animal, which means if she gets loose, run for your life. Or climb a tree and scream for help, because anteaters can't climb."

They looked disappointed, so as an example, I explained that it took thousands of years for Man to domesticate the dog. "Cavemen only allowed the less dangerous of wolves to hang around their encampments, otherwise the young children would get eaten. Those more docile animals would breed, so down through the centuries the tamest of the wolves evolved into semi-dogs. That new species became even tamer over the years until we wound up with the Pekingese."

Everyone laughed, but the redhead asked, "What happened to the wolves the cavemen didn't turn into pets?"

"They remained wolves."

Before the troop left for Africa Trail, the redhead came up to me and confided that, yes, we were related. "My mom said to be sure and tell you if we ran into each other that my grandmother is your father's great aunt. That makes us cousins. Cool, huh? I'm going to be a zookeeper, too."

As Deborah Holt had pointed out earlier, yes, it was a small world.

After a brief chat with Liza, my newly discovered cousin, I left her with her scout troop.

From the giant anteater's enclosure I moved toward Down Under, but on the way I passed the construction zone where Colder Climes was being built. The vast, frigid exhibit was scheduled to open early next year, with one side specializing in animals such as caribou, polar bears, puffins, and arctic foxes, while the other side—already dubbed Little Antarctica—would host several species of penguins. Besides offering the obvious animal attractions, Colder Climes was certain to be popular during the hottest days of summer.

Further on I came to Gunn Zoo Lake, where the prosimians lived on Lemur Island, just off shore. These "before monkeys" included the always-popular lemurs, slender loris, aye-ayes, and sifakas. The zoo's designers had wisely located a large picnic area on the mainland shore, complete with telescopes through which visitors could view the antics of the playful, long-tailed creatures.

I hadn't yet eaten lunch, so I bought a veggie burger with extra cheese at the refreshment stand, and retired to a table where I had a good view of Lemur Island. Even without the telescope I could see Marcus Aurelius, my favorite ringtail, pulling the ear of a lemur twice his size. He had once been featured on *Anteaters to Zebras*, but because of a loose sphincter, his appearance hadn't been a success.

Remembering that my television segment was on hiatus reminded me that I had been branded as a person of interest in the murder of Bambi O'Dair. My attorney had assured me that nothing would come of it but I was still worried, less for myself than for Caro. There was no use in wishing for Joe's speedy return. He might not be back for another week, and by then, anything could have happened.

As I munched through my veggie burger I couldn't get Mr. Rat out of my mind. It didn't put me off my feed, I was too hungry for that. But envisioning the threatening note attached to him sure took the shine off the day. There was no way I could put the case out of my mind, so I gave up and took my notebook out of my cargo pants pocket to do some thinking on paper, an old habit of mine.

I started a list of questions with the appearance of Mr. Rat.

Question No. 1: Did the bad spelling on Mr. Rat's threatening note prove Victor's killer was uneducated? Or had it been written by an educated person taking pains to appear uneducated? Probable answer: the spelling was too poor to be genuine.

Question No. 2: Did the same person who killed Victor also kill Bambi? Probable answer: yes. Although the murder methods were different, the fact that Bambi was Victor's daughter was no coincidence. At least I didn't think so.

Question No. 3: Had Victor been murdered because he was a blackmailer? In other words, had Scarlet, Woodstock, Aloha, or Taxi—whoever they were—killed him? Answer, maybe, maybe not. Anyone who found out Victor had fraudulently married them to their intended spouse might have been angry enough to kill him, especially if large amounts of marital money were involved. But Victor was a convicted killer and his victim's survivors included a wife and a child. Had that child, now an adult, hunted him down and killed him out of vengeance? If so, why kill Bambi?

Question No. 4: Who did I know who might have a reason to be blackmailed? For starters, Deborah Holt, Judd Sazac, and Melissa Keegan. Who else? I'd once read somewhere that everyone had a secret which under certain circumstances they might kill in order to keep. Look at my own life, for instance. Despite my constant denials to the Feds, I had always known my father's whereabouts, as well as the identifying numbers of his various hidden bank accounts. I would never kill to protect his money but I might kill to protect him or Caro. For that matter, I suspected they would both kill to protect me, too. Recognizing the darkness in my own soul, I had to admit that few saints dwelled among my relatives and friends. Under certain circumstances, we all were capable of desperate acts.

But murdering two people?

I shook my head and looked out once more at Lemur Island. As my eyes focused, I saw Marcus Aurelius bite another ringtail on the leg. It bit back. There was an immediate dust-up, with the second ringtail emerging as the winner. The animal's pink, yellow, and white collar identified her as Pompeia, Marcus' sister.

Just another dysfunctional family.

Back to my notebook. Blackmail victims seldom advertised their moral or legal failings, which is what made them vulnerable to blackmail in the first place. Who did I know who could have possessed a secret big enough to kill over? Determined not to let personal feelings cloud my judgment, I wrote out another list, this one starting with my fellow liveaboarders at Gunn Landing Harbor.

I was just writing down Deborah Holt's name when more screeches from Lemur Island interrupted me. Marcus Aurelius, not having learned from experience, had a second lemur's tail in his jaws. The other lemur didn't like it. Twisting around like a circus contortionist, he grabbed Marcus by the ear and twisted. Marcus screamed and let go. The fight wasn't finished. Pompeia joined in the fray; so did Calpurnia, the duo's mother. Soon all four lemurs were rolling on the ground, pinching, biting, and slapping.

The rest of the lemurs gathered around to watch, but like most lemur dust-ups, it came to an abrupt end when Julius Caesar, the leader of the troop, barged in and bit everyone within biting distance. Put firmly in their respective places, the brawlers scattered into the trees.

If only human interactions were that simple.

Which reminded me of Victor Emerson's murder and my suspect list. Like it or not, Deborah Holt needed to be at the top for several reasons. One, because Victor had performed her marriage to Phil, the reptile keeper, and two, because she was working the Faire the night Victor was killed. She possessed both motive and opportunity. She'd attended one of the crossbow demonstrations, along with just about everyone else working the

Faire. As far as strangling Bambi went, any zookeeper had enough arm strength to strangle a woman, and as her Facebook page had declared, she was out to get "Deer Woman." Deborah's earlier warning struck a sour note, too, as did her familial relationship to the head of Demonios Femeninos. A familial propensity for violence? Something else bothered me about her. The first time we had discussed the fact that Victor had officiated at her marriage, she'd acted nonchalant, but the second time she'd been furious. How much about Deborah did I really know?

Then again, what about Walt McAdams? I hadn't checked up on him yet, but doubted the firefighter had a motive for killing Victor. Then again, Walt had always been a carouser, so it was easy to imagine him falling into trouble. Plus, as a security guard at the Faire, he was the first to arrive on the crime scene. Handy, that. He was also…

A loud crack, followed by a shriek from Lemur Island.

Then a splash.

I looked up to see Marcus Aurelius struggling in the water several feet from a broken eucalyptus branch.

Lemurs are not aquatic animals, which means most can't swim. Instead of doing the smart thing and struggling toward the branch, the panicked lemur floundered off in the opposite direction, toward the open lake where he was almost certain to drown.

Leaving the notebook on the table, I grabbed my radio off my belt and punched in 999 while running toward the water. Without waiting for an answer, I yelled, "Lemur in water on the southwest side of the island. Send help!"

Screams from the other lemurs accompanied me as I threw the radio aside and plunged into the lake. The few yards were warm and shallow, and as I struggled toward Marcus, the mud sucked the shoes off my feet. I didn't mind. Bare feet would make my swim easier, if not pleasant. This area of Gunn Zoo Lake was brackish, and as I stroked along, algae and debris of every sort slopped around me. By the time I reached the deeper portion of the lake where I had last seen the lemur, I was covered in filth.

And Marcus had gone under.

Fully aware that in cloudy water my chances of finding the lemur were slim to none, I took a deep breath and dove under anyway.

First dive, nothing.

The water stung my eyes—God only knew what kind of bacteria was floating around in there—and all I could see were greenish-gray shadows within shadows. Stretching out my arms, I grasped at them, but they swirled away, unsubstantial as air.

I surfaced, took another breath, and dove in another direction. There!

A darker shadow. Moving. Twisting. Long tendrils—legs?—trailing from it.

I stroked toward the shadow, reached out...

And grabbed a limp, furry arm.

I surfaced.

Rolling onto my side, I tucked Marcus' head under my left arm, and with the right, swam for shore. Although less than twenty yards away, it seemed like a mile as I stroked one-handed though the algae-thickened muck. Finally, my feet touched mud and I staggered ashore.

Not worrying, for once, about being gentle, I placed the lemur down on the ground belly first and pressed three times on his back, expelling the water in his lungs. Then I turned him over and gave him mouth-to-snout respiration for ten seconds.

Then I began the chest compressions.

I was still working on Marcus when help arrived via the zoo's animal ambulance. A vet jumped out of the passenger side and ran toward us carrying an oxygen tank and a snout mask. As I continued the chest compressions, she fitted the mask over the lemur's face.

"Keep going," she said, feeling for a pulse in his neck. "Don't stop. Not for a second."

I wasn't about to stop.

Compress.

Compress.

Comp...

"Eooowow!"

Marcus was alive. And very unhappy with what I was doing.

By now the vet and I were surrounded by other keepers who had heard my emergency call, and they sent up a loud cheer. Marcus might have been a pest, but he was one of the zoo's favorite animals. To lose him, especially in this way, would have been hard on us all.

Before I could turn him over to the vet's care, Marcus rewarded me for saving his life by giving me a blood-drawing bite on the hand.

◇◇◇

I spent the next half-hour in First Aid, getting cleaned off and having my eyes and lemur-bit hand cared for.

"Hope you didn't hurt that lemur," the nurse said, as she gave me yet another painful shot. "He's a sweetie. Wouldn't hurt a fly."

"I'm not a fly, as my bit hand can attest."

Dumping the used syringe in a medical waste box, she said, "Well, that's it. You're good to go, but you might want to keep an eye on that hand. If the redness doesn't go away and it gets more tender, go straight to the ER. Same thing if you start coughing up anything strange. Oh, and while you were showering off, your buddy Deborah came by with a clean uniform for you. And shoes. Hope they fit."

The shoes turned out to be a little tight, but other than that, I was—as the lemur-loving nurse had proclaimed—good to go.

So I went.

After stopping by the animal hospital and checking on Marcus Aurelius, who appeared to be doing fine after his soggy adventure, I made my way to Down Under. Fortunately, I'd had the presence of mind to retrieve my notebook and radio from lakeside, so I didn't have any worries on that front and was able to pick up my day where it had left off.

The residents of Wallaby Walkabout were in fine fettle. Abim, another former star on *Anteaters to Zebras*, hopped over to meet me. When I doled out pre-packaged wallaby feed—mostly grains mixed with dried fruit—into their dishes, they crowded around like pigs at a trough. Because of their placid nature, the mini-kangaroos made popular pets, but not necessarily appropriate ones. Ever try to paper train a wallaby? It can be done, but not easily.

After Abim sated himself on his entrée, he came back begging for dessert. I didn't disappoint him. Like many wallabies, he was partial to banana slices, so I sneaked him a couple until the others figured out what was going on and swarmed around for their share. No problem, since I'd brought enough for all.

It didn't take long to clean the entire enclosure and freshen their bedding, so soon I was in the koala habitat where I found Wanchu asleep again. Adorable though they may be, koalas don't make better pets than wallabies but for an entirely different reason. Due to their low protein diet, koalas doze seventy-five percent of the time, thus providing their owners with less companionship than usually desired. Wanchu's coma-like slumber enabled me to take care of her enclosure without being poked or clawed, but I did miss her company. When I left a few minutes later, she was still sleeping the sleep of the innocent.

Several stops later it was almost closing time, which was a good thing. The shoes Deborah so kindly loaned me had rubbed blisters on my heels. But as I prepared to leave Down Under, I noticed a small crowd around the bowerbird habitat. Most birds are kept in the aviary or nearby surrounds, but our New Guinea natives' mating rituals were so unusual that Dundee, Sheila, Evelyn, and Marsha were given their own large space with the rest of the southern hemisphere animals.

A middle-aged woman left the fence and approached me with a bewildered look on her face. I knew exactly what she was going to ask.

"What in the world is that bird doing? He's got, he's, well, he's collecting piles of things. I swear to God they're color-coordinated!"

"That's his way of wooing the ladies," I replied.

I walked back with her to the exhibit to explain in detail. "He's already built his bower," I pointed out. "See those two large, perpendicular sticks? He's using them as columns to support the roof he's built out of small twigs and leaves."

"But it must be six or seven feet across—and he's not that big a bird!"

"No, but he's a busy bird. See what he's doing now? This morning I dropped off a mixed pile of bright-colored objects— bottle caps, big buttons, rocks, shells, small fruit, even flower petals and macaw feathers. Right now he's rooting through the pile, hoping to gather more blue for the blue stack he's started. Once he thinks it's big enough, he'll start on a red stack, then a green one, then purple, each color in turn until he's gone all the way through the color spectrum. He'll go after those shiny black stones I brought for him, too. Lady bowerbirds always prefer a well-decorated estate, one with some flash."

"I thought animals were supposed to be color blind."

"Not as many as science once theorized."

"How long will it take him to finish?"

I watched as Dundee scuttled back and forth, carrying blue objects in his beak. "At the rate he's going, several more days. Then, if he's done a good job, one of the females will join him in his color-coordinated love nest."

From the eager expression on her face, I knew which question was coming next. "Do bowerbirds make good pets?"

"Only if you can give it an entire room of its own. And if you want to spend the rest of your life collecting bottle caps and rose petals."

She smiled. "Guess I'll just have to enjoy him here in the zoo, then."

I smiled back. "That's what we're here for."

Later, while ushering the squirrel monkeys into their night house, I thought about Dundee's nest building and smiled again because the bowerbird reminded me of Joe. Once I agreed to marry him, he had gone into a frenzy of rebuilding. First he erected a mother-in-law apartment for Colleen on the back of his property, a lovely self-contained cottage she liked so much she could hardly wait to move in. Just before he left for Virginia, he'd started a new wing on the east side of the house. The extension boasted an enormous master suite with his and hers bathrooms, and a walk-in closet big enough to live in. When I'd protested such extravagance, he'd said, "Nothing's too good for my girl."

As soon as Joe came home, I'd introduce him to Dundee. They had so much in common.

When I finished caring for the squirrel monkeys, one final chore remained before clocking out, and that was the chore I most looked forward to: returning Alejandro to Friendly Farm.

Alejandro greeted me with a surprised chirp as I walked into the Quarantine barn. And when I actually led him out of his stall and into the evening air he danced with delight.

"Maaa!"

"Yes, I know, my sweet boy," I said, as we walked along the back trail toward Friendly Farm. Doves cooed above us, while in the distance, the squirrel monkeys chattered. The evening breeze smelled of honeysuckle. "You're free for the night, Alejandro, but tomorrow morning I have to take you back to Quarantine."

"Ipe?"

"Bummer, isn't it?"

Once I turned him loose in the barnyard, I took a pitchfork from the tool shed and shoveled some bedding into the corner, but the llama wasn't ready for sleep. After being cooped up for so many days, he wanted to move around. He took several circuits of the area at a gallop before calming down enough to bleat greetings to his old pals.

A horse neighed back from the barn. A cow mooed. Chickens clucked sleepily.

Relieved to see my friend happy again, I returned the pitchfork to the tool shed and clocked out.

◇◇◇

When I arrived at the jail, Caro had good news, and it showed. Her makeup was perfect, her hair was perfect, her manicure was perfect. She even glowed as she announced, "Soledad's been released!"

"How'd that happen? I thought the judge considered her such a danger to the public that he ordered her held without bail."

"A misunderstanding, which her new attorney cleared up, pointing out that there was insufficient evidence to hold her."

"Did the new attorney happen to be Albert Grissom, your own attorney?"

She inclined her head regally. "I told Al if he wanted our relationship to progress further I expected him to help my friends. See what a woman can accomplish when she plays her cards right?"

A beautiful woman, maybe, but not us plain Janes. "How nice," I said, only partially meaning it. While I felt happy Soledad Rodriguez was once more free to litter San Sebastian County with her uncle's fliers, the specter of Duane Langer's murder was worrisome. For a while she had been the chief suspect, and I wondered how Duane's friends in Viking Vengeance would view her release. If only half the rumors about the gang's viciousness were true, Soledad had better watch her step. Or leave town, change her name, and get face-changing plastic surgery.

I pointed Soledad's peril out to Caro, but she pooh-poohed my concerns. "Demonios Femeninos has her back."

"Maybe so, but I can't help but wonder how a group of women might fare going up against a heavily armed White Power gang. What are the Femeninos planning to do, bat their eyelashes in unison?"

"Sexist."

"What?"

"You heard me, Theodora. That was a blatantly sexist remark and I'm appalled to have raised a daughter who has such a Victorian view of women."

"Who are you and what did you do with my mother?"

She sniffed. "Like all sexists, you've always underestimated a woman's powers of persuasion."

"Such as, 'Please don't shoot me, Mr. Viking Vengeance, it might hurt?'"

"You're such a snip."

I managed to stop myself before replying, *I'd rather be snippy than self-deluded.* Somehow my mother always brought out the worst in me. "Sorry, Mom."

"Caro!"

I lowered my voice in a conspiratorial whisper. "Sorry, Caro. Okay, so now that Soledad's been sprung, where's she staying? Not at her apartment, I hope. She'd be a sitting duck."

"She's staying at my house."

I felt my mouth drop. This was such a bad idea on so many levels it took me a while to speak again. "Are you nuts?" I finally hissed. "You've got a maid who's married to an ex-con, and now you've opened your house to a gangster!"

Somehow she managed to purse her collagen-plumped lips into a thin line. "Don't be so judgmental. I know what I'm doing."

"Your jewelry. Your furs. Your antiques. Soledad's not just a gangster, she's a *gang leader!* She'll call her buddies and they'll strip that house clean."

"There's gangs, and there's gangs." She was lucky the Plexiglas separated us, because her smug expression made me want to wring her neck.

"Oh, really, Caro? Then what kind of a gang is Demonios Femininos?"

"A social group. The women don't do drugs, let alone sell them. They don't knock over banks or convenience stores, and they don't go in for breaking and entering."

"Oh, really?" I couldn't help repeating myself.

"Really. Soledad told me."

"Which means you're taking the word of a murder suspect!"

Her eyes narrowed. "In case you haven't forgotten, Theodora, I'm a murder suspect, too. So are you. Surely you're not under the impression that Al Grissom didn't tell me about you being handcuffed and dragged in for questioning after you found Bambi's body."

Affronted, I said, "Whatever happened to client confidentiality?"

"Stop being so naive. Because of the jailhouse grapevine, I'd heard about your situation before Al did. We get the news faster than the *San Sebastian Gazette,* so when he stopped by for a visit I only needed him to fill in the blanks. Now I don't want to hear any more about Soledad, understand? Cell mates have to stick together. It's the jailhouse code."

Since there was nothing intelligent I could say to that, I clomped away in my borrowed shoes.

◇◇◇

On the way back to Gunn Landing Harbor, I drove by Joe's house. It was dark. Colleen must have already turned in. From the outside nothing looks lonelier than a dark house so I didn't slow down, just kept on going.

I felt better once back at the *Merilee,* where my furry friends, already fed and walked by Linda Cushing, welcomed me with unrestrained joy. Once I took care of their petting needs, I changed out of my borrowed clothes into more comfortable sweats and nuked a TV dinner. I read the notes I had made before Marcus Aurelius fell into the lake, then began to add to them.

Dr. Willis Pierce, San Sebastian Community College's favorite drama teacher, could easily have a guilty secret because pretty young co-eds were the standard professorial temptation. Willis' former relationship with Bambi and the revelation he'd been married before, proved that despite his dandified ways, he had an eye for the ladies. Maybe Victor caught him having a dalliance with one of his students, a real no-no in these more enlightened days. I placed a star beside his name as a reminder to Google him.

Among my non-liveaboarder friends and acquaintances I listed the people working the Renaissance Faire.

Due to Yancy Hass' experience as a stunt man in action films, the Faire's Black Knight had a good working knowledge of all sorts of weapons, including crossbows. He was also probably the person most capable of violence. Given the wild lifestyles so many Hollywood people led, Yancy could have easily wound up in Victor's blackmail ledger.

I put a star next to his name, too.

There was one more person I needed to add to the list: Suspect X. The child, now grown, of the man Victor killed in the convenience store holdup. Had he or she discovered Victor's whereabouts and wreaked a belated justice? The person would have been around Bambi's age—but so were Deborah and Phil Holt, Walt McAdams, Yancy Haas, and both Keegans.

As I stared at my lists of questions and suspects I realized I had left someone out, someone who spelled badly, had criminal connections, and whose children had been impacted by Victor's faux-marriage chapel. Regretfully, I added Eunice Snow, my mother's maid. Come to think of it, she was the right age to be the child of Suspect X, and so was her husband Bucky.

I sat back and sighed. While I realized that we can never fully know other people, I had a hard time believing any of my liveaboarder friends would kill anyone. The same went for my coworkers at the zoo. Two of the men on my list—firefighter Walt McAdams and stuntman Yancy Haas—were the more physical of the group, possibly more likely to become involved in violent situations. But committing premeditated murder?

I didn't think so.

Still, someone had killed Victor Emerson and his daughter Bambi, so I opened Victor's blackmail ledger and studied it again. The payments began little more than a year back, starting low, then gradually escalated, proving that even blackmailers get affected by inflation. From the condition of his trailer, Victor was barely scraping by, so discovering blackmailable secrets must have thrilled him to no end.

I reexamined the last page in his account book.

05/15—r'cd Taxi—$250
05/16—r'cd Scarlet—$125
05/18—r'cd Woodstock—$125
05/25—r'cd Aloha—$100
05/29—r'cd Taxi—$250

Compared to the month of April, everyone was up by twenty dollars a month. Judging from the amounts, I doubted if any of Victor's victims were worth serious money. Added together, though, the steady income made a significant difference to a man living at near-subsistence level. The most financially comfortable of his victims appeared to be Taxi, whoever he was. A local cab driver? Probably not, because not only did Taxi fork over the highest amount, he paid twice a month. His secret must have been a big one, because in contrast, someone called Aloha paid Victor a lowly one hundred per month.

For several reasons, that particular code name made me uncomfortable. Fellow zookeepers Phil and Deborah Holt had honeymooned in Hawaii. So had the Sazacs and the Keegans, but because of the low amount Victor charged Aloha, I immediately ruled the Sazacs out; they were rolling in dough. That left Deborah. Or Phil. Even zookeepers could afford to fork over one hundred dollars a month, if they didn't have many other bills. But I remembered Deborah once telling me their adorable little daughter needed orthodontia because she'd inherited her father's big teeth and her mother's small jaw.

And then there was Woodstock. Did the code name refer to the legendary music festival in upstate New York and Victor had used it to describe a blackmail victim who had attended it? The only person on my suspect list old enough to have been there was my friend and fellow liveaboarder, Linda Cushing. She hadn't made my suspect list because she had been taking care of my pets when the murder occurred. Besides, Linda was too feisty to allow herself get blackmailed in the first place.

Scarlett was probably a woman, which made me think of Jane Olson, Caro's auburn-haired friend. Jane had led a colorful life, if she had done something dastardly at some point, Victor would certainly have hit her up for more than five hundred a month. Since Jane's marriage to the Gold King, her bank account was bigger than Caro's.

This left Taxi, Victor's chief financial supporter. The nickname conjured up movement, which could describe Walt McAdams or Yancy Haas. Neither was a refugee from the poorhouse, but a five-hundred-a-month blackmail tab wouldn't be welcome, either. On second thought, since Taxi was the only person on the list paying Victor twice a month, did the double dip really reflect a bigger secret or merely a bigger pocketbook?

My brain hurt.

I looked at my watch. Almost midnight. If I didn't turn in now, I wouldn't get enough sleep to comfortably get through my highly physical job tomorrow. Problem was, I wasn't sleepy.

I looked at my phone. The last time my father called me, I'd neglected to ask his bedtime. I had, however, saved his number.

"Hi, Dad," I said, when he answered on the first ring.

"You sure stay up late for someone with your job."

"Are you, ah, alone?"

"Meaning are either Aster Edwina or Mrs. McGinty sharing my cold, lonely bed? I'm sorry to tell you that neither of them are."

"Excellent, because I want to tell you what I found out today." Leaving nothing out, I told him everything.

When I was done, Dad gave a low whistle. "Victor was a nasty piece of work, wasn't he? But he was what my friends call a Small Time Sam, a guy who wastes his talents on piddly stuff. Speaking of my friends' usage of slang, there's something you mentioned in his ledger you should think about. You say someone named Taxi was paying Victor twice a month? Well, in certain circles the word 'taxi' is used for a certain kind of prison inmate."

I sucked in my breath. "Are you sure?"

"I've heard Long Louie use the word when referring to men he did time with, those he counted on for certain favors, such as getting the right drugs or weapons or hooking somebody up with the right lawyer. Basically, a taxi is a guy who arranges things. A fixer."

"That puts a different slant on things, doesn't it?"

"Possibly. But maybe I'm wrong and Taxi is just a guy who drives for a living, like a chauffeur or a trucker. Or, and here's something to think about, someone who owns a cab company."

The city of San Sebastian had no cab company. Anyone needing taxi service had to call Yellow, Associated, or Coastal, all operating out of Monterey. There were a couple of independents floating around, but no one I know used them, not even Victor. He owned a seven-year-old Taurus, which the police had towed to the crime lab. Maybe it was parked next to my pickup.

While I was still thinking about taxis and towed cars, Dad mused aloud, "Yes, the cab theory is interesting, but let's consider this. When an inmate successfully escapes from prison, he always has help. Remind me how Victor escaped."

"The newspaper accounts said he hid in a laundry bag and rode out with the laundry truck. At some point along the way, he exited the truck and hid out until someone picked him up. The driver was later fired, but no charges were brought."

"You see? He'd need help to arrange that, both in prison and on the outside."

The question was, if Taxi could help Victor escape, why didn't Taxi escape along with him? The answer might be that unlike Victor, who was a lifer, Taxi was a short-timer due to be released soon. This scenario raised another question: if Taxi had helped Victor escape, why would Victor pay him back by blackmailing him? When I asked my father, he had a ready answer.

"Life situations change, Teddy. Maybe Victor fell on hard times. There used to be quite a bit of money in the wedding chapel racket, but these days, with all the short term shack-ups and hook-ups the younger generation prefers, marriage has lost its popularity. I read somewhere that marriage ceremonies are down twenty percent, proving that not everyone's as fuddy-duddyish as you and your mother. Now, think about this. Victor lived in a trailer. What was it like? One of those big doublewides? They can be fairly nice, I'm told. Not that I would ever live in one."

"Yeah, you prefer your Costa Rican casita. And Dominga."

I thought about Victor's battered singlewide with its thrift shop furniture. Even his wedding chapel, once you went beyond the public area, needed work.

"Victor's trailer was ready for a major overhaul," I told my father. "Or the junk heap."

"There you go. The guy was hurting financially. I'll bet he…" Suddenly he began to whisper. "Gotta go, Teddy. I hear the pitter patter of bare female feet approaching my bedroom door."

Dial tone.

I sat there for a few minutes, thinking about honor among thieves. The friendships developed in prison might not hold once the freed prisoner moved on to a new life. Especially when hard times came calling.

There was something about this entire scenario that bothered me, although I couldn't put my finger on it. But thinking about jailhouse friendships turned my mind toward Caro's unlikely friendship with her own cell mate, Soledad Rodriguez.

How would that play out?

There being nothing more I could do at this time of night, I went to bed.

Chapter Eighteen

The first thing I did Thursday morning was to call my father again. He wasn't as quick to pick up the phone this time and when he answered, his voice was raspy with sleep.

"It's not even five o'clock, Teddy. What's the matter with you?"

"Ask your contacts if they can find out the name of Victor's cell mate."

"Will do, but never call me this early again."

He hung up.

Once at the zoo, I had enough work that I didn't think about Victor, Bambi, or Mr. Rat until I made my way to Monkey Mania, where Central American squirrel monkeys ran free and intermingled with zoo visitors. James Dean, one of the juvenile monkeys, was playing Hide and Seek with Marlon, the alpha. Instead of getting irritated, as the feisty Marlon was prone to do, he was enjoying the game. Both monkeys took turns being "it," hiding in the underbrush or behind trees. When discovered, the hider would make a mad dash for the rock designated as "home."

This back and forth hiding game reminded me of something, but it wasn't until I arrived at Africa Trail that I figured it out.

Marlon was like Victor Emerson—mature, cagy, a better hider than James Dean. But James Dean had his triumphs, too, and at one point had been cheeky enough to reach out from his hiding place and pull Marlon's tail.

Two monkeys hiding from one another.

I realized what had been troubling me about the entire Victor blackmail scenario. Regardless of the man's lack of funds, he was much more suited to be someone else's blackmail victim, not the other way around. During the convenience store holdup, he committed murder, and before his escape, was serving twenty-five to life. If law enforcement had learned of his present whereabouts, he would have been sent back to Nevada to serve the remainder of his sentence.

The fact that Victor had been the blackmailer, not the black-mail*ee*, could mean his victims knew nothing about his past. If they had, one of them would have turned him in.

Unless the intended victim had more to lose than Victor.

I thought about Victor bleeding out at Alejandro's feet from a mortal crossbow wound. I thought about Bambi's swollen face, the stocking wrapped around her neck.

I thought about Mr. Rat.

For the first time I truly understood how foolish it was for me to remain on board the *Merilee,* where a vicious killer knew where I lived.

My hands began to shake.

◇◇◇

Somehow I finished out my day at the zoo, but as soon as I made it home to the *Merilee* I packed a suitcase. An hour later, Bonz, Feroz, Miss Priss, and I were ensconced in my old bedroom at Caro's house.

Dinner was a strange affair. Soledad Rodriguez, who occupied the bedroom next to mine, sat at the long table across from me. Next to her sat Bucky, Eunice Snow's ex-con husband, enlisted by Caro to guard us from Viking Vengeance and other assorted killers. The couple's twins were upstairs asleep, leaving us adults to entertain each other. As Eunice served up heaping portions of lasagna, we tried talking about the weather but that lasted about three minutes. Once you've described coastal fog, there's nowhere else to go.

"I love fog," Eunice said, sitting down next to her husband. "I just wish it wasn't so damp."

"Fog's damp, no two ways about it," Bucky observed.

"At least it burns off by ten," Soledad threw in.

"Fog isn't so bad inland," was my contribution.

"Nope."

"No."

"Nah."

Having nothing else in common but fog and lasagna, we stared silently at our plates.

"How's the lasagna?" Eunice finally said.

We all agreed that the lasagna was really, really delicious and fell silent again.

About five minutes later, Bucky said, "I saw a good movie the other day."

"Tell us about it," I asked, desperately.

"It was this Italian thing, subtitles and all. *The Bicycle Thief.* Anyone ever hear of it?"

Eunice and Soledad shook their heads, but I raised my hand. "Saw it a few years ago." In Rome, with Caro.

Bucky grinned, revealing a missing front tooth. "I found it depressing but somehow uplifting. It revealed man's inhumanity to man, and the difficulty of rising above one's given station in life. But at the end the shared tragedy drew father and son closer together."

This surprising speech made me study Bucky more closely. Thin, pink-skinned with white-blond hair and pale blue eyes, he resembled a poorly nourished Angora rabbit, not a pundit.

"You got all that from the movie, Bucky?"

He shrugged. "When the guy from San Sebastian Cinema called and offered me the job as an usher, I thought it might be a good idea to read up on film, so I went to the library and got a book."

"That's where they keep them," Soledad muttered.

"They've just begun a series of old classics, so they're showing *Wings* next week. The book I checked out, *History of Cinema,* describes it as a 1927 silent movie about these World War I fighter pilots. Clara Bow, Gary Cooper, and even that old Hollywood gossip columnist Hedda Hopper, were in it. *Wings* won the very first Oscar for Best Picture. Is that cool, or what?"

Eunice beamed at him. "Bucky's real smart."

"He can read, too," Soledad muttered again.

I shot her a dirty look. She caught it and threw it back. With her black lip liner and thin black eyebrows she looked pretty scary so I let it pass.

"I really, really like this lasagna, Eunice," I said.

The others agreed again that they really, really liked the lasagna, too.

◇◇◇

In my room later, I opened my laptop and renewed my acquaintance with the Google gods.

I started with stunt man Yancy Haas, and what I found raised the hair on my arms. Stunt man Yancy Haas had so violent a history I had no trouble believing he could easily kill a dozen people.

Ten years earlier, while living in a Hollywood apartment, he had been booked for assaulting his roommate, a fellow stuntman. When the victim, one Dave Mason, didn't show up in court to testify, nothing happened with the case. Yancy's trouble didn't end there. Not long afterward, he was popped for two DUIs less than three months apart. He had been sentenced to six months in jail and his driver's license had been suspended for two years. A year after his release from jail, and while still living in the Los Angeles area, he had been found guilty of attempted homicide when he attacked his girlfriend with a knife. A man in the neighboring apartment heard the commotion and broke in and saved her. Once the woman had been transported to the hospital, it took ninety-three stiches to close her wounds. That crime, ostensibly Yancy's last to date, earned him a five-year stretch in California State Prison in Centinela. He was paroled twenty-eight months later for good behavior.

Curious, I looked up Centinela on GoogleMaps. It was in the far southeast corner of the state, nowhere near Nevada's Ely State Prison. Not that it would matter, Victor having escaped from Ely years earlier. Still…

I moved on to Willis Pierce. At first glance I found no newspaper articles linking the drama professor to old crimes or questionable relationships with students, but having already learned that the nicest people sometimes had the dirtiest pasts, I kept looking. Eventually I discovered that before moving to San Sebastian County more than a decade ago, he had taught acting for a few semesters at Atlantic Cape Community College in Mays Landing, New Jersey. When I looked up Mays Landing on GoogleMaps I saw it was just a hop, skip, and jump inland from Atlantic City. Mob ties? Gambling debts? There was no way of knowing. I found no mention of the marriage I'd heard him make a disparaging remark about. Maybe that had happened later. After Atlantic Cape, he left to direct a community theater group in South Africa. Two years later, his wanderlust apparently slaked, he returned. After a brief vacation, took the job in San Sebastian.

What was his ex-wife's name? Ah, yes. Serena Sue.

When I typed in "Serena Sue+Pierce+New Jersey" nothing came up, but when I dropped the Pierce part, photographs of two Serena Sue Tagilossis popped up. One was a wizened Serena Sue celebrating her one-hundredth birthday at the Egg Harbor Retirement Home. The other Serena Sue Tagilossi, possibly the centenarian's great-granddaughter, turned up in a blurry wedding snapshot taken in front of the Egg Harbor United Methodist Church. It showed a newly minted Mrs. Serena Sue Tagliossi Moss standing next to her beaming, clean-shaven groom, one Anthony James Moss. The accompanying article described him as an employee of the Lucky Lady Casino in Atlantic City, New Jersey. Although the quality of the photograph was poor, Moss resembled Willis enough to be his cousin. Reading further I found Willis listed as Best Man. The two men didn't have last names in common, since they were probably related through their mother's side of the family.

Willis must have married his cousin's cast-off. The idea seemed a bit creepy to me, but it certainly wasn't creepy enough to be blackmailed over. One of my cousins had married his own former sister-in-law, for Pete's sake.

Letting the quasi-incest slide, I continued searching but never found a story announcing Serena Sue's remarriage, which meant little. Second, third, and fourth marriages rarely made the papers unless the beautiful bride was Gunn Landing socialite Caroline Piper Bentley Hufgraff O'Brien Petersen. Every time Caro married it made headlines on the society page of the *San Sebastian Gazette.* Her divorces always made the papers, too.

Next up on my suspect list came Walt McAdams. Walt and I were such good friends I felt guilty checking up on him, guiltier still when I found a short newspaper article about a barroom brawl he had once been involved in. He'd broken a man's jaw when the man slapped his drinking partner, a woman. Walt had a short temper, but he was no killer. Especially not a killer of women.

Or was I in denial?

◇◇◇

The puzzle being impossible to solve given my limited computer skills, I gave up on Serena Sue for the time being. I was getting tired, anyway, and needed to get some sleep for my next grueling day at the zoo. Then I remembered that Zorah told me that since I would be staying late playing the star of the Great Escape, I didn't have to come in until noon. Good. That would give me more time. Now that I knew what information I was missing, I could concentrate with a fresh mind after breakfast.

A glance at the clock showed it was after eleven. I had been up since five, so no wonder I'd begun to droop.

"Just a few more," I said to Bonz, who watched me from the foot of the bed. "The easy ones."

He wagged his tail. It hit Miss Priss across the snout, but after a perfunctory hiss, she fell back to sleep. Feroz never stirred.

A renewed search came up with little on my harbor neighbor Linda Cushing, just a mention that she'd once been questioned in the suspicious death of another Gunn Landing Harbor live-aboarder. Since the real killer had been caught and sentenced to life without parole, Linda was off the hook. Other minimal finds included a society column announcement of Jane Olson marrying her Gold King, and a photograph of family law attorney Frank Turnbull receiving a plaque for his volunteer work with the San Sebastian Food Bank. That last being the only clear photograph I had found so far, I breathed a sigh of relief that Frank was wearing clothes, not his Speedo.

Before turning in for the night, I went down the hall to Caro's bedroom and took a quick inventory. Her jewels still there, so were her furs. Next I walked downstairs and checked off the more valuable pieces of furniture. Louis XV ormolu-mounted bibliotheque basse, still there. George III painted satinwood secretaire, still there. Seventeenth-century Flemish open arm-chair, ditto. Sixteenth-century Portuguese side table, ditto. Eighteenth-century Russian ormolu-mounted bergère, ditto.

Even the nineteenth-century settee that once belonged to Czar Nicholas II was still there, although it did look less elegant now that the scrawny form of Bucky lay snoring on it, a baseball bat clutched in one hand, a book on classic films in the other. He hadn't bothered to take off his shoes.

When I nudged him, he continued to snore.

I nudged him again, this time more strenuously. More snores. Some bodyguard he was.

I leaned over his prone body and yelled in his ear. "Yo, Bucky!"

He sat up so fast I had to jump out of the way of his flailing arms. "Whazzat!"

"Aren't you supposed to be keeping watch?"

He rubbed his eyes. "That's what I was doing until you startled me."

"You were…Oh, never mind. But could you at least please take your shoes off if you're going to sleep on my mother's settee? It's…" I almost told him its provenance, then changed my mind. "If you get it dirty it'll take Eunice forever to clean it."

"Right, right. Sorry. Don't want to put the poor woman to more trouble than I already have." He untied his sneakers, tucked them under the settee, and sat up straight, facing the door: the very picture of an alert bodyguard.

"Thanks, Bucky."

"Anything you need, lady, just ask. I sure appreciate everything you've done for me and Eunice, what with the job at San Sebastian Cinema and all."

"And I appreciate your standing guard. It's very thoughtful."

Minutes later, when I left to go back upstairs, he was snoring again.

Chapter Nineteen

Bucky must have been a better bodyguard than he appeared because when I woke up the next morning we were all still alive. The crossbow killer hadn't murdered me and Viking Vengeance hadn't rubbed out Soledad.

After a quick shower—I had to admit it was nice not to have to trudge across the parking lot to the harbor's community showers—I walked downstairs, trailed by my pets. The dogs immediately availed themselves of the doggy door, but Miss Priss stalked over to her bowl and scowled at me through her one eye.

At the table, Eunice was dishing up an avocado omelet to Soledad.

"Where's Bucky?" I asked, parceling out dog and cat food into separate bowls.

"Still sleeping," Eunice replied. "He sat up all night guarding you girls."

Soledad startled me with a smile and a wink. Minus her gang-gal makeup she looked like a normal person. Acted like one, too. "I appreciate Bucky's sacrifice, Eunice," she said. "It was very gallant."

Gallant? Accent on the second syllable? Heck, she didn't even sound like her former self. I would have thought more about that, but whatever was going on with Soledad would have to remain a mystery. For now, at least. Something had occurred to me in the shower this morning, so as soon Eunice served my own omelet I gobbled it down, excused myself, and ran back upstairs. I needed to hang out with Google again.

Just as I fired up my laptop, I heard a knock on my door. "Come on in," I called.

"Teddy, I think we should talk."

Soledad. The gangster wore a nervous smile.

"Sure." I hit the screensaver command and a picture of Lucy, the giant anteater, filled the screen. "Pull up a chair."

Soledad sat down with her hands folded primly in her lap. "First of all, just to get things clear, I'm not going to steal anything from this house. Secondly, I'm not going to steal away your mother's affections, either."

The woman had the power to render me speechless.

"I know this is a difficult situation for you, Teddy, but it's difficult for me, too. I'm used to being with my *chicas*, yet here I am, staying in the house of a woman I met under less than optimum circumstances who was kind enough to get me out of jail when no one else could. She offered me sanctuary in her own home, with all this…" She waved her hand around, taking in my tacky teenage four-poster bed and Bon Jovi posters. "…all this this grandeur. You need to know that whatever I can do to pay her back, I'll do. But you also need to know that right now I'm intimidated as hell, both by her and by you, and when I get intimidated I tend to act extra scary to make up for it. Sorry about that."

I finally found my voice. "Optimum?"

She grinned. "Sociology major, English minor."

"Have I been had?"

"Not really. The tough *chica*, that's exactly what I used to be and still am to a certain extent. Old habits die hard. When I was younger I got in a lot of trouble, mostly petty stuff, thank goodness, so with my 3.8 grade average I was still able to get a full ride scholarship to UCLA. Now I'm back and helping my *chicas*, but after my recent legal troubles I'm beginning to think I'd serve them better as a defense attorney, not a free-lance social worker. So law school's next."

I shook my head. "You're a surprising woman, Soledad."

"So are you, Teddy." She stood up and walked to the door. "Anyway, that's what I wanted to tell you. With all the weirdness happening around here these days, you have enough problems of your own without having to worry about me ripping off your mother. Same for Bucky. Last night I took him aside and told him what my *chicas* would do to him if Caro came up with so much as one fork missing. Ever see that TV program, *Scared Straight?* That's what I laid on him."

"I'm more into the *Penguins of Madagascar*, myself." As she opened the door, I asked, "How will you pay for law school?"

Another big grin. "Manicures?"

After we got through laughing, I thought of another question. "Soledad, do you know who killed Duane?"

She gave me a long look. "Not yet. But I'm in the process of finding out. A woman owes that much to the only man she ever loved."

◇◇◇

As soon as she left, I opened up my laptop again, cruised onto Google, and continued snooping into the personal lives of my friends and neighbors.

Deborah Holt's crimes of violence appeared to have ended with her graduation from college, but there was no way to be certain. Google was mute on that. Another search for Linda Cushing's possible misdeeds came up empty, too. Same story with Jane Olson.

I did start to have some luck when, remembering Willis Pierce's cousin, the first husband of the lovely Serena Sue, I typed in "ANTHONY JAMES MOSS"+NEW JERSEY. I found a legal announcement that Serena Sue Tagliossi Moss was no longer responsible for the debts of Anthony James Moss. Well, well. Usually, when a couple is divorcing, it was the man who put that sort of notice in the paper. Regardless of the social strides women have made, males were still the major family breadwinners, and had the most to lose if they ran up big debts. Then I remembered that the wedding announcement said that Willis' cousin worked for a casino. Dollars to doughnuts, he had a gambling problem.

Finding more information turned out to be tricky. Another search using the state and full name turned up nothing of relevance. Same for "ANTHONY MOSS" and "JAMES MOSS." When I tried "TONY MOSS," there were so many hits I almost gave up. The professions of the sixty thousand or so Tony Mosses ranged all the way from janitors to a father-son team of circus acrobats. After a quick scan of some possibilities, I narrowed my search to "TONY MOSS"+NEW JERSEY and came up with only six thousand. Making progress. Then, remembering a possible gambling connection, I typed "TONY MOSS"+NEW JERSEY+COURT.

Bingo!

I took another look and realized I had patted myself on the back too soon. This was a different Anthony James Moss and he lived in Reno, Nevada, not Egg Harbor, New Jersey. So why did it come up on my NEW JERSEY search? Damned Google.

Frustrated—I'd been working the laptop for more than an hour—I stood up and paced around while Bonz and Feroz went downstairs and urged the two outside through the doggy door. After a few minutes pacing, I was still restless, so I walked downstairs to find the two dogs back in the kitchen, arguing over a rubber bone.

"Play nice, you two," I scolded. I helped myself to a cup of coffee, and wandered through the house. Eunice was in the entertainment room watching a daytime rerun of *Real Housewives of New Jersey* with Bucky and Soledad. Bucky, who still clutched his baseball bat, was enthralled but the leader of Demonios Femeninos had returned to her *de rigueur* sneer.

"Interesting program?" I asked, just to be saying something.

Eunice: "I really admire those women!"

Bucky: "They're smokin' hot!"

Soledad: *"Que pedazo de mierda."*

I don't speak Spanish, but I doubted it was anything complimentary. Not wanting to share their viewing pleasure, I continued wandering the house, sipping my coffee. Sanctuary isn't all it's cracked up to be; it's mainly boring. I still had four hours to kill before I left for the zoo and the Great Escape. I went into my mother's library, a smaller, less grand version of Aster Edwina's, and looked for something to read. Caro's collection leans toward best-selling biographies of famous people. I wasn't interested in anything written by the cast of *Jersey Shore*, but I was able to find a copy of Alison Weir's *The Six Wives of Henry VIII*. I took the heavy tome back to my room and began reading.

Wrong choice.

Although the book was well-researched and written, it remind me too much of Victor Emerson clad in his Henry the Eighth cloak, lying murdered at Alejandro's feet. From there my thoughts traveled to Bambi's bedroom and the ghastly sight of her dead, staring eyes. Anything, even Google, was better than this, so I put the book down and returned to my laptop.

The link to "TONY MOSS"+NEW JERSEY+COURT was still up on the screen. With nothing left to do, I clicked on it…

…and saw a clear mug shot of "TONY MOSS."

After that, I couldn't get to the phone fast enough.

Chapter Twenty

Joe was still on voice mail, not that I was surprised. Homeland Security could be ruthless in their phone confiscations.

But my old friend Deputy Emilio Gutierrez was on voice mail, too.

There being no other choice, I called Acting Sheriff Elvin Dade. He wasn't on voice mail and sounded more than happy to talk to me.

"Ready to confess to the murders of Bambi O'Dair and Victor Emerson, Teddy?" he asked. Without waiting for my answer, he continued, "Good for you! Hey, I'll send a car over right away to bring you in so's you can give your statement. We'll even brew up a fresh pot of coffee. Or do you want tea? I'm sure we can find a bag around somewhere. There's a nice clean cell waiting for you, right next to your mother's! Ya know, Teddy, offenders are always relieved once they confessed, like weight has been lifted right off their shoulders."

"There's no weight on my shoulders," I snapped, then proceeded to tell him what I'd found out.

Before I finished, he began to laugh. "You think I'm stupid or something?"

Yes, I did think Elvin was stupid or something, but admitting it would be foolish. I started all over again, walking him slowly, very slowly, through the timeline, even giving him the URLs of the web sites I found so he could double-check my information.

The only thing I left out was my break-in at Victor's wedding chapel and trailer.

Elvin still didn't get it.

"You think I have time to play these games? I'm warning you, Miss Theodora Bentley. If you keep pestering me or any of my deputies, I'll have you arrested again."

"On what charge?"

"I'll think of something."

There's nothing worse than the combination of stupidity and smugness. It's brought down many a politician and was now in danger of letting a double murderer go free. I swallowed my pride and asked if he knew when Joe would be back.

"If I knew, I wouldn't tell you."

"How about Emilio?"

"Your old buddy? His mother wound up in the hospital last night, something to do with her heart, I think, or maybe it was her gall bladder, I can't remember, so Emilio and his family flew down to L.A. to be with her. My guess is that they'll stay for a couple of days, keep her cheered up and stuff like that. They say happy people live longer. Come to think of it, why do you need to know where Deputy Gutierrez is? Gonna complain about me? Don't think I'm not aware of what goes on around here, all the bitchin' and carpin'."

The man was beyond stupid. Instead of a brain he had a vast echo chamber where one was supposed to be.

He was still talking. "…and if you and your mother would behave yourselves and stop poking into other people's business, San Sebastian County would be better off. The both of you are a disgrace to decent, God-fearing people."

He paused and I heard a man's voice in the background saying something about a car. Coming back on the line, he said, "Gotta go. Some idiot's parked in a fire zone over at City Hall. Anyways, I got more important stuff to do than listen to your crank calls. If you know what's good for you, Teddy Bentley, you won't call me again."

Click.

It took me several minutes of heavy breathing and clenched fists before calming down enough to think rationally. Not that it did any good. Due to Dade's intransigence, there was nothing I could do until Joe—an eminently sane, intelligent man—came back from Virginia.

Or Homeland Security returned his cell phone and he saw all his messages.

Glancing at my watch I saw there were still a couple of hours left before I was due at the zoo, but given everything that had happened, I decided to start work early. Aster Edwina wouldn't pay me for it, but working with the animals would take my mind off my frustration with Elvin.

On second thought, leaving the safety of Caro's house might not be a good idea. Maybe I should call in sick.

I was reaching for my cell to call Zorah and tell her I wouldn't be coming in before remembering that this was the day of the Great Escape. The press would be there. So would ex-Marine Ariel and a mob of cameramen, plus every zookeeper and park ranger on the Gunn Zoo payroll. Despite Bucky's trusty baseball bat, today the Gunn Zoo would be the safest place in San Sebastian County.

After making another call—this time to New Jersey—I put on my zoo uniform and headed to work.

◇◇◇

Once at the zoo I became so immersed in caring for the animals that the hours flew by. It seemed like only minutes before I found myself in Zorah's office, slipping my lion costume over my zoo khakis and two-way radio. The lion head was heavy, but it looked authentic, at least from a distance.

"Fits great," Zorah announced as I pranced and preened in front of the mirror. "Just comb that mane and straighten out that tail."

I combed my mane and flipped my tail. "Meow."

She laughed. "Try to sound more like a killer, Teddy."

No laugh from me, the word "killer" having a vastly different connotation.

"Ready to hit the trail, girlfriend?"

"ROAR!" I was getting in the mood.

"I'll take that as a yes." She took me by the paw and led me out the door.

Ariel, mike in hand, was waiting behind the big cats' night house. Being interviewed by the anchor was Aster Edwina, dressed in Renaissance finery for some reason. She wore a long gold and purple gown studded with so many jewels it was a wonder she didn't fall over. To add to her grandeur, a large bejeweled crown rested atop her white hair.

I hated to admit it, but she looked fantastic.

Behind Ariel and Aster Edwina stood a full complement of park rangers with their nets and tranquilizer guns held at the ready. Gary, one of the rangers, assured me they were unloaded and no one would shoot me.

"We'll just pretend to shoot," he said, keeping his voice low enough so it wouldn't be picked up by the mike. "They add to the reality of the event, don't they?"

They sure did. So did the portable lion cage standing nearby. When Zorah led me in, I prowled around, snarling, threatening the camera's red light with a flurry of paws.

"Run fast, but not too fast," Zorah whispered, as she partially closed the cage door. "You have to make the escape last for a half hour, the time slot allocated for the TV coverage. That includes your ten-minute rest stop near Down Under. In that outfit you can't check your watch, so I'll radio you when it's time to start again. When you come running past Monkey Mania, the cameras will pick you up and follow you all the way to the night house. Act feisty. We don't want our runaway lion coming in looking half dead. It needs to be full of piss and vinegar so it can put up a big fight when it's netted."

"You want the media to pass me while I'm taking my break?"

"No, silly. By the time you reach the bottom of Africa Hill, they'll be traipsing across the middle trail on a shortcut to Down Under. The media will get some nice shots of the wallabies, the koalas, and that crazy bowerbird. He's started two new

piles—one turquoise, the other orange. His display will look great on camera. After that, everyone will head for the animal cafeteria to see the bugs."

Zorah continued giving me tips until Ariel's interview with Aster Edwina ended, then left to join the rangers.

"As I was saying in my introduction earlier," Ariel said, smiling at a camera, "this year the role of escaped lion is being played by our old friend Theodora Bentley, the zookeeper who weekly brings us the delightful segment, *Anteaters to Zebras*. While animals seldom escape their enclosures, staged escapes such as the one we're about to witness help train emergency personnel in case such a problem ever occurs. Ms. Bentley, do you have anything to say to our viewers before the chase begins?"

She stuck the mike through the cage bars into my lion face.

I was so startled at the glowing introduction that at first I didn't respond. Wasn't my television program supposed to be on hiatus until my innocence was proven? Or had some figure more powerful than the station itself—Aster Edwina in all probability—intervened in my behalf?

"Roar, for cryin' out loud!" Ariel hissed, breaking my train of thought. She shoved the mike so close it bopped me on the nose.

"ROOOARRR!!!" I replied.

I tried to bite her, too, but my lion head didn't have teeth.

"You see how dangerous these big cats can be," the anchorwoman said, after making a big show of jumping out of biting range. "If that had been a real lion, I'd have lost my hand."

"ROAR!!!" I swiped at her again.

With a satisfied smile, she continued, "And now a word from our sponsor, the Gunn Landing Renaissance Faire. Have a good time and help the San Sebastian County No Kill Animal Shelter grow, because all of the proceeds from the Faire go to benefit homeless animals until they can either be fostered out or adopted into forever homes. For a few dollars, you can have a great time and save an animal's life. Huzzah!"

Aster Edwina rushed over and grabbed the mike. "Faire-goers who arrive in costume get in free, but donations will be gratefully accepted," she said. "Huzzah!"

Close on the heels of Aster Edwina's huzzah, I heard the faint sound of a lute, its strings plucking a revved-up version of that Renaissance favorite, "Greensleeves."

Huh?

"Since we are covering the entirety of the Great Escape," Ariel said, grabbing the mike back, "and the event will last a full half hour, we've asked several featured entertainers from the Faire to showcase their talents until the lion gets netted. Here they come!"

A blast of trumpets and then, to my horror, a full contingent of Renaissance Faire actors came trooping up the hill. Leading the throng was Willis Pierce, in full King Henry the Eighth regalia, followed by his entire Royal Court. A jester danced behind them, every now and then and then bumping into the twig-bedecked Green Man, who underneath all his greenery looked much different than the actor I'd first seen portraying him at the Faire. A substitute? Also in the crowd were Deborah Holt and her reptile keeper husband, Caro's friend Jane Olson and her Gold King, comedians Ded Bob and the Silly Slatterns, crossbow vendors Melissa and Cary Keegan, the battling Sazacs, Speaks-To-Souls with three leashed greyhounds, Yancy Haas in his Black Knight armor, and a gaggle of monks and peasants. Even Howie Fife, no longer limping, had put his court minstrel costume back on.

They looked spectacular, but the killer outshone them all.

Because of my lion mask, no one noticed my alarmed state. Actors all, they played to the cameras, tossing around "thees" and "thous" and "zounds" and "forsooths" like so many beach balls.

Cameras!

My panic eased somewhat when I remembered the media was present. Television hosts, radio announcers, print reporters, bloggers, everyone. No matter how desperate, the killer would not dare try anything now. Besides, the killer had no way of knowing I had figured everything out. For the next thirty minutes, at least, I was safe.

After that, I would hurry back to Caro's house and not emerge until someone, anyone, listened to my story. Maybe the State Police, maybe the…

"Escaped lion!" Zorah bawled, nearly deafening me. "Code Red! Code Red!"

With an adrenalin-charged roar I sprang out of the cage and charged down the path toward the steep hill alongside Africa Trail, cameramen and park rangers in full pursuit.

Encumbered as I was in my lion suit, I wasn't as fast as usual. The rangers weren't so hampered, and as we rocketed along it looked like they might catch up to me and bring the chase to a premature end. Just before they caught up, I picked up the pace.

The descent down the Africa Hill worked to my advantage, and by the time I made it to the huge giraffe and Watusi cattle enclosure, my pursuers were left far behind. Giraffes, gentle but curious creatures, wandered over to the fence to see what was going on. I looked like a lion but I didn't smell like a lion, so as far as they were concerned, I didn't count. The Watusi cattle didn't care, either, and merely kept grazing. Far to the back of the enclosure, Big D, our cantankerous male ostrich, stuck his head up and gave me the once-over, but when he saw the fake lion wasn't the bearer of food, he went back to doing whatever he'd been doing.

The zebras weren't as relaxed. As soon as the male Grevy's zebra saw me speeding along, he rounded up his harem, stood protectively in front of them, and sent me a challenging bray.

"Don't have time to fight right now," I huffed back. "Take a rain check."

On and on I ran, cutting across the big central plaza and turning into California Habitat, where the coyotes were interested enough to stop yipping at each other as I crossed the lane bordering their enclosure. By the time I reached the border of Down Under I could no longer hear my pursuers. Good. After my mile-long sprint, I needed a rest.

Zorah had told me to take a ten-minute break once I reached this point, so I halted. If everything went according to plan, my pursuers had already cut across the middle of the zoo to get some fuzzy-cute photographs of the koalas and wallabies in Down Under, and were now moving on to the animal cafeteria to take video barrels of termites and worms. My watch was hidden underneath my costume, but she had promised to radio me as soon as it was time to head for Monkey Mania, where the cameras would pick me up again. I patted my rump to make sure my radio was still secured to my belt. An answering hiss told me it was.

Now all I had to do was wait.

The perimeter of the Gunn Zoo is ringed by a wide paved trail, the better for visitors to walk along pushing strollers or wheelchairs, but the zoo's interior is forested with eucalyptus and live oaks, interspersed with colorful exotic plants. Hidden by the heavy undergrowth are the narrow keepers' paths leading to the back of each species' night house.

Knowing the temperature would be cooler in the shade, I moved away from the main trail and onto a keeper path. I was just about to take off my lion's head to breathe the fresh air when someone stepped out of the undergrowth.

The killer.

This time, the killer had a gun.

Chapter Twenty-one

"Prithee, fair maid, where goest thou?" asked King Henry the Eighth, resplendent in blue velvet robes. As impressive as they were, the gun in his hand commanded more attention.

Act dumb. Pretend you didn't figure it out. Stalling for time, I took off my heavy lion head and shook out its mane.

"Oh, hi, Willis," I said, as casually as possible. "I see they roped you into the Great Escape, too. They even gave you a fake gun!"

My ploy didn't work.

"Why couldn't you leave it alone, Teddy? Now I have to kill you, too, and that was never what I wanted." The cultured veneer of the drama teacher had vanished, and now he sounded like who he really was—Anthony James Moss, a remorseless ex-con who had murdered three people, including his cousin, the real Willis Pierce.

"Kill me? What the heck are you talking about?"

"Nice try, Teddy, but that fool Elvin Dade told me all about your crazy phone call this morning while he was writing me a ticket for parking in a fire zone at City Hall."

"Elvin *told* you about my phone call?"

When the man I'd known as Willis Pierce laughed, his gold-and-blue cloak rippled merrily. "How dumb can a man get, right? I was just in City Hall for a mere second, paying yet another ticket—I really am going to have to do something about my parking practices—so I didn't think anyone would make a fuss.

But the next thing you know I was surrounded by cops, led by our chatty Elvin. He couldn't wait to tell me how stupid you are. What did you do to make the man hate you so much?"

"It's Caro he hates, not me. When they were teenagers..." Oh, what did it matter now? I gave up all pretense. "You're Taxi."

"Guilty as charged, dear lady." Returning to his former Henry the Eighth persona, he rendered an elegant bow.

Vying for time, I said, "The other Faire actors will notice you're missing, and when I'm found dead, they'll point to you!"

"*Au contraire.* Not long after the TV cameras spent a few minutes sharing our dance with all of San Sebastian County, Aster Edwina ordered our bells and motley crew to depart forthwith, and so we did. I bade farewell to the others in the parking lot. Once they'd driven off, I made haste to return to your little Eden. But so much for that. You know what galls me about this entire thing? I actually saved Victor's life by orchestrating the little snitch's escape from prison. How did he repay me for favors rendered? The villain blackmailed me. No honor among thieves, apparently."

Or killers.

I wondered how long I had. In a few minutes the tour of the animal cafeteria would be over, allowing the Great Escape to resume. Zookeepers, park rangers, and the media would assemble near Monkey Mania, waiting for my reappearance. If I could just keep him talking his attention might wander and I'd be able to...Well, I didn't know exactly what yet, but I'd come up with something.

Playing to his vanity, I feigned admiration. "I really underestimated you, didn't I? I should have known better. After all, a man who could come out of prison and assume a Ph.D.'s identity has to be incredibly bright. *And* talented."

He actually preened. "People always said my cousin and I looked enough alike to be twins. When Cousin Willis returned from Johannesburg, he accepted the job offer from San Sebastian Community College, but before picking up stakes and moving again he wanted to have a weekend ramble down the

Appalachian Trail. Erroneously believing that blood was thicker than water, he asked if I'd like to come along."

"That's where you killed him, then. On the trail."

His gentle smile seemed wildly out place in the circumstances. "Correct again, Teddy. With this very gun. Since he'd only flown out here one time for his interview, taking his place at the college was easy, especially since I knew as much about theater as he did. More, actually. My dear cousin was no big loss to Broadway, you understand, and he was only a run-of-the-mill scholar. As the Bard said, 'Nothing in his life became him like the leaving it.' *Macbeth,* Act I, Scene IV. By then most of our relatives were dead, so there was no one to raise the alarm when the boy dropped off the face of the earth."

In the distance, a howler monkey began his nightly serenade, and another howled in answer—an off-key symphony that usually made me smile. I didn't feel like smiling now, but I made the effort.

"Impressive, Willis. Or should I say Tony? All you had to do was drop a few pounds and grow a beard like his. Maybe you can tell me how you...?"

"Trying to extend your life by keeping me busy bragging about my misdeeds?"

Considering how terrified I was, the calm in my voice amazed me. "That, too, but I really am interested. I still can't figure out why you let Victor blackmail you since he had more to lose than you did. I don't understand why you had to kill Bambi, either." A big lie there, since I already knew, but I had to keep him talking.

Once again his vanity overcame his determination to kill me. "Given Victor's murder conviction, he had more to hide than me, so you're right there. I pointed this out when he first hit me up for the money and said I should be the blackmailer, not the victim. Know what? He had the gall to laugh! He told me the marriage business was in the toilet and that he was too old to start another scam, but he couldn't exactly apply for Social Security, could he? Not living under an assumed name, he couldn't. Did you know that for a tiny fraction of a minute I actually felt sorry for him?"

"If you felt so sorry for Victor, why kill him? And why with a crossbow, since you obviously own a gun?"

"Answer part A, because of the money, of course. I don't like being blackmailed, especially now, when the balloon payment on the *Caliban* was due. Answer part B, because the crossbow was quieter, and would give me more time to get back to the harbor, leaving a Faire full of suspects to be questioned by that stupid Elvin Dade. My plan would have worked, too, if Alejandro hadn't shrieked his head off. As a lifetime animal lover, I do feel bad about scaring the llama, but it couldn't be helped." He looked at his handgun. Stroked it.

I had to interrupt that perilous chain of thought. "Okay, Tony. I understand. You love your life in Gunn Landing. Heck, who wouldn't? So you played along with Victor for a while and made the payments. Then the economy went to hell. I happen to know that SSCC salaries aren't that great, and what with harbor's slip fees going up and the *Caliban's* payment due, your budget was stretched to the breaking point. And so were you. Am I right?"

"You should have been a psychologist, Teddy."

"Then came the Renaissance Faire and its lavish display of Medieval weaponry. You seized the day."

"No moss on this stone. When I saw that tart Melissa sucking face with Yancy Hass behind the armory stall, I snatched up the crossbow and a couple of darts and hurried away. Later, I took Victor aside and told him I'd hand over my usual payment near Llama Rides at two a.m., and…Well, you know how that turned out, don't you? I donned the leper's costume I'd also had the foresight to swipe, just in case I was seen, and did the dirty deed."

He sighed. "Alas, dear Teddy, you're such a fine conversationalist, I hate the thought of putting an end to all that wit, but your time runneth out. I need to get over to the college for the final rehearsal of *Much Ado About Nothing* before anyone notices I'm late." Heaving a theatrical sigh, he said, "Don't worry. I've always liked you, so I'll make it quick."

He raised the gun.

Before I could dodge out of the way, the thick brush to the left of me rustled and the Faire's Green Man stepped out. His leafy costume perfectly matched the surrounding foliage.

"Surprise! You should have known I wouldn't miss the Great Escape, Teddy!"

It was Dad. And he didn't see the gun in Tony Moss' hand.

The shocking interruption took Moss' attention off me for a half-second, but that was all I needed.

I threw the lion's head.

The heavy mask knocked Moss' gun hand aside enough that the bullet plowed into a nearby tree. Unfortunately, he hung onto his weapon.

"Run!" I screamed at my father over the loud gunshot.

Dad had always been quick on the uptake and he didn't disappoint me now. Before Moss could swing the gun around for another shot, Dad and I plunged into the heavy undergrowth. With me in the lead, we ran, not back down toward the wide visitor's lane, but deeper into the foliage where the bushes slapped at us as we headed toward Monkey Mania. If we could make it there, we'd be close enough that our screams for help might be heard by the park rangers. But for now we had to save our breath and just run.

"You can't get away, Teddy!" Moss yelled behind us. "You've been running too long and I'm fresh. Whoever that is with you, he's no spring chicken. Stop now and I'll make this quick, just like I promised. If you don't, when I catch you, you'll get it in the gut and he'll get it in a much worse place."

"Did that Henry the Eighth guy kill…?" Dad puffed.

"Yes. Shut up and run."

Moss was right about one thing. Despite my adrenalin rush, my physical exhaustion became more and more evident as we plunged through the heavy undergrowth. Dad's age—he was in his sixties—and sedentary lifestyle were handicaps, too. With growing despair I realized we might not make it all the way to Monkey Mania and help.

But I wasn't going to let Tony kill us without a fight.

Desperate, I grabbed Dad's hand and wheeled us into a nasty growth of black hawthorn bushes. Their sharp thorns slashed our faces and ripped much of the cloth leaves off Dad's Green Man costume, but I didn't care. If we could reach the equipment shed at Friendly Farms where I'd stashed the pitchfork after mucking out the barnyard, we'd have a chance.

From the noise behind us in the undergrowth, Moss was catching up. His bulky Henry the Eighth costume didn't seem to bother him at all, although it would look like hell afterwards. When he turned up at the Renaissance Faire tomorrow in ragged robes, someone—maybe even the dense Elvin Dade—might figure it out. Then again, Moss had a creative mind and he'd probably think of something. When Joe got back, though…

Don't think about Joe.

Think about that pitchfork.

"Teddy, let go of…of my hand." Dad's breathing had grown more and more ragged as we plunged through the hawthorn thicket. "We can't out…outrun him…together. We need to… to separate…Let me…stop and I'll…I'll distract…him while… you go ahead."

When I glanced at him I saw bloody scratches marring his dear, patrician face. Clenching his hand even harder, I snapped, "You're not sacrificing yourself for me!"

"But he'll…he'll kill us…both. Better me…than you. I've had…a long life. You…you haven't."

"He's not going to kill either of us," I lied. "I have a plan."

It wasn't much of one—pitchfork against gun never is—but it was better than sacrificing my father. As the crashing noises behind us drew nearer so did our possible salvation. I had begun to see flashes of clearing through the dense undergrowth. The barnyard lay only a few yards ahead, and at the other end of it, the shed. I was trying to figure out how many seconds it would take to open the latch when I dragged my protesting father across the paved lane that led past Friendly Farm and saw…

Alejandro.

Standing in the middle of the barnyard, where I'd left him earlier.

A better plan formed in my mind. I helped my winded father under the fence and then pushed him down behind the big water trough.

"Sit perfectly still," I whispered. "Once Moss goes for me, I want you to crawl to the other side so he can't see you."

Dad was too exhausted to argue.

His momentary safety thus accomplished, I fell to my hands and knees, and with waif-like cries, crawled toward the llama.

As Tony Moss emerged from the brush and vaulted the fence, I could see that evil little gun pointed at me. If this didn't work, Dad and I were both dead.

Then I heard a familiar, blessed sound.

Alejandro.

Screaming in rage.

Wheeck! Wheeck! Wheeck!

Believing rightly that his little human friend was in danger, Alejandro galloped forward and hit Moss with his shoulder just as the man fired. A clod of dirt kicked up near my heel as I rolled away.

Wheeck! Wheeck! Wheeck!

Alejandro rushed Moss again, this time knocking him fully to the ground. Then, as Moss lay sprawled on his back, Alejandro began to stomp him with those big, clawed feet. If I had been a better person I would have stopped the attack once the blood started to flow, but I just stood there and watched.

And God help me, I enjoyed it.

◇◇◇

Fortunately—or unfortunately, depending on your point of view—help arrived before Willis Pierce, a.k.a. Anthony James Moss, bit the big one. My talkative delay had worked, and everyone had made it out of the animal cafeteria and started toward Monkey Mania. The sound of Moss' last shot had carried over the hill, alerting my waiting pursuers that someone was hunting the escaped lion for real. They all came running, park rangers, zookeepers, the media with their cameras, taking pictures and shooting video as they ran.

Someone else ran, too.

Dad.

As soon as he saw help was on its way, he blew me a kiss and skedaddled back into the undergrowth.

Moss was a mess. His royal finery was ripped, his lip was split, and his nose appeared broken. But I'll give the man this; while the hastily summoned EMTs loaded him onto a stretcher, he maintained his sense of the theatrical.

Before he was carted away, he waved a bloodied hand at the cameras and said, "This is what happens when you quote from the Scottish play."

Chapter Twenty-two

Another thing happened that night to reaffirm my belief in miracles.

As I sat in the same interview room where Acting Sheriff Elvin Dade had once given me the third degree, who should interrupt his repeat performance of accusations but Joe Rejas, the real sheriff of San Sebastian County.

Paying no attention to Elvin's order to remain seated, I wrapped myself around Joe and wouldn't let go. He smelled of sweat and travel and man, all man. Once he got through kissing and otherwise mauling me, he peeled me off and set me back down.

"Elvin!" he barked. "What the hell's been going on!"

To complete the miracle trifecta, Albert Grissom, my defense attorney, rushed through the door with the same question.

The unfortunate Elvin merely sat there, mouth agape.

With Grissom's approval, I started talking. I told Joe everything that had happened, from the Google hits to Willis' attempt to kill me. The only things I kept quiet about were my adventures in breaking and entering.

At one point Joe stopped me. "How did you find out Victor was a blackmailer, Miss Bentley?" He had segued from loving fiancé to inquisitor.

Unhappy at the prospect of lying to the man I loved, I replied, "There was, ah, a rumor going around that, um, you needed to watch your step around him or he might, ah, use your indiscretions against you."

Joe narrowed his eyes. He wasn't buying it. "You're telling me that based on a mere rumor, you started snooping around to see who might have secrets?"

"Everyone has secrets, Joe."

Grissom cleared his throat. "Sheriff, instead of worrying how Miss Bentley came into certain information, why not just ask her what she knew and when she knew it."

An expression of relief flitted across Joe's face, and he became the loving fiancé again. "Sounds good to me. Go on with your story, Teddy."

After a nod from Grissom, I complied. "As I was saying, once I saw Tony Moss' mug shot, I realized that Willis wasn't really Willis, so I called Elvin and, well, he didn't believe me. I decided I needed more proof, something concrete that would convince even him."

I snuck a look at the former acting sheriff. He seemed to have shrunk.

"Anyway, I took a chance that Willis'…I mean *Tony Moss'* ex-wife might be still around, you know how these small towns are, nobody ever leaves, so I called Egg Harbor information and asked for the phone number of Serena Sue Moss, but she turned out to be listed under her maiden name of Tagliossi. I called her and once I told her that her ex-husband was living in Gunn Landing Harbor, she was more than happy to talk to me, especially about what a bad husband he'd been, never paying attention to her good advice, always buying things they couldn't afford, and finally running them into bankruptcy. She heard that after the divorce he moved to Reno to work in one of the casinos, but she didn't know he'd been caught siphoning money until he called her and begged for money to hire an attorney. She did—still a flame there, I think—but he was found guilty anyway and wound up in Ely State Prison. That's the same place Victor Emerson—well, the guy who called himself Victor Emerson—was incarcerated."

At this, Elvin Dade could no longer contain himself. He sat up straight and barked, "You're trying to convince us some two-bit blackjack dealer was able to masquerade as a college teacher? What do you take us for—idiots?"

"Try to act like a professional for once, Elvin," Joe said, giving him a frigid look. When he turned to me, his expression softened. "Deputy Dade does have a point, Teddy. Can you explain that?"

I smiled back. "I'd been puzzled about that myself, but Serena Sue said that she met Tony Moss when they were studying drama at Princeton University. Like the real Willis Pierce, he loved the theater." Remembering my own little red-headed cousin who wanted to be a zookeeper when she grew up, I added, "Sometimes these things run in families."

Defeated, Elvin sank back into his chair.

"At first it was all good. They got married right after he directed her as Titania in *Midsummer Night's Dream*, but problems soon cropped up. She told me he went out and bought a flashy car when he didn't have enough money to pay the rent, and they got evicted. That kind of thing continued until he was forced to drop out of Princeton to take a job at the Lucky Lady Casino in Atlantic City, and she found work at a cocktail lounge. Unlike her, he kept current with what was happening on and off Broadway; she was too disheartened. When he bought a sailboat instead of helping her pay bills, she had enough and filed for divorce. At that point he split for Nevada, where he got caught skimming from the casino there, and wound up in Ely State Prison."

In a way, I felt sorry for Tony Moss. At the very least, he would be spending the rest of his life in another prison cell, far away from the *Caliban*, his forty-five foot sloop. I hoped a police search of the sailboat would find the crossbow that killed Victor, but doubted it. After using the crossbow for a second time for skewering Mr. Rat, Tony was smart enough to have dumped the murder weapon into the Pacific during one of his afternoon sails.

Who would own the *Caliban* next? Someone who could love her as much as he did, I hoped. I wondered if my defense attorney would be interested. Mother loved to sail.

"Teddy? I mean, Miss Bentley, you didn't answer my question." Joe's voice interrupted my chain of thought.

"Sorry. Could you repeat it?"

"As I was saying, I can understand why Mr. Moss would kill Victor—I mean the late Glenn Reynolds Jamison—but why did he kill Bambi O'Dair?"

This is where the truth became touchy again. Dad's inquiries had gleaned the information that Victor was Bambi's father and Moss was probably afraid the phony minster had shared his knowledge about him, but I couldn't tell Joe that. Fiancé or not, he was still an officer of the law. If he knew Dad was in town, he'd be forced to look for him. Given Joe's native son knowledge of Gunn Landing's love affairs and scandals, he would start at Caro's house, then move up to Gunn Castle, and Dad might wind up sharing a cell with Tony Moss.

"I haven't the slightest idea," I answered.

Joe narrowed those beautiful brown eyes at me again. "Are you sure you're telling me everything?"

I crossed my fingers. "Absolutely. Now you know everything I know." *Except for the part that would harm my father.*

He stared at me for a moment, then shrugged and shifted his attention to Elvin Dade. "Where's Moss' gun, Elvin?"

"Oh, ah, it's…it's…" Elvin turned to Emilio, who stood in the doorway, still dressed in his civvies after his return from Los Angeles. "Deputy, what happened to the gun?"

"You mean what happened to the gun after I hear the crime techs had to wrestle it away from you?" Emilio drawled. "I sure hope you didn't get your fingerprints all over it when you picked it up off the ground with your greasy hands. Oh, well, maybe the techs can still get a partial. Not that they were ever able to do anything with that crossbow bolt you wiped off with your handkerchief."

Joe glared at Elvin. "You handled evidence with your bare hands? Again? After all I've warned you about?"

Elvin shifted in his seat. Sweat popped out on his forehead. "Well, I couldn't leave the gun on the ground, could I? It...it could get covered with manure."

Joe muttered something in Spanish and it didn't sound like a prayer. "You didn't happen to wash the gunshot residue off Mr. Moss' hands for him at the same time, did you?"

"Of course not. That would be unprofessional."

Emilio snorted. So did I.

At that, Joe cleared everyone out of the interview room except for Elvin. The rest of us couldn't have waited in the hallway for more than two minutes before Elvin came rushing out of the interview room, his face as red as a baboon's behind. He said nothing as he passed us, just hurried for the exit as fast as his stubby legs could carry him.

Epilogue No. 1

Three months later

First, in this forest, let us do those ends
That here were well begun and well begot:
And after, every one of this happy number
That have endured shrewd days and nights with us
Shall share the good of our returned fortune,
According to the measure of their states.
Meantime, forget this new-fall'n dignity
And fall into our rustic revelry.
Play, music! And you, brides and bridegrooms all,
With measure heap'd in joy, to the measures fall.
—William Shakespeare's *As You Like It,* Act V, Scene IV

It was a perfect September Sunday. A sea-born breeze blew gently through the tall eucalyptus trees shading the large crowd gathered in San Sebastian Civic Park. Birds sang. Children laughed.

Joe and I were sitting on a blanket with a picnic basket, waiting for the festivities to begin.

When the San Sebastian Community College Marching Band struck up Mendelssohn's "Wedding March," two dozen wedding-gowned and tuxedoed couples filed arm in arm across the stage of the band shell. They would shortly be re-united in marriage—for real, this time—by the elderly Reverend Isaiah

Smithfield, once known as "Brutha Ike" by his pot-smoking friends in the Haight. Clad in his clerical robes, the Reverend Smithfield stood on a dais beaming down at the couples as they slowly formed a choir-like arrangement facing the audience. It looked like a high school graduation, if the graduates were between twenty and seventy.

Leading this charge toward connubial respectability were Mayor Jimmy Murano and his soon-to-be-wife-again Evelyn, along with two city council members and their giggling again-brides. Behind the politicos came everyone the phony Victor Emerson had married.

Well, almost everyone.

Liveaboarders Deborah and Phil Holt marched up happily, taking their place in the crowd with their five-year-old daughter, who was decked out in flower girl finery. Following them, to everyone's surprise, were Deanna and Judd Sazac, who for once, weren't arguing. Jane Olson, Caro's great friend, was remarrying her dashing Gold King. I spotted my friend Emilio Gutierrez, looking devastatingly handsome in his dress uniform, eager to remarry his adored and adoring Elena.

"Everyone looks so happy," I whispered to Joe.

He nuzzled my ear. "Just like we're going to look soon. Now, shush. If there's one song I love, it's the 'Wedding March.'"

Also tying the knot again were my mother's former maid Eunice Snow and her husband Bucky. The seven-months-pregnant Eunice could have looked like a hippo in her flouncy white dress, but the joy in her eyes made up for her expanded girth. The couple had plenty to celebrate. Bucky had been so determined to make a success of his job at the San Sebastian Cinema that he spent the last three months devouring books on film. In a payment-in-kind deal with the local TV station, Bucky's boss wrangled him a segment on *Good Morning San Sebastian*, where in addition to hyping the coming attractions, Bucky held forth on cinematic history. The segment, "Bucky Goes Hollywood" was now as popular as my "Anteaters To Zebras," which was back on the air. To add to the couple's joy, Eunice finally found a well-paying job. Aster Edwina, merely to spite her old enemy Caroline Piper Bentley Hufgraff O'Brien Petersen, hired Eunice to work at Gunn Castle at twice her previous salary.

My memory of Caro's chagrin when Eunice defected to the castle was interrupted when someone tickled my ear again.

"Stop it!" I hissed at Joe. "Grown-ups aren't supposed to be making out at dignified rituals like weddings."

"They do if they live in San Sebastian County. We're not big on dignity here. Know what, Teddy? This might be hard to believe, but I feel kind of disappointed that your mother isn't on that stage today. She would have been the star of the show."

I shook my head. "Caro would sooner wear clothes from Walmart than take part in a group wedding."

A month earlier, sporting a new six carat marquise-cut diamond solitaire, my mother had married Albert Grissom in a lush garden ceremony at her Gunn Landing mansion. As a wedding present, the two men she had once married at Victor's wedding chapel and later divorced, promised not to demand repayment of their generous settlement. Touched by her ex-husbands' generosity, Caro indulged in some charity of her own. With the help of my new stepfather, she set up a small educational foundation, which was sending several members of Demonios Femeninos to the Monterey College of Cosmetology. Soledad, Caro's former cellmate, received enough foundation money to make her dreams of law school a reality.

Always a sucker for my felonious father, Aster Edwina's cold heart softened enough to loan him her private jet and pilot. The day after the faux Dr. Willis Pierce was formally charged with double homicide, Dad flew back to Costa Rica and into the waiting arms of Dominga.

Not retying the marital knot today were Cary and Melissa Keegan. Rumor has it that Cary had been willing, but as soon as the Gunn Landing Renaissance Faire ended, Melissa followed stuntman Yancy Haas to Los Angeles. Good luck to them both, I thought. Given their propensity for violence, they'd need it.

Former sheriff's deputy (now retired) Elvin Dade and the very righteous Wynona weren't here today, either. Their own pastor had quietly remarried them in a small private ceremony in their church. As soon as the sale on their house went through, they were moving to Florida.

As for Joe and me, we passed on the group wedding for our own reasons. I'll tell you more about that later.

In a plea bargain designed to escape the death penalty, Anthony James Moss confessed to the murders of Victor Emerson and Bambi O'Dair. He also revealed the whereabouts of the body of his cousin, the genuine Dr. Willis Pierce, whose bones were finally given a decent burial. In an odd twist, Serena Sue, Moss' ex-wife, moved from New Jersey to California so she could more easily nag him during visiting hours at Folsom Prison, where he was serving a life sentence without parole. I guess there's no accounting for twisted love. The last I heard of Tony Moss, he was planning to stage a prison production of *Julius Caesar*.

Et tu, Brute.

Within a week of being back from Virginia, Joe—urged on by Soledad Rodriguez—had solved the murder of Duane Langer. Finding the real killer had not been that difficult; just too difficult for ex-Acting Sheriff Elvin Dade. As it turned out, Duane had been shot to death by Kenny Guy Hayward in a bid for leadership of Viking Vengeance. Not only is there no loyalty among thieves, there was none between racists, either.

"How's Kenny Guy doing?" I asked Joe, who wouldn't leave my ear alone. "A little bird told me he's trying to organize another white power group while awaiting trial."

Joe left my ear alone long enough to answer. "Not well. The other white power thugs hate him because he killed their precious Duane, and everybody else hates him simply because he's Kenny Guy. I figure his life expectancy at about three months after he arrives in Folsom."

"Hmmm."

"Yeah, hmmm." Back to the ear.

After a while, he said, "Those other blackmail victims. Who do you think they were?"

"I don't know."

Here's the problem with lying: the more you do it, the easier it gets. I had a good idea who Scarlet, Aloha, and Woodstock were, but since their misdeeds were more embarrassing than criminal, I wasn't about to set myself up as the moral enforcer of San Sebastian County. We'd already had one of those.

To take Joe's mind off blackmail, I said, "There's something I've been meaning to ask you."

"Ask away, you sexy animal, you," he whispered.

"Considering the fact that your week-long absence played holy hell with folks hereabouts, did you at least learn anything important when you were out in Virginia with Homeland Security? You know, enough to make all that misery worth it?"

"I'd love to tell you, honey, but if I did, I'd have to kill you." Snicker.

A few minutes later, Joe having turned his attention to the other ear, I caught sight of two more friends in the audience. I poked Joe in the side with my elbow. "There's Ada and Howie. Should we go over and say hi?"

"Maybe later." He nibbled his way down to my neck.

Because of the national publicity about the phony college professor's arrest, Ada Fife, mother of the one-day marine biologist Howie, was outed as the runaway wife of Gerard Eversleigh Howard, producer of New York's prestigious Caballero Opera. When Howard received word of his ex-wife and son's whereabouts, he flew to San Sebastian County with lawyers in tow. They were met at the airport by Joe and his new second-in-command, Deputy Emilio Gutierrez, the county commissioner having finally seen the error of his "seniority above merit" rule. After a few harsh words from Joe, who produced the photograph of a severely-battered nine-year-old Howie that Ada had given him, Gerard Eversleigh Howard slithered back into the slime from whence he came. He hasn't been heard from since, although Ada is now receiving child support—retroactively, enough that Howie is now commuting to college in a new Mustang convertible.

Speaking of slithering, the week after the Renaissance Faire folded up its tents for the year, Sssbyl slithered back to the zoo on her own one fine morning. Just yesterday she sent out a tweet that she had just given birth to "42 sssweet Mojave rattlesssnake babiesss," and that she was in "ssseventh Heaven." But Sssbyl hasn't forgotten her fans. She still tweets daily, holding forth on subjects ranging all the way from marriage advice to barbeque sauce. She has become one of the Gunn Zoo's major attractions, teaching thousands of children that snakes aren't as bad as they're reputed to be.

The only animal more popular now than Sssbyl is Alejandro. The *San Sebastian Gazette*, not exaggerating for once, declared the llama a hero. Reports of his life-saving attack made him an overnight media star. He now gives frequent interviews with the California media, as well as stringers from the *New York Times* and the *Chicago Tribune*. Alejandro doesn't usually have much to say, so I "interpret" for him.

Just as Zorah had been interpreting for Sssbyl all along.

One more thing. In the white hot glare of all the media attention, Ernest Dalrymple dropped his lawsuit and entered rehab. I hear he is doing well.

The amped voice of Reverend Smithfield interrupted my reverie as he began the marriage service.

"Dearly beloved, we are gathered here to…to…to be married…Whazzit? Oh, yeah, hey, everybody, we're gathered here together for something, to…to…"

Joe stopped the delicious thing he was doing to my neck and stood up, his eyes on the reverend. "Teddy, is that preacher stoned?"

I stood up with him and squinted my eyes toward the band shell. The Reverend Smithfield's eyes were bleary and his hair mussed. Underneath his cassock, where his breast pocket would be, I thought I saw the outline of a candy bar. Or maybe it was crackers.

"Stoned as a goose," I said.

"Then maybe I should go up there and arres…"

When I shot him a look, he sat back down. "On second thought, maybe not."

Giving him a peck on the cheek, I said, "Oh, Joe, I really really *really* love you!"

But I promised to tell you why Joe and I weren't among the merry throng gathered at the park to exchange vows. That is, if the Reverend Smithfield ever remembered them.

Here's why we're holding off.

As soon as Joe and I heard about the upcoming group marriage ceremony, I brought up the possibility of joining our fellow San Sebastianites. He hung back.

"You don't think it would be fun?" I asked.

"Fun, yes, but on our wedding day I want you all to myself," he had whispered as we snuggled on board the *Merilee*. "Besides, I won't be finished with the master bedroom extension for at least two more months, and I don't want you to spend the first days of our marriage breathing in sawdust and plaster. What color do you want?"

"Color?"

"You know, for me to paint the bedroom."

I knew men well enough not to answer, *any color you like, honey*, so I said, "Yellow. It's the happiest color there is."

He gave my ear a gentle bite. "Agreed. But there are a million shades of yellow. Daisy, buttercup, sunshine…Tell you what. I'll pick up some paint chips from the hardware store. No, make that several hardware stores, and let you choose. How about some blue accents? Or orange, if you want to stay with the warm tones. Turquoise is in now, too, and would look nice with yellow. Maybe lots of plants to get some green in there? Oh, and a home-made quilt from that Amish catalog we were looking at the other day? I want everything perfect for you."

My fiancé, the color-coordinated bowerbird.

Epilogue No. 2

@Sssbyl: That Ssshakessspeare dude sssaid it bessst—all'ssss well that endssss well, even for usss sssnakesss.